HIS CURVY FRIEND

A SMALL TOWN CURVY GIRL ROMANCE

BOOK BOYFRIENDS WANTED
BOOK ONE

MARY E THOMPSON

BOOK BOYFRIENDS WANTED

Welcome to MacKellar Cove, a sleepy little town nestled in a quiet cove on the St. Lawrence River. Grab a drink at the bar where all the locals hang out. Join the women for a talk about life and love at the local bookstore. Just be careful because it's still a small town so everyone knows everything about everyone else. Which is why the most popular dating app doesn't include pictures.

Grab a drink, and a slice of cake, and meet your favorite book boyfriend. We want them all!

BOOK BOYFRIENDS WANTED
His Curvy Secret (subscriber exclusive)
His Curvy Friend
His Curvy Wife
His Curvy Treat
His Curvy Frustration
His Curvy Gift
His Curvy Outcast
His Curvy Nurse
His Curvy Ex

His Curvy Craving
His Curvy Genius
His Curvy Fantasy
His Curvy Boss
His Curvy Infatuation
His Curvy Stranger
His Curvy Muse
His Curvy Surprise
His Curvy Distraction
His Curvy Sunshine
His Curvy Fascination
His Curvy Happiness

SUBSCRIBE NOW AT MARYETHOMPSON.COM

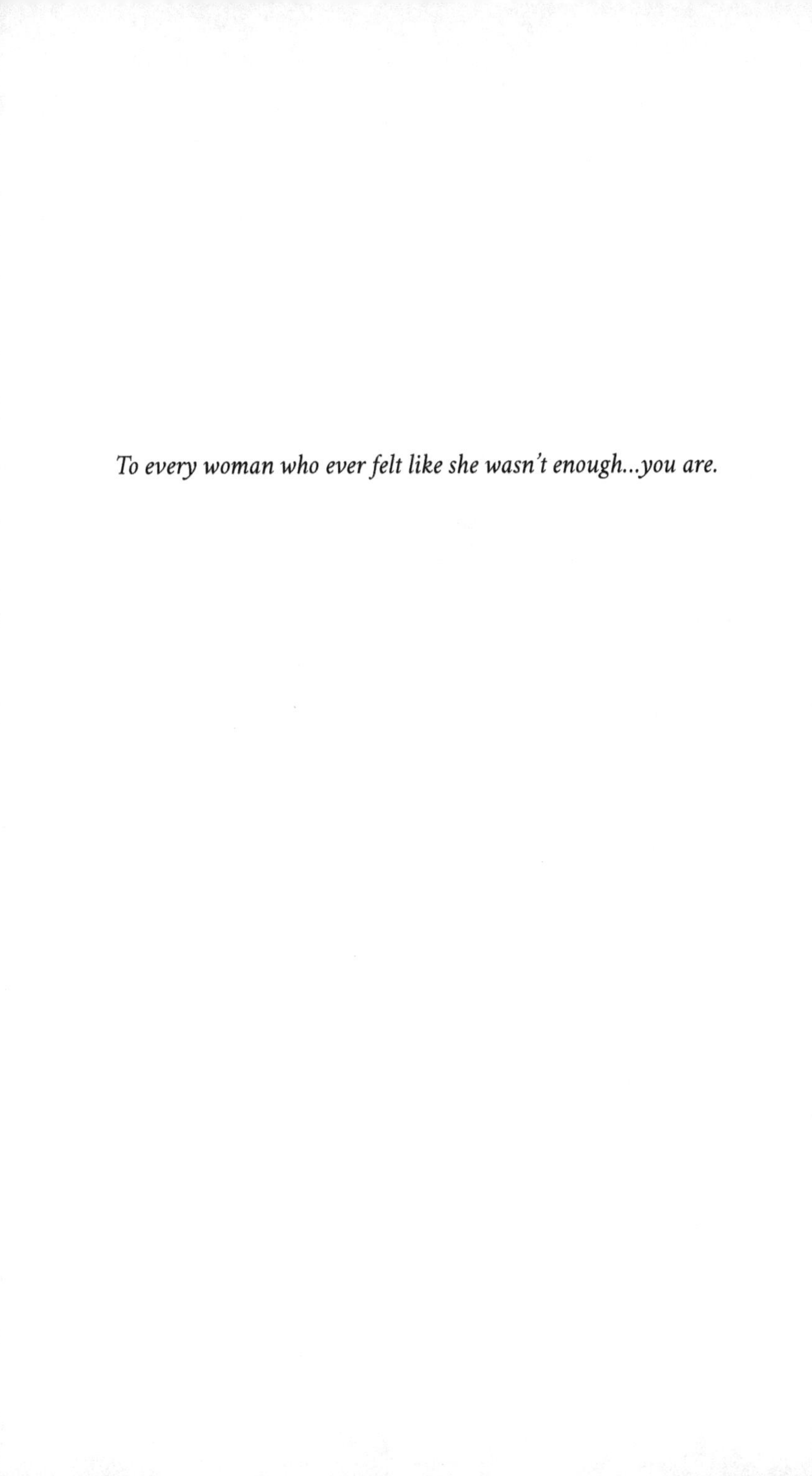

To every woman who ever felt like she wasn't enough...you are.

BLAKE

I was already staring at the ceiling when my alarm blared. The sun hadn't woken up yet, but I had. I'd been up for over an hour and dreading the day for months. I would get through it, but it wasn't going to be a good day.

I slapped the screeching alarm and climbed out of bed. I took a fast shower to help me wake up then got dressed in my normal uniform of jeans and a black tee with *Cracked* scrawled over my large left breast and a bigger version of the logo on the back.

I tied my hair up into a ponytail and added a touch of mascara and a little lipgloss. Not that I was trying to impress anyone, but it helped me feel a little more prepared to face the day. When I admitted to myself I couldn't delay any longer, I took a deep breath and left my house.

The walk to Cracked only took a few minutes. Even a curvy girl like me made the trip quickly, but when the heat of summer finally moved in, it would take me a little longer if I wanted to avoid being drenched in sweat all day.

Megan, one of my coworkers, was coming from the other direction when I walked down Caroline Street. We met in front of Cracked and hugged. It was going to be a tough day for all of us.

Lights were on inside, and the kitchen was already bustling. We had an hour before we opened, but biscuits were going in the oven, batter was being mixed, and coffee was brewing.

"Hey," Jean, another coworker, said, giving Megan and I both hugs. "This day sucks."

We nodded in agreement. Of all the things Georgia asked us to do before she died, none of us thought celebrating her sixtieth birthday with a celebration of her life would be hard, but now that the day had arrived, it was almost impossible.

Earl, the owner of Cracked and our boss, called out from the kitchen and waved with his spatula. We waved back and set to helping Jean while Earl cooked breakfast. We'd all agreed to have breakfast together this morning. It was a chance to share the start of the day with the people who saw Georgia daily.

Earl came out of the kitchen with a plate of pancakes, Georgia's favorite, and lots of bacon and sausage. We grabbed one of the full pots of coffee and sat down.

We held hands and all said a private prayer or blessing or whatever. I asked Georgia to give me strength to be there for Karissa, her daughter and my friend, and to hold out for the kind of love she had with Eddie.

We squeezed hands and dug in to the food. Customers would be knocking on the door right at six if we didn't open on time, so we ate quickly, sharing stories about Georgia.

"Did you ever hear about her first day here?" Earl asked.

I turned to look at him and shook my head. "Were you here?"

He nodded. "I've been here forever, baby girl. I hadn't bought the place yet, but I was in the kitchen. Ms. Georgia was a new mom the day she walked in here. She had that sweet baby girl of hers strapped to her chest and she marched in that door and demanded she talk to the manager."

"No," I breathed. Georgia was always confident, but even I struggled to imagine her having that kind of gall.

Earl chuckled, his teeth bright against his dark brown skin. His shaved head and face made him look younger than he was. I guessed he was pushing seventy, but I really had no idea.

"Oh, she did. She said that she was going crazy at home with a new baby and she needed to work. Kathy was our manager then and she asked if Georgia had any experience. She said no, but she would learn quickly as long as she was given a shot and plenty of breaks so she could nurse her new baby," Earl said with a laugh.

"She demanded breaks and to bring Rissa with her?" I asked.

Earl nodded. "She was always a pistol. I never thought she'd be gone from here before me."

The overwhelming sadness slapped me across the face. It stole my breath and had me closing my eyes.

"None of us ever thought we'd be here without Georgia," Jean said. "It's not the same without her."

I forced a smile and tried to fake that I felt it. "You guys are all coming to the party Saturday night, right?"

They all nodded back. "Wouldn't miss it," Jean answered for everyone.

"Thanks. You know it'll mean a lot to Rissa to have as many people there as possible."

"How is she doing?" Megan asked. Megan was a few years older than me, but we'd become friends over the last year. She started working at Cracked when Georgia got sick and had to back off her hours. When Georgia found out she wouldn't be back, Megan agreed to take the job full time and got to know the woman she was replacing. It wasn't easy to have someone else step into Georgia's shoes, but Megan honored Georgia with everything she did.

I shrugged. "I haven't talked to her in a couple days. She's been working on a new app and is really busy. I don't know if she's trying not to think about today or if she's just under a deadline."

Karissa was a brilliant programmer and had a knack for developing apps that quickly went viral. She'd been secretive about her latest project, but she was close to finishing it last I heard.

"If today is this hard for us, I can't imagine how she's feeling," Jean said.

I nodded in agreement.

We finished our breakfast and cleaned up our seats. Earl went back into the kitchen while Jean, Megan, and I set the dining room up and refilled our own coffee cups.

Megan opened the door just before six to let in the customers waiting for breakfast. All the regulars knew it was Georgia's birthday and walked in with solemn faces and little fanfare.

I took orders and shared Georgia stories. For the first hour, it was hard to keep it together as everyone wanted to talk about her. A few of the guys who'd been her regulars for years got choked up.

By the time the early morning group headed out, I was ready for my five hour shift to be over so I could hide under my covers and cry instead of having to smile. I cleared tables and stocked creamer, sugar, and jelly. When the door opened again, I turned to tell the new guest to sit wherever they wanted and saw Ian Jameson.

Ian's sister had been my best friend forever, and Ian was…he was Ian. We were friends, too, but he'd become more in the months since we lost Georgia. I'd known him forever, and he was sort of like a brother to me also.

Except for the fact that he starred in some of my fantasies lately. Okay, all of my fantasies.

"What are you doing here so early?" I asked him with a teasing grin.

Ian didn't get up before ten most days. When he did, it was major. For him to be walking into Cracked just after seven in the morning was a shock.

"I wanted to check on you," he said softly once he reached my side. He kissed my cheek and lingered, pulling me into a hug.

I wrapped my arms around his neck, enjoying the embrace almost as much as I enjoyed the strength I got from him. "I'm okay," I said.

He pulled back and studied me carefully. I tried not to think about what he saw. My ponytail was likely messy by now, maybe even with something in it. My shirt had been clean two hours ago, but it had a smear of butter at my waist where my belly brushed over a plate without me realizing it and something sticky on my right breast that was probably syrup. And I was sweaty, because chubby girls were sweaty girls.

"Are you sure?"

I nodded. "Yeah. It's not easy, but I'm okay. Why are you really here?"

He shrugged. "I hear breakfast is the most important meal of the day."

I laughed and rolled my eyes at him. "Are you staying or are you on your way somewhere?"

"I'm staying. If that's okay."

"Of course. You can sit wherever you want."

"Where's your section?" he asked.

I pointed. "Any of those tables and the counter is mine."

He squeezed my hand and winked. "I'll grab a seat at the counter."

I nodded and finished what I was doing then went back to where he sat. I didn't want to appear too excited to see him, but it wasn't every day Ian stopped in when I was working. Still, I knew his order without asking.

"The usual?" I asked him when I made my way over. He already had a cup of coffee with one creamer and his menu was closed next to him.

He nodded. "Always. Thanks, babe."

I smiled, put his order in with Earl, grabbed plates from the window for another table, and checked in with customers who'd finished eating. When I made it back to Ian, he was watching me.

"What?"

He shook his head. "Just impressed with how you do this."

"What?"

"Talk to people all day. I couldn't do it."

"You talk to people," I argued.

He shook his head. "I talk to one customer at a time, then they go away and I work on their boat for a few weeks. You're dealing with multiple groups at once and always have a smile for everyone."

I shrugged. "I'm used to it, I guess. I don't really think about it."

The door opened and I glanced up with an automatic smile. I froze, my eyes going to Ian before going back to the man at the door as he walked closer.

I dated William Hogan for almost five years. It had been almost nine months since he dumped me, all because he thought I slept with the man he was about to take a seat next to.

"Hey, Blake. Can I get a coffee?" William asked, sliding onto the stool one away from Ian.

I nodded, turning away from Ian to grab the coffee.

"Willie," Ian said, using the nickname he'd given William, even though he knew William hated it.

"Ian. I guess I should have expected you to be here," William said.

I poured his coffee and played chicken, carrying the pot around to the rest of the restaurant filling mugs for everyone I spotted with less than a full cup.

By the time I made it back to the counter, William was scowling and Ian looked pissed.

"I'd like to order," William said.

I nodded and pulled my notepad out of my apron pocket.

"Two poached eggs. Dry rye toast with butter, not margarine, on the side and grape jelly. Four slices of bacon."

I wrote it all down and looked up. "Is that everything?"

"Yes," William said.

I nodded and put his order in. Ian's was ready, so I grabbed his plate and set his food in front of him.

"Looks great, babe. Thanks," Ian said.

I didn't think anything of him calling me 'babe,' but apparently William did. He grunted and huffed a laugh. A part of me wanted to explain to him that Ian called me that for years, but I didn't owe William anything anymore. He broke up with me.

I busied myself with other customers until William's food was ready. I set the plate in front of him and asked if he needed anything else. He looked around and said no, then dug in to his breakfast.

Ian's plate was empty so I took it and set it in the dish bin and asked if he wanted anything else.

"Another cup of coffee would be great," he said with a grin.

I nodded and poured him another cup, sliding a creamer in front of him to add to it. I put the pot back and leaned against the counter, watching the mostly empty restaurant.

The low moments were always the moments I talked to Georgia. She was constantly sharing wisdom and advice. She had an encouraging word for everyone and a smile and joke whenever you needed one.

The emotion got to me for a second, and I needed to get away. I tore off the bills for both men and set them on the counter, then left the floor. There was nowhere to hide, but the bathroom was a single stall and, thank God, it was empty.

I stuffed the back of my hand in my mouth to stifle the sob that wrapped around my throat and tried to push its way out. I sucked in a breath through my nose and blew it out again, over and over, until the need to cry passed.

I washed my hands and took a deep breath, then unlocked the door and started to leave.

Only to be pushed right back into the bathroom, the door closed and locked behind us.

"Ian, what are you doing?" I demanded.

"You're not okay, babe. Come here." He wrapped his arms around me and tucked my head under his chin.

I wanted to resist him, but he was there and he cared. I slid my arms around his waist and held on tight. Five minutes. I could take five minutes.

I let the emotions run, crying hard. My nose ran and my eyes flooded. The sobs I choked back a minute ago rushed right back to the surface and erupted from me.

Ian just held me, his warm hands gliding up and down my back in smooth, even strokes. I hated that he felt the ripples of my chubby back under his perfect palms. I couldn't hide my curves, but I did everything I could to mask them.

I pushed all thoughts of my excess of curves away and tried to slow my tears. After a few minutes, I finally calmed enough to pull back from Ian.

He wiped the tears from my lashes and cupped my jaw, tilting my head up to look at him. "Feel better?"

I smiled and nodded.

"Good," he said, pulling me back in and kissing my forehead. "I wish I could take this pain from you."

"Me, too."

He chuckled. "Willie's gone."

I laughed softly. "Did you run him off?"

He shook his head. "I didn't do anything."

I nodded. It didn't matter either way. William was a customer, nothing more. I didn't want him to be more. We were over, and I was okay with it.

Ian finally let us out of the bathroom, and we nearly ran into Jean. Her dark brows went up, but she didn't make a comment. I would definitely hear about it later, though.

Ian paid for his breakfast and kissed my cheek before he left, putting a huge tip down with his bill. I started to chase him out, but I could give half of it back to him another time. He knew I hated when he gave me a massive tip.

The rest of the morning went by quickly until a dark-skinned woman with wide, excited eyes walked in just after nine. The expensive purse on her shoulder and the MacKellar Cove sweatshirt said she wasn't a local, but she definitely looked like she knew where she was.

"Are you here for breakfast?" I asked her, holding a menu.

She nodded and gave me a kind smile. "I am. Thanks."

"You're welcome to sit anywhere you'd like," I said with a return smile.

She zeroed in on the stools at the counter and sat on one of them. I set her menu in front of her and offered her coffee.

"Oh, yes, please. I left really early this morning to get here. Can I ask you a question?"

I nodded. "Of course."

She drew a deep breath and smiled. "I was here a year

ago, and there was a woman working here. We talked for a while about, well, a lot of things. Her name is Georgia. Is she here by any chance?"

I sucked in a breath and smiled. It wasn't the first time a customer asked if Georgia was around. Everyone knew her. With visitors, I rarely told them the whole story, though. Just that she wasn't around.

"I'm sorry, but she's not here."

"Oh," the woman said, her face falling. "She promised me she'd be here today."

"She did?" I asked. That didn't sound like Georgia. She loved her customers, but she didn't usually schedule time to see them again. Even the regulars knew Georgia took a day off once in a while and didn't work seven days a week.

The woman nodded, her tight curls bouncing with the movement. "Maybe it's silly, but today's my birthday. She told me it was hers, too. When I was here a year ago, I told her I'd love to live here. She convinced me I should, and I finally made it happen. I have everything I own in my car outside, and I move into my new condo today. I was really looking forward to telling her I did it. And having a familiar face in town since I don't know anyone."

Well, shit. I had to tell her the whole truth after that confession…and it was going to hurt.

I drew a deep breath and smiled. "I'm Blake," I started.

"Hi, Blake. Trinity."

"It's nice to meet you, Trinity. I'm friends with Georgia's daughter. Her name is Karissa."

"Oh, would she know where her mom is? I brought her something. Maybe you can give it to Karissa to give to her mom?" She dug into her purse. "It's a necklace. I make jewelry and she commented on the piece I was wearing last year. I wanted to thank her for talking me into following my heart and living my dreams."

My breath stuttered as I inhaled. "Trinity, I'm sorry, but Ms. Georgia died a few months ago."

"What?" she asked, her smile crumpling. "No."

I nodded. "She had breast cancer. She didn't know how bad it was until it was too late."

"No," she said again.

I nodded, choking back my own tears as Trinity's raced down her cheeks.

I stepped around the counter and hugged the other woman. Trinity turned into my embrace and held on to me. I hugged her, knowing I couldn't provide the same comfort Georgia would but doing my best to console the sobbing woman in my arms.

"She okay?" Jean asked softly, stopping behind me.

"Georgia," I replied, knowing nothing more needed to be said.

Jean patted me on the shoulder and continued on.

Trinity hiccuped and drew in a breath. "I'm so sorry."

I shook my head as I stepped back. "Trust me, I've had more than my share of moments doing the same thing. Georgia never wanted us to cry over her, but she was an amazing woman. It's impossible not to miss her."

Trinity smiled. "I only knew her for a few hours, but she was so nice to me. She really made me want to live a better life. To be happier."

"Georgia had a way of inspiring people to do things they didn't even know they wanted to do."

Trinity chuckled. "That's exactly what she did with me. Now I feel like a fool for moving up here because of a woman I knew for a few hours who isn't here anymore. I hated the city because I didn't know anyone, and I'm in a new town and still don't know anyone."

"Well, you know me. And a few blocks down is a bar called O'Kelley's. Have you seen it?"

She nodded. "It's by my new condo, I think."

"Oh, you're moving in to Waterfront Villas? Nice. Karissa and our other friend Finley live in one of those. Anyway, Saturday night, we're having a party for Ms. Georgia at O'Kelley's. Starts at seven, but we'll probably be there until they close. You should come."

Trinity shook her head. "No, I couldn't impose."

I smiled and put a hand on her arm. "I promise you, we'd love to have you join us. Please come."

Finally, Trinity nodded. "Okay, I will. Thanks, Blake."

I grinned. "It's always good to have friends."

---

2

*B*y the time my shift was over, I was feeling better. I'd made a new friend, helped her feel welcome in MacKellar Cove, and I'd seen Ian.

If I was being honest, seeing Ian was always the highlight of my day, but I couldn't tell anyone that part.

I went to the back to grab my bag before heading out, but Earl stopped me.

"Hey, let me talk to you a minute. Come here and flip pancakes with me," he said in his gruff, affectionate tone. Earl was the kind of guy who hated to get emotional but always was. He loved all of us like we were his own kids even though he'd never had any. He'd never gotten married and never dated as far as I knew.

I took the spatula from him and flipped the row of pancakes in front of me while he added more to the griddle.

"I have a proposal for you. I've been thinking it's time to update that big wall overlooking the square. And I want you to do it," he said, not looking at me.

I couldn't look at him either. Cracked was the first building west of the town square, which was really a huge park that took up three full blocks in the center of MacKellar Cove. The square was where everything in town happened. It was iconic for visitors, but also a meeting place for locals. Adirondack chairs sat on a small hill overlooking the water with pathways that ran into town. A wide sidewalk from the square led up and down the waterfront behind the businesses that lined the small cove set off from the St. Lawrence River. The square was the centerpiece of MacKellar Cove, and overlooking the square was huge for business at Cracked.

And Earl was trusting me to create something that would help bring in that business. Wow.

"Are you serious?" I blurted, unable to stop the words.

He chuckled. "Of course. Who else would I get? The other muralist in town?"

My heart cracked just slightly that he was hiring me because I was the only one around.

Then he said, "You're my one and only choice, Blake. Because you're the best, and you love this place as much as I do. I can't imagine trusting this job to anyone else. And it will be a job. I'll pay for the paints and supplies and your time. Starting today. Work up a few ideas and we can talk whenever you have them ready for me."

Wow. I really couldn't believe it. I'd painted a few small murals around town, but nothing the size of Cracked. It would be huge for me, for my career. And it was the kind of challenge I'd been looking for. Something other than nondescript water scenes that I painted on a regular basis to sell in the local gift shops. They paid the bills, but they didn't always inspire me.

"I'd be honored," I finally told Earl. "I...thank you."

"There's one more thing," Earl said. He shuffled his feet and flipped pancakes, avoiding my gaze again.

"Spit it out, Earl," I said with amusement.

He grinned and said, "I want Ms. Georgia in the painting."

"What?" I breathed.

He shrugged and met my gaze with his own warm, sad one. "She was the heart and soul of this place for more than thirty years. I want people to know about her for another thirty or more. Eddie agreed to it. He said Georgia would have been honored."

"What did Rissa say?" I breathed.

Earl avoided my eyes again.

"You didn't ask her?" I half-shouted.

He shrugged. "I thought you could."

"Oh, jeez, Earl. You know you should have talked to her."

"I know, but I thought it might be easier coming from you. Will you talk to her?"

I nodded. We were all getting together that night to have our own quiet celebration for Georgia. I told him I'd figure out how to mention it to Rissa then headed out.

Instead of going straight home like I should have, I walked to the square so I could see the wall. I sat down in the middle of the first block, behind the Adirondack chairs on the grassy area that was a haven for young parents, and stared at the wall.

Ideas filled my head immediately, one flooding in after another. My fingers itched to start sketching, but I didn't have a book with me. I didn't even have a receipt from breakfast. I just had my mind, and I let it wander.

It wasn't long before it was wandering toward Ian. More and more my thoughts were consumed by him. Ever since our trip to Hawaii where Georgia and Eddie got married, I couldn't stop thinking about Ian. The way he held me close when we danced. The way his fingers teased my bare skin when he touched me. The way his eyes blazed with something dangerously close to need when I walked in on him in the bathroom.

I could still see the look in his eyes from that night. I didn't realize he was in the bathroom when I got back to the room we shared. I'd been in the hotel bar with the rest of the girls, and I thought Ian wandered off in search of someone to spend the night with. The room was silent when I let myself in, and I assumed the housekeeper left the bathroom door closed for some reason. I never imagined I'd walk in on Ian, water from his shower still running in rivulets down his chest. My gaze tracked those drops until they disappeared in the thick patch of hair surrounding his semi-erect cock. He yanked his towel around his waist, breaking the spell I was under.

Then my eyes snapped to his and every cell in my body tightened with an undeniable craving. His hazel eyes were stormy. Lust filled. Soaked with as much desire as my panties.

I backed up and closed the door, figuring someone else was in there with him. Why else would he have that look in his eyes?

But he was alone. No one else walked out minutes later when he did, wrapped in that towel, to get clean clothes. I was already in bed, covers pulled up to my neck, wishing I was alone so I could slide my hand into my panties and take care of the throbbing ache.

That was the moment I knew I needed to break up with William. He'd never looked at me like that. And I knew my friends were right saying it wasn't worth being with someone who didn't ignite that instant yearning in me.

The fact that William beat me to the break-up just meant I didn't have to be the bitch who dumped him after five years of dating and a proposal gone wrong.

I repeatedly tried to think of a time William made me half as turned on as Ian did with that one look and couldn't come up with one. It really wasn't fair that the only man who sparked my desires that much was a man I couldn't have. Even if he wasn't my best friend's brother, Ian wasn't a commitment kind of guy.

I sighed and told myself I needed to forget about Ian Jameson. He was a friend, but he didn't want to be anything more, so I needed to stop thinking about him as more. It wouldn't do me any good, and neither would fantasizing about him in public.

The sun was warm on my back as I walked home, letting me know summer was coming quickly. By the time I reached my door, my tee was sticking to my back and my thighs were chafed and sore. I stripped everything off in my room and tossed it all in the laundry basket in the corner. I needed a cold shower and some painting clothes so I could get some work done.

A FEW HOURS LATER, I jumped back in the shower to wash off the paint, then dressed in a loose pink top and jean shorts. We were having a mid-week girls' night at Book Boyfriends Unlimited, Finley's bookstore. It was a few blocks from Cracked on Riverview Road. She had a prime spot, right on the water where boaters could pull up to the nearby pier or anyone walking along the water could stop in. Finley was a die-hard romance fan and only sold romance novels, which worked out well for all of us since it was the only romance we had in our lives.

Finley already had the closed sign flipped when I got to the store. She locked the door also, since under normal circumstances, she would be open for business. I knocked and waited for her to let me in.

"Hey, hun," she said, wrapping me in a hug. Finley was like the sister I never had. We were opposites in many ways, but we always got each other. And no matter what else was going on in our lives, we were always there for each other.

"How are you?" I asked her. Ms. Georgia was like a mother to all of us, and I wasn't the only one struggling with the day.

She shrugged. "It's been tough. I had a reminder on my phone that I'd forgotten to remove. And I set up the display to showcase her favorites, but it was tough to walk by it all day."

I looked at the table front and center. Finley liked to ask locals what their favorite books were and maintained a display through the busy season with those selections. It gave everyone a chance to try out new authors. Ms. Georgia always participated. She was the one who got most of us into reading romance. She wisely told us the men in books weren't real, but we needed to wait for men like them in our lives. Men who would say sweet things and do whatever it took to make us happy.

I was finally ready to listen to her.

"How was your day?" Finley asked after a minute.

I shrugged. "Pretty good. Earl wants me to paint a mural on the side of Cracked."

"What?" Finley yelled. "Blake, that's awesome. That's not just pretty good."

I smiled and added, "He wants Ms. Georgia to be in the mural."

Finley's eyes narrowed. "Karissa hasn't mentioned this."

"That's because she doesn't know yet. Earl asked Eddie, but he wants me to talk to Rissa."

Finley huffed a laugh. "That was nice of him," she added with a dash of sarcasm.

I grinned. "Yeah, tell me about it."

Another knock on the door interrupted our discussion. Laura waved from the other side of the glass. She held up a plate that made my stomach rumble even though I didn't know what it was.

"Hey," Laura said once Finley let her in. "It's Oreo cheesecake. Ms. Georgia's favorite."

Finley and I hugged Laura and the three of us headed toward the back where Finley hosted book clubs and our group of friends every week.

Laura uncovered her cheesecake just as there was another knock on the front door. Finley went to see who it was while Laura and I talked.

"How are things at the clinic?" I asked.

Laura gave me a sad smile. "Today was tough. We had all hoped Ms. Georgia would ring the bell."

I nodded. "We did, too. How was Dr. Allison?"

Laura had a thing for her boss, who was Ms. Georgia's oncologist. Dr. Allison was brilliant and kind, but he was stiff and cold. He never joked or laughed with his patients. He was all business, which was fine, except people needed to feel like they were still human and not just a diagnosis.

"He was his usual self," Laura said softly. She defended him constantly, but there was only so much she could say about him when he acted like nothing bothered him.

"I guess you have to be detached in his world. Otherwise he couldn't do his job," I said, trying to be kind to the man. He did try to save Ms. Georgia, and he was well regarded locally and within the cancer community.

Laura nodded and looked up when Finley came back with Elise and Karissa. Karissa held up two bottles of wine. "I need to celebrate tonight."

"What are we celebrating?" Laura asked.

Karissa's grin was wide and bright, showing off her white teeth and the one with the slight turn to it. "I finished my app today. I think my mom inspired me. There was one thing I was working on, and she helped me get it straight today. It'll be live in a few days, and I'm so excited about it."

Karissa's fingers flew over her phone before she turned it around for us to all see what looked like the front of a bookstore.

"Book Boyfriends Wanted," Elise said.

Karissa nodded. "Yep. We're always talking about how cool it would be if we could wave a magic wand and turn the book boyfriends we love into real men. Well, this will do it."

"Your app is a magic wand?" Finley asked. One brow went up with her skeptical tone.

Karissa shook her head. "No, but it's close. It's a dating app, except everyone is going to be known because of their favorite characters. The questionnaire I developed has a lot of questions about who you are, but I added in a bunch that tell others who you are in a relationship and who you're looking for. If you want a guy like Mr. Darcy, you'll get paired with him. If you'd rather go for a Mr. Grey, you'll get him. It takes everything we love about romance novels and puts it into the real world so we can find real men who act like book boyfriends."

"Holy shit," Elise said. "This is perfect."

The rest of us murmured our agreement.

"Excellent," Karissa said happily. She opened her wine and grabbed one of the cups on the table. "Because you're all going to sign up and help me test it."

We looked at each other and nodded. "Okay," Finley spoke for us.

"Seriously?" Karissa asked. "I really thought it would take a lot more to convince you guys to give it a shot."

"A chance to meet a man who's going to love me like this guy?" Elise asked, holding up the book we've been reading. It was a new friends to lovers story with a dirty-talking, alpha hero. I totally understood her desire to find a guy like that.

Karissa nodded.

"Can I sign up now?" Elise asked.

Karissa laughed. "As soon as it's live! I'll let you guys know. And thank you."

We dug in to Laura's cheesecake and shared stories and advice we'd gotten from Ms. Georgia over the years. We drank Karissa's wine and celebrated her app and Ms. Georgia.

It was a perfect night.

"I met someone today," I told them after we'd finished the wine and eaten the entire cheesecake.

"Is he cute?" Elise said.

I shook my head. "Not a guy. A woman. She knew Georgia. Met her last year. They have the same birthday, and Trinity moved here today. She came in to Cracked and wanted to tell Georgia she finally followed her dreams and moved up here." I pointed at Finley and Karissa. "She moved into your building today."

"I remember Mom mentioning her. It was the first time she met anyone with her same birthday. She couldn't believe it took fifty-nine years," Karissa said with a smile.

"I don't think I know anyone with my birthday," Elise said. "That would be cool."

"Yeah," we all murmured.

"I invited Trinity to the party Saturday. I hope that's okay," I said.

"Of course," Karissa said. "Mom would have wanted her there. Did you tell her?"

"That she died?"

Karissa nodded.

"Yeah, I did. She kind of freaked out that she moved to a strange town and the only person she knew wasn't there. I told her we'd be her friends and invited her. I feel bad for her."

Finley and Karissa exchanged a glance. "We'll look for her in the building," Finley said. "I wasn't home all day so I don't know where she moved in. There are still a few vacant units."

"I was buried in my app and didn't leave until I came here. I don't know either," Karissa said. "But we'll meet her Saturday if we don't figure it out before then."

We were all a little quiet after that, thinking about Saturday and the party we were throwing. We were going to O'Kelley's, but we knew most of the town would show up. Everyone loved Georgia, and they all wanted to celebrate her birthday.

We talked a few more minutes, then everyone cleaned up and headed out. I yawned and stretched, knowing I was going to be exhausted the next day. I was running on fumes already and would be even worse in the morning. But it was good to see my friends.

We all walked out together after Finley made sure the store was locked. We hugged in front and said goodbye then all walked off in the direction of our homes.

I thought about how happy Karissa was about her app and wondered if I should have said something to her about the mural. It was chicken of me to keep my mouth shut, but maybe once I had a few concepts, she could help me pick something.

That was what I told myself, at least. I hoped it was true.

3

IAN

The steady hum of the sander in my hand soothed me. The vibration tingled up my arm, but the earplugs I wore and the sound of the sander blocked out everything outside my head. Too bad they couldn't block out everything inside my head, too.

Blake. It was always Blake.

I didn't want to block her from my mind, but I needed every last bit of energy to focus on work instead of thinking about her like I usually did. Especially since I saw her the morning before. With Willie.

She didn't look surprised to see him there, but she didn't look particularly happy to see him, either. When she ran off, I waited a few seconds for him to follow her, but he was clearly not interested. It fucking gutted me to hold her while she cried, but she let me comfort her so it was worth it. I hadn't had my arms around her since we danced together in Hawaii. Too damn long.

A knock on the side of the boat had me ready to rip someone's head off. I hated when people did that. It wasn't like they didn't know I was under there, working.

I stopped the sander and set it on the concrete next to me, then rolled out from under the brand new twenty foot boat to scowl at whoever was there.

Thankfully, I hadn't taken off my mask so the owner of the boat I was working on, Robert Mallory, couldn't see the look on my face.

I swiped off my mask and the shitty look and gave the guy a grin. The customer was always right, so I couldn't tell the guy he risked me putting a hole in the side of his precious boat if he kept doing that shit, but I really wanted to.

"Morning," I said cheerfully. Or as cheerfully as I could manage when my day was barely started and already being interrupted.

"It looks amazing," Robert said with a wide smile. He slid his hand over the side of the boat where I'd already spent days sanding the wood to be soft as Blake's skin.

"Thanks. It's going to be beautiful on the water."

Robert nodded. "I can't wait to take it out. It'll be ready for the Fourth, right?"

"Absolutely. Should be ready by the middle of June," I said. In my head, I added, "if I can get any work done," but I didn't push it. Not with a guy like Robert. Some of my other clients would understand, but Robert was the kind of guy who liked to be the smartest person in the room. Since he was paying me a hell of a lot of money to build him a large custom wood boat, I was going to let him believe anything he wanted.

"Sounds great. I can't wait to take her for a ride. The new girlfriend is excited to see it."

I nodded, knowing no words were necessary. Robert wasn't really paying attention to me, he just wanted me to know he had a young, hot girlfriend. He was pushing sixty, and with a girlfriend too young for me, he thought he was hot-shit. At thirty-six, I wasn't interested in dating twentysomethings anymore, but that was mostly because Blake was thirty-one.

"Have you come up with any names yet?" Robert asked.

I hated when owners asked me to name their boat. The name was the most personal part of a boat. The people who came to me without a clear idea of what they wanted to call it were always frustrating clients. They were wishy-washy about the whole thing, and once in a while, they backed out of the deal when the boat was done and the final bill came out.

Robert had more than enough money to pay for his precious boat, but if he had no connection to it, he wouldn't hold on to it for long.

"You could name it after the new girlfriend," I suggested.

Robert shook his head. "Nah. Then she'll start to think she has a place."

I bit my tongue to keep the words I wanted to say inside. I hated dealing with guys like him. Guys who thought women were disposable and could be recycled. Fucking assholes.

"What about naming her for your mom or your favorite fish?" I offered.

He scowled. "I'm glad you're better at building boats than you are at naming them. Keep thinking. Let me know when you come up with a good idea. I'll be back next week to check on things."

I nodded and waved as Robert turned and walked out of my shop. Having the place open was the only way I could work since cooling it would cost a small fortune, but it meant dealing with clients and douchebags like Robert whenever they felt like dropping by.

I was not looking forward to coming up with a name for his boat. If it were my boat, I'd be naming it for Blake. I almost named my boat for her, but she was dating Willie at the time and I didn't have the right. I still didn't, but I was going to earn the right.

I got back to work, letting the sander work the tension Robert created out of my body. Laying on my back and sanding the bottom of the boat above me was tedious, and after a while, my arms were throbbing and in need of a break.

As soon as the sander flipped off, two feet appeared next to me. I recognized the shoes immediately and grinned.

"What the hell are you doing here?" I asked.

"Had to see the master at work," Ramsey Holland said. Ramsey and I grew up together. We were rivals in high school for no other reason than we were in the same grade and competed for the same girls. Once we went to college and Ramsey got married, we found a way to be friends and laugh about the stupid shit we did when we were younger.

"Why are you really here?" I asked him.

He grinned. "Is this Robert's boat?"

I nodded, making note of the fact he was avoiding my question. "Yep. He just left. Had to come check in on me. Make sure I was taking care of everything. And seeing if I had a name for his boat yet."

"What a dick. Why would he want a boat if he isn't going to name it?"

I rolled my eyes. "To impress the newest twenty year old he's screwing."

"He should name it for her."

I shook my head. "He said then she'd think she has a right to something."

Ramsey scoffed. "He's such a piece of shit."

"No argument there. So, what's going on?" I asked again, hoping he wouldn't dodge the question a third time.

Ramsey shook his head. "I just wanted to go somewhere I would be welcome."

I nodded toward the office for Ramsey to follow me. I took a seat at my desk and stretched my back before reaching into the fridge for two bottles of water. "Not a beer, but better than nothing."

"It's going to be a hell of a summer," Ramsey said, untwisting the cap on his water and draining half of it.

It wasn't even Memorial Day yet, and we were sweating our balls off. He was right about summer, but that wasn't why he came to see me.

"I have a/c in the back. And a spare couch," I told him.

He blew out a breath and nodded. "Hopefully I don't need them. Melody hasn't mentioned throwing me out lately."

"What's going on with you guys?" I asked. I'd never worked up the courage to come out and ask the question, but I really wanted to know. If for no other reason than he was my best friend, and he and Melody were perfect for each other. She'd been a year behind us in school, and way too good for both of us, but she had a crush on Ramsey. A crush he returned. They'd been married almost ten years, but lately, things weren't going well.

"She wants another kid," Ramsey admitted with a hand on the back of his neck. "We talked forever that we were done trying after we lost the last one. We don't need more than one kid, but now she wants to try again."

"Shit," I breathed. Melody lost their second child when she was almost twenty weeks pregnant. It was the hardest thing I'd ever been through, and it wasn't my kid. Sitting on the outside and unable to do anything to help two people I cared about cut me up inside. They had a five year old who would be starting kindergarten in the fall, but she was their only kid.

Ramsey nodded. "Yeah, that's how I feel. Amber is perfect, but Melody said she's ready for another baby."

"And you're not?" I asked.

He shook his head. "I can't go through that again. Losing another one. I almost lost Mel when we lost Steven. She barely spoke to me for the better part of six months. She was so depressed, and she refused to talk to anyone. I can't do it again."

I drew in a breath. Melody wasn't the kind of woman who would take no for an answer. She was a woman who knew what she wanted and wasn't afraid to get it, no matter who stood in her way. Whether they tried again or not, Ramsey was at risk of losing her.

"I'm sorry, dude. I guess I'm as good at helping you as I am at naming other people's boats."

Ramsey chuckled at that one. "You'd have no issue if you were naming your own boat. *Blake's Dream.* Or maybe *I love Blake.* How about *Blake's Fantasy*? Big, long, wet wood? It would definitely be a fantasy since she'll never get anything that big from you."

"Fuck you," I said with a laugh. Ramsey was the only one who knew how I felt about Blake, and he was happy to take as many jabs at me as possible. He also encouraged me to tell her I loved her, but I was a chicken shit.

"No, that's what you want to do to Blake. You should, too. Maybe at the party this weekend you can corner her in the bathroom and tell her how you feel."

I rolled my eyes. "Yeah, that's a great idea. Hey, Blake. Let me treat you like all the other women I've fucked and press you up against this wall right here."

"You haven't been with that many in O'Kelley's have you?"

I scoffed. "No, but that's not the point. Blake's special. She's different. She's—"

"Everything," Ramsey said.

Our eyes met and we both nodded. Love definitely sucked. Especially when you weren't on the same page.

Ramsey and Melody would get there, but I wasn't sure if Blake and I ever would.

"I gotta head back to work. Just wanted to stop by. Work on those names. Maybe *Twenty-Something*? Then he can just say it's for whichever woman he's screwing at the time," Ramsey suggested.

I snorted. "Sounds perfect to me, but I'm not sure he'll go for it."

Ramsey grinned. "You should mention it to him. See if he bites."

"Yeah, I'll make sure I do that," I said sarcastically.

"It's a damn good idea," Ramsey said, walking out into the sunshine and waving.

I chuckled and shook my head. It was a good idea, but something told me the client wouldn't find the humor in it. Which meant I was back to work, and back to thinking of names that weren't Blake.

O'KELLEY'S WAS ALREADY CROWDED when I walked in Saturday night. Everyone in MacKellar Cove loved Ms. Georgia, and half the surrounding towns felt the same. Her funeral was insane, but her birthday was a celebration. We got the word out as much as we could, and it clearly worked.

I searched the stuffed bar and scanned the wooden booths until I saw the mousey brown hair I wanted to wrap around my hand and headed toward Blake.

"Hey," Finley said when I got close enough. "Blake saved you a seat."

Blake smiled up at me. "You said you were coming."

I winked and sat on the chair next to her. "I wouldn't miss it. Thanks."

She grinned, her cheeks pinking up. I wondered how far

that blush extended beneath the collar of her teal top. My gaze strayed to the exposed curves of her breasts and lingered until Finley cleared her throat.

I looked up at my sister, but she wasn't looking at me. Still, staring at Blake in a crowded bar wasn't a good idea. Someone would definitely notice, and even though my deadline was up, I couldn't have someone else telling Blake I wanted her. She was skittish, and she needed to realize on her own that I didn't hang around their group because of my sister.

Eddie and Karissa walked over carrying two pitchers of beer and two bottles of wine.

"Piper started us a tab," Karissa said. "Just for our table, though."

"There are a lot of people here," Eddie said as he set the beer down.

"Everyone loved Ms. Georgia," Blake said. "She's very missed."

Eddie nodded. He and Georgia were only married a few months, but he loved her almost all of his life. He told me once that he would never regret the life he had with his first wife, but he would always wish he had more time with Georgia. I couldn't help but wonder if Georgia told him about our deal and the promise I made her.

"Georgia loved everyone, too. She'd come home every day with new stories about the people she talked to. She knew what was going on with everyone in town. Whether they needed prayers or just someone to talk to, she was always thinking about everyone else. She told me I had to watch out for all of you," Eddie said with a grin.

The group was quiet as Eddie's words sunk in. Blake drew in a deep, shaky breath. I wanted to wrap her up and make her forget about every sad moment of her life.

Instead, I poured drinks for the table, handing out beer

and wine to each person without having to think about who wanted what. When we all had a glass, I lifted mine and said, "To Ms. Georgia. The mom we all loved as our own. The woman we all counted on for a laugh. And the friend we all had when we needed one."

"To Ms. Georgia," the others said with me.

We clinked our glasses together and drank to Ms. Georgia.

I watched Blake over the rim as I drank. Her tongue darted out to lick the edge of her glass before she pressed it to her lips. As the amber liquid eased to the top, her tongue darted out to taste it before it filled her mouth. I wondered if she kissed the same way she drank beer. Unable to wait for the kiss to start before she was licking her way inside. Excited and ready for more.

If I kept my promise to Georgia, I'd find out soon enough. Shortly after her wedding, she stopped by my shop and told me it was time to shit or get off the pot. Her words exactly. She said I'd loved Blake long enough, and since Willie had just dumped her, I needed to tell her how I felt before someone else asked her out.

I promised Georgia I would do something by her birthday, and seeing as how we were at her birthday celebration, my deadline was up. I had to either tell Blake I wanted her or walk away.

I fucking hated it, but Georgia was right. I couldn't keep wanting Blake forever. I never had trouble telling any other woman exactly how I felt, but with Blake I couldn't imagine telling her the truth.

Maybe it was because she was the only one I ever truly cared about.

That probably made me an asshole, but there was no one like Blake. There never had been and I doubted there ever would be.

People from town stopped by our table to share stories about Ms. Georgia with Eddie and Karissa. They laughed with them and offered condolences to the people who were still upset by her passing. The rest of us chatted quietly about summer coming and plans for the nice weather. After the bitterly cold winter, we were ready for some sunshine and bare skin.

Or maybe that was just me.

"Hopefully some hot new guys come to town this summer," Elise said with a smirk. "I could use a little excitement."

"Oh, please," Finley said, "you never have any trouble finding excitement."

Elise was definitely the friendly one of the group. She hooked up like I did, with no attachment and plenty of fun. She hit on me a few times, but I couldn't sleep with a friend of Blake's. I preferred to keep my one-night stands at a little more of a distance than that.

"I enjoy sex," Elise said. "And summer men are usually rich and willing."

"How do you know they're not married?" Laura asked.

Elise shrugged. "I don't always. I'm not into cheating, so I ask, but if they lie to me, it's on them. If I see a tan line from a ring or texts from a woman, I'm done, but if there's no reason to think a guy is married, I'll take his word for it."

"I'd be so paranoid," Blake said. "But I also don't hook up with strangers."

"You really should try it sometime," Elise said. "You still haven't slept with someone since William, have you?"

Blake glanced at me quickly then shook her head. My dick twitched at the thought. Not of Blake and Willie together, but of being the one to end her dry spell.

"Hello, Blake," he said from right behind me. Fucking Willie. Of course he had to appear right then.

She turned and smiled up at him. "Hi, William."

"How are you?" he asked, his gaze sliding around to the rest of the table.

Blake turned in her chair so she could look at him. Her knees brushed my hip. She apologized, then focused on Willie again.

Fucking Willie. Just looking at him and knowing he once had the right to touch her made my blood boil. Blake was mine. She didn't know it yet, but she was mine. She was going to be mine. And it was time for Willie and everyone else to know it.

4

———

"I'm good," she finally said to him. "Thanks for coming."

He nodded. "Of course. Ms. Georgia was always important to you."

The way he said it made it sound like he was there for her. Like he should be the one taking care of her. He lost that right.

I leaned closer to Blake and made sure Willie noticed me. I nodded up at him. "Good to see you again, Willie."

The twitch in his jaw made me smile. I loved pissing him off.

"Yeah, you, too," he replied through gritted teeth. "I seem to be seeing you everywhere with Blake these days."

Blake stiffened next to me. I put my hand on her thigh, drawing Willie's attention. I rubbed my thumb over the soft skin at the edge of her shorts and said, "She's a tough woman to stay away from."

Willie drew in a breath and stood straighter. "I see. Well, it was good to see everyone."

I stared after him until he was at the bar and not looking

our way. Then Blake shifted in her seat, dislodging my hand from her thigh. She spun around to face the rest of the table.

"I still don't know how you stayed with him so long," Elise said. "I guess he's cute, but he just has no personality. No passion. No excitement."

Blake shrugged and didn't answer.

"We're not here to dissect Blake's relationship," Finley said. "Let's give her a break tonight."

Blake offered her a grateful smile and relaxed a tiny bit. She was still stiff in her seat, but when her gaze strayed to the bar, she drew in another ragged breath.

Willie was watching her. Dammit. I knew what that look meant. He still wanted her.

I leaned closer to her and rested my arm on the back of her chair. She turned to look at me and smiled. I tugged her closer, and she sank against me. I kissed the top of her head and rubbed her bare arm.

The asshole in me pulled my gaze to the bar. Willie was watching us. I caught his gaze and nodded at him, a *fuck you* and a *thank you for being a dumbass* all at once. He scowled and turned away. And I just grinned.

"Why aren't we dancing?" Karissa asked. "This is a party. We should be dancing. Who's up to it? Eddie?"

Eddie chuckled and shook his head as Karissa stood and offered her hands to him. "No, honey. I'm going to pass on this one. Let you kids enjoy the dance floor."

"Who's with me?" Karissa asked, looking around the rest of the table.

Elise, Finley, Laura, and Blake all stood. They wore matching happy smiles.

Blake moved to get around her chair and lifted an eyebrow at me. "You coming?"

I didn't have to be asked twice. I stood and followed her to the dance floor, positioning myself behind her.

The women danced in a small circle. Other friends joined us, some pairing off. Blake glanced over her shoulder more than once at me. Her hips taunted me with every shift, and her smile teased me. She was happy. Carefree. Beautiful.

The song shifted and something slow came on. Karissa went to grab Eddie's hand, and Finley turned to another friend. Elise and Laura paired off, which left Blake and me.

"Want to dance?" I asked her from behind.

She nodded and spun to face me. Her arms went around my neck, her body close to mine. I slid a hand around her waist and pulled her closer. I brushed her hair back from her face with my other hand and smiled at her.

"You look happy."

She smiled. "I am. It's always fun to be out with my friends."

I nodded, wishing I was a part of what was making her happy.

"And you," she added softly.

I smirked. "I'm not one of your friends?"

She rolled her eyes and scoffed. "You know what I mean."

I nodded and eased her closer. She didn't fight me as our bodies touched. We shifted together, letting the music flow through us and dictate our moves. We didn't speak, just moved as one. As the song played, we grew closer and closer until there wasn't any space between us.

All of my attention was on Blake. The beautiful smile on her face. The happy look in her eyes. The soft feel of her skin. Then she scowled.

"What's wrong?" I asked.

She forced a smile. "Nothing. Just William is watching us."

I turned her so I could see Willie instead of her. His gaze was locked on us, his eyes straying down to where my hand rested on Blake's lower back.

"He still wants you."

She shook her head. "No, he doesn't."

I nodded. "He does. But we can end that now if you want."

Her gaze snapped to mine. Those big, brown eyes open and trusting. "How?"

"He'll back off if I kiss you."

She opened her mouth to say something then shook her head and looked away. "It's okay. You don't have to do that."

Every cell in my body tightened. This was my one chance. If she refused, I had to accept it and let go of her forever. I couldn't let her say no.

I tilted her chin up. She tried to look away, but I wouldn't let her.

"Blake, kiss me."

"Ian, really, you don't have to. I know how you feel about William, but I can handle him."

"Blake, kiss me."

"No, it's fine."

"Wow, you really know how to hurt a guy. I'm practically begging you to kiss me and you're refusing," I teased.

She huffed a laugh. "It's not that. I don't want you to feel you have to."

I eased closer to her, holding her chin up as I pressed my body to hers. "Blake," I whispered, "kiss me, Blake."

Without breaking eye contact, she nodded. Her hands tightened around my neck, drawing me down to her.

Everything moved in slow motion. The slick of her tongue over her lips. The soft inhale of her breath. The way her breasts lifted and pressed against my chest. Her fingers locking around my neck. Her curves cushioning my body.

Then my lips touched hers. Everything inside me exploded. Desire lit me up. The softest touch of her lips turned me inside out and had only one thought going through my head, the same word pulsing through my veins.

Mine.

I let Blake take the lead, holding back my desire for her. If I pushed too far too fast, I'd lose her before I even had her. Losing Blake wasn't an option, which meant she was in charge.

She kissed me like it was her first kiss. Tentative and questioning. Her lips parted, and her soft tongue darted out, just like it did when she was tasting her beer. I tilted my head to the side and slicked my tongue alongside hers.

She groaned and her kiss grew more bold. Her hands tightened, pulling at the hair on the back of my neck. Her tongue plunged into my mouth, then retreated like she realized what she did.

I pressed my hand into the small of her back, keeping her close, and she did it again. I stroked my tongue with hers, and teased the velvet soft skin under the edge of her top.

I wanted more, but Blake pulled back and took a deep breath. She chewed on her bottom lip and took a step back. "Maybe we should sit for a minute."

I nodded, hating that she was already pulling away from me. "Okay. If that's what you want to do."

She nodded and started walking toward the table. When we were halfway there, she stopped. "Um, I need to use the bathroom. I'll meet you at the table."

I stared after her as she rushed away. I made my way to the table and glanced back when I was at our seat. Blake was talking to a beautiful woman with spiral curls and dark brown skin. She pointed to our table, and I waved so the woman knew where Blake was pointing.

The woman grinned and nodded, then walked toward me as Blake turned toward the back where the bathrooms were.

I sat and caught a smirk from Finley. I gave her a questioning look, but she ignored me as the woman walked up.

"Hi. Blake said I should come sit here. I'm Trinity," the woman said.

"Oh, it's so nice to meet you," Karissa said. "I'm Karissa. Georgia was my mom. Blake said you met her. Thanks for coming."

Trinity grinned and waved as everyone else introduced themselves. Then she took Blake's seat next to me.

"Hi," she purred at me.

"Hey," I said. "I'm Ian."

"It's really nice to meet you."

I nodded. I didn't want to make her think I was interested, but if Blake wanted her there, I wasn't going to be rude either.

"Do you live here?"

I nodded. "Uh, yeah. I grew up here. Lived here my whole life."

"Wow. I just moved here this week. Maybe you can show me around sometime," Trinity said.

I forced a grin and nodded. "Maybe, but really, it's not that big of a town. If you drive around for five minutes, you'll see the whole town."

Trinity laughed, her dark curls slinging over her shoulder. "You're funny."

"Blake," I said, noticing she was standing at the edge of the table.

Blake just gave me a tight grin. "You guys all met Trinity."

Everyone nodded. Blake avoided my gaze. Without a place to sit, the wheels in her head were turning. She was getting ready to bolt.

"Come here, babe," I said, waving her over. I stood so she would think I was giving her my seat. Once she got closer, I tugged her to me and pulled her onto my lap.

"Ian," she breathed.

I slid one hand onto her thigh and the other over her back. "Just sit with me, babe."

"I'm too heavy," she said quietly.

"You're perfect," I told her.

She didn't fight me, but she didn't relax either.

Finley smirked again, but she didn't say anything. The others barely acknowledged what was happening. Except Trinity.

Trinity leaned closer to me. "I'm sorry. I didn't realize you two were together."

"We're not," Blake said quickly.

I glanced at Blake, then at Trinity. She smiled and winked at me, clearly picking up on exactly what was going on.

"Blake said you just moved here," Finley said to Trinity. "Where did you live before?"

"I grew up in Syracuse. When I was here a year ago, Georgia told me I should move up here. It took me a year, but I finally did it," Trinity said with a proud smile.

"I moved here a little over two years ago," Laura said. "I love it. I lived outside Buffalo, but I can't imagine living anywhere else now."

"Was it hard to find your place?" Trinity asked.

Laura shook her head. "Not really. I work at the oncology clinic so unfortunately, I met a lot of people quickly. And Georgia, of course, introduced me to these ladies who welcomed me in right away and became close friends of mine."

"She was amazing. I'm still having trouble wrapping my head around her being gone," Trinity said.

Blake drew in a breath, her body shifting against mine. With the height difference between us, her shoulder was against my chest. I pulled her closer to me and whispered, "Are you okay?"

She nodded and straightened, pulling away from me.

The mixed signals were killing me, but I wasn't about to give up yet.

"Hey, what do you call a grumpy cow?" I asked just loudly enough for Blake to hear.

She glanced at me and raised an eyebrow.

"Moooo-dy."

She snorted a laugh. "You're so corny."

I shrugged. "At least it made you laugh. That's the whole point."

She finally relaxed and leaned against me. Her arm went around my neck and her breast rested on my chest. I had to focus on my sister so my dick didn't make an appearance against Blake's hip.

"Let's dance," she said after a few minutes. "I need to move."

I followed her and the others to the dance floor. She danced with her friends, alternating between shaking her hips with them and singing along to the song and checking that I was still there.

I watched her the whole time, my gaze rarely drifting from her. She shimmied and shook and tempted and teased. By the time a slow song came on and she moved toward me, my entire body was wound tight.

"Dance?" she asked me with a tentative eyebrow raised.

I slid my arms around her waist and pulled her close. She took a deep breath and tucked her head under my chin. From the outside, we looked like we'd been together forever. We held each other close, our bodies moving in sync. And when she leaned back and looked up at me, I couldn't resist the urge to press my lips to hers again.

She reached up on her tiptoes to meet me halfway. Her breath tickled my face half a second before I tasted her again. I kept our kiss tame, sweeping through her mouth with my tongue but not taking things deeper. I ached to grind myself against her, to let her feel what she was doing to me, but I kept my hips shifted away, leaving a separation between us.

The song changed to something fast and Blake spun out of my arms. She danced and laughed and sang the songs at the top of her lungs. I took advantage of every opportunity I had to touch her, drawing her close to me and easing my arm around her waist as much as possible.

Blake had no clue how sexy she was. Every sway of her hips and shift of her body against mine had every inch of me tightening.

When we danced before, it was different. Her body brushed mine, but the air between us wasn't charged with lust and desire and opportunity. At least not on both sides. I couldn't remember not wanting Blake, but I also couldn't remember thinking she might want me.

She looked up at me, those eyes she thought of as boring and mousy nearly bringing me to my knees. I'd do anything for the woman in my arms. Her shy smile said she was okay with the way I kissed her, the way I held her. I wanted every man in the room to know she was mine, and if they even thought about touching her, they'd have to answer to me.

But Blake wasn't mine. Not yet. It was do or die time, and I needed to know if we had a chance. For years, I sat on the sidelines and waited for her to dump that loser, Willie, but he was the one who broke up with her. What a dumbass. He had no idea what he gave up. But he screwed me in the process. I didn't know if she was pining over him or not. Blake didn't tell me those things, and I couldn't exactly ask my sister.

Her arms around my neck teased the hair at my nape. Her fingers on me turned me on in ways I never thought possible. I shouldn't be ready to blow with all my clothes on and only a few kisses between us, but it was Blake. Everything about Blake was better, stronger, more.

"You okay?" I asked.

She nodded. "I'm perfect right now."

Well, damn. If that didn't give me a hard-on, nothing

would. I tilted her chin up again and brought my lips down to hers. I couldn't resist kissing her. I had my first taste, and I wasn't sure I'd be able to stop. It was everything I hoped it would be and more. Sweet and sensual with a hint of trademark Blake humor underneath.

Her lips parted under mine and I slid my tongue along hers. She moaned, a sound just loud enough to reach my ears. I'd never been one for public displays of affection, but with Blake in my arms, I couldn't stop myself from kissing her like she was the only thing keeping me alive. I sealed my body to hers, letting her feel the bulge in my shorts. She gasped again, and I thrust my tongue in deeper. She groaned and wrapped her arms tighter around my neck, bringing me closer to her.

Fucking heaven right there.

The music changed to something fast that had the other people on the dance floor jumping and moving and bumping into us. Reluctantly, I pulled back from Blake and drew in a steadying breath.

Everyone in the room was watching us, but I only cared about her. She was the only one that mattered to me, and if she was okay with me kissing her, then I was happier than a zebra mussel in the river.

5

BLAKE

"Can I walk you home?" Ian asked. His hand rested low on my back, possessive. There was no mistaking the hand.

Unless you knew it was all for show.

I nodded and let him lead me out the door. It wasn't unusual for us. We both lived in town. We both walked home from O'Kelley's most of the time. Ian sometimes walked with me, sometimes not. But with William inside watching us leave, there was only one reason Ian was walking me home.

Just like there was only one reason Ian kissed me.

I drew in a breath of fresh, cool air and shivered. I loved spring in MacKellar Cove, but it wasn't warm. Summer would be nice, but summer wasn't here yet.

"Are you cold?" he asked.

I shook my head. Not with his arm still around my waist and his body pressed against my side. Who would be cold with a man like Ian brushing against them with every step?

"I didn't know Willie was going to be there tonight," Ian said.

I could feel the edge in him as much as I could hear it in

his voice. I shrugged. "It wasn't a private party. He probably heard about it from someone we invited."

"You didn't invite him?"

I huffed a laugh. "Uh, no. I haven't spoken to him in months."

"Except the other day when he was at Cracked?"

I sighed. "Well, okay, if I have to serve him, I talk to him there, but we don't talk about anything other than how he likes his eggs cooked."

"You don't know how he likes his eggs cooked?" Ian asked.

I shrugged. "No. I don't know everyone's order."

"You know mine," he said, his voice low and husky. It rumbled through me, alerting every nerve in my body. Like they didn't already know he was right there, pressed against me and twisting my mind with his sexy alphaness.

"I've been serving you for years," I said. It was complete shit, and we both knew it. I'd been serving William for years, too. I couldn't explain why I knew Ian's order without thinking about it but had no idea what my boyfriend of five years liked to eat.

"So, if you don't talk to him, why did he come over tonight to say hello?"

I shrugged again. "I don't know. It's a small town. Maybe he wants to be nice."

"I think he still has a thing for you," Ian said, his fingers pinching into my side.

We reached my door, and I turned to him. "Yeah, I know. That's why you kissed me."

His hazel eyes held mine prisoner, not letting me look away. "That's not why I kissed you, Blake."

I laughed. "Yeah, okay. Why else would you kiss me?"

He tilted my chin up, his eyes blazing with something that looked like desire.

I swallowed roughly and drew in a sharp breath. "Ian?"

"Me kissing you had nothing to do with Willie, Blake."

"What did it have to do with?"

"You, babe. All you."

"Ian?"

"Invite me inside, Blake."

"Why?" I stammered.

"Because I want to kiss you some more."

I ran my tongue over my lip and drew it into my mouth. I bit down, hard, because I had to be dreaming. No way was Ian Jameson standing on my doorstep and asking to come in so he could kiss me.

But he was still there. Still looking at me with that same look he gave me when I walked in on him in Hawaii.

Sharing a hotel room was supposed to be simple. William decided not to go, and Ian decided to go, both at the last minute. It was easy since I had a hotel room to myself and everyone else was already paired up.

I never thought it would spark fantasies about my best friend's older brother for months.

"Blake," he said again, firmly. He wasn't taking no for an answer. And I didn't want to give him that answer.

I dug my key out of my pocket and unlocked my side door, letting us in. Ian kicked the door closed behind us and followed me through the dark house. His hand tugged my shirt up, his warm fingers brushing my bare skin. I nearly groaned at the sensation.

"Blake, where are you going?"

"Couch. I don't think I can stand if you kiss me again. Not now."

He chuckled, a sound full of male pride. He knew he was hot. Hell, everyone in town and half the towns on the St. Lawrence River knew he was hot. Ian was well-known, and not just for the amazing wooden boats he built and restored.

I wasn't going to think about that at the moment. I wasn't going to sleep with him. But I'd happily make out with him for a while and add it to my mental fantasy video.

Once we were out of the hallway, he wrapped his arms around me and pulled me flush against him. We walked together, our steps synced as our bodies moved toward the couch.

Ian knew my home as well as I did. He turned on the lamp next to my couch and turned me toward him. "Blake."

"Hmm?"

"Breathe, babe."

I sucked in a breath and tried to draw another one.

"Blake, breathe. Calm down, babe."

I nodded and tried to force myself not to hyperventilate. Ian ducked down, catching my gaze and breathing deep. I imitated his breaths, feeling my heart rate calm down and my breathing level out.

How was the man who caused the problem also the solution?

"Blake?"

"I'm okay."

"Do you want me to go?"

"No!"

He chuckled and swiped his thumb over his lower lip.

"Sorry, I mean, no. I'd rather you didn't."

"Good," he said, his voice slipping back into that deep, husky tone that lit my nerves on fire and made my panties wet.

He earned his reputation. Without even trying, he had me desperate for him to kiss me or touch me or something.

He took my hand and led me to the couch. He sat and pulled me down next to him. "You're in charge here, Blake."

I shook my head.

"No?"

"I think you need to be in charge."

He raised an eyebrow at me. "Are you sure about that?"

I nodded. I wasn't sure about anything, but I knew I'd embarrass myself if I tried to initiate anything. My experience paled in comparison to his.

"Come here, babe," he said gently, wrapping his arm around my back and lifting me onto his lap.

I straddled him, sinking onto his lap. I jerked up when I felt a firm ridge at my core.

"You're not running from me, Blake."

"I didn't run," I argued.

He pressed his fingers into my back, just above my waistband, guiding me down onto him.

"Ian?"

One hand trailed down my throat, drawing goosebumps from every inch he touched. His fingers grazed back up then speared into my hair and tugged me down to him.

He didn't kiss me slow. Not like he did on the dance floor. Oh, no. This kiss was anything but slow. All of a sudden, his tongue was in my mouth, licking my tongue, thrusting, tasting me. The hand in my hair tilted my head to the side, and he plunged in even deeper.

He withdrew just enough for me to whimper at the loss, then thrust in again. In and out, gentle and firm, kiss and nip. He drove me crazy. Every time I thought I could keep up with him, he changed what he was doing and made me guess again.

His hand on my back pressed me closer to him until my entire body was plastered to his. My breasts squished to his chest, my curves tight against his planes. I wanted to hide my body from him, but he slid his hand up and down my back, over my side, and down my thigh, touching all the curves that I hated.

I wrapped my arms around his neck and told myself to

enjoy it while it lasted. Ian wouldn't hang around long. He wasn't the kind of guy who stuck, and I wasn't a one night stand type of woman.

I lost myself in Ian, enjoying the feel of him between my thighs and his kisses making me crazy. When he left, I was going to have plenty of material to fuel my fantasies.

Just when I thought I could get a few more minutes of pleasure, a knock on the door echoed through my house. I jumped back, my breath freezing in my throat.

I climbed off of Ian and dragged him to his feet as the knock came again. "You need to go," I said, shoving him toward the side door.

"What?"

"Go. Now. I'm sorry, but you can't be here right now."

"Why the hell not? Who is that?"

"Please, Ian," I begged, tugging on him.

He didn't budge. He stared at my door, then took in my expression, and his hardened. "I kissed you on the dance floor at O'Kelley's. In front of the whole fucking town, Blake. Who's at your door at two-thirty in the damn morning?"

"Ian, just go."

He shook his head and shook my hand off him. "Hell, no. I'm not going to sneak out the back so your late night booty call can come in. If he wants to come in, he can see me here. I'm not a warm up, Blake."

"Ian, don't!" I shouted as he walked to my front door and yanked it open.

"Oh, hi," my mother purred from the front porch. Thankfully, she didn't fall inside when he opened the door.

"Ms. Dewitt?"

She laughed. "Oh, honey, you don't need to call me that. I'm Nadine, gorgeous."

"Mom," I hissed.

"What?" she blurted. Then she looked at Ian. "My

daughter is no fun. She's always telling me to stop drinking and sleeping with men I don't know, but why would I do that?"

"Mom, please," I said, moving toward her. I pulled her inside and closed the door behind her. I managed to get her to the couch, where she sank down in the same spot Ian and I had just been.

"Blake, you should sleep with that sexy man I just saw. I don't know where he went, but he was h-o-t, Blakey."

My cheeks heated from embarrassment. I couldn't look at Ian. I never should have let him come in. She always showed up on Friday and Saturday nights. Thankfully, she didn't do this during the week, but weekends were when she 'let go.'

"Okay, Mom. Let's get you to sleep," I said.

"You really need a better couch," she grumbled as she laid down. "Or a bed for me to crash in. You should really take better care of me."

"Or you could stop drinking and go home," I said softly. It wouldn't matter if she heard me or not. She wasn't going to quit. She'd been doing this off and on since I was in high school. I spent nights at Finley's house on the weekends so I didn't have to live with it, but Finley never spent the night at my house. Not after the first time Mom came home drunk and Finley worriedly asked if she was okay. I'd hoped my mom would have outgrown getting drunk most weekends, but so far I was the only one bothered by it.

Her soft snores were the only response I heard from her. I covered her with the blanket on the back of the couch and went to my kitchen. I took the vinyl tablecloth out of the trash can in my pantry and carried both back to the living room, painfully aware of Ian's silent stare following my every move.

I moved the coffee table away from the couch and laid the

tablecloth on the floor. I set the trash can in front of her where she wouldn't miss.

Then I forced a smile and looked toward Ian. "You should go."

"Blake," he said softly, his tone gentle and questioning.

"It's fine."

I swallowed the emotion in my throat and squeezed my eyes shut. I grew up in MacKellar Cove. I went to college in Syracuse, but I moved back home once I was done. I lived with Mom for a few years, but as soon as I could afford my own house in town, I moved out. On my own. And during all those years, I kept my mother's drinking from my friends.

Having Ian witness my biggest shame doused any chance of flames.

He moved around the couch and approached me. I wanted to run from him, but it wouldn't change anything. Better I face it head-on and end whatever this was before it got started.

"Thanks for walking me home," I said when he reached me.

"Blake, babe. Look at me." His tone pried open all the walls I built around my feelings about my mother.

"I don't want to talk about it," I said softly. I couldn't trust my voice. Any louder and it would shake and he'd know how upset I truly was.

"I'm not going to make you talk."

"I'm not really in the mood anymore, either."

"Do you really think I'm trying to get in your pants after your mother just tried to feel me up and then told you to sleep with me?"

I closed my eyes as a fresh wave of shame washed over me. All the times I hated dealing with her paled in comparison to Ian seeing it.

He pulled me into his arms, enveloping me in a warm hug

that undid every shred of my resolve. I wrapped my arms around him and drew in a ragged breath. I wanted to cry, but I couldn't. Not until he was gone.

"This isn't the first time she's done this, is it?"

I shook my head.

"How long, Blake?"

I shrugged.

"Oh, babe. Years?"

I hesitated then nodded.

"Blake," he groaned. "Why didn't I know about this?"

I laughed and pushed out of his embrace. "Because no one knows. I don't tell anyone. Finley doesn't even know. Do you really think I want everyone to look at me like you are right now? She holds it together well enough when she's out so people don't really know how much she's drinking. She's never passed out in public or gotten sick. She saves that pleasure for me."

"You shouldn't be dealing with this alone," he said softly.

I laughed mirthlessly and gestured around the room. "And who do you think is going to help me? I'm an only child. I have no father. And the only man I've been involved with in the last decade thought I cheated on him with you in Hawaii."

"What?"

I sighed and dropped my head into my hands. "Forget it."

"Willie thinks we slept together? Why?"

"I don't know! It doesn't really matter, though, because he broke up with me months ago. And after tonight, he's convinced he was right the whole time about us."

"Do you still love him?"

I snorted. "I don't think I ever loved him."

"What do you mean?"

I shook my head and walked into the kitchen. I needed water, and it seemed Ian wasn't leaving any time soon. I poured us both waters and handed his over. I drank mine, stalling for time.

"What do you mean you never loved him, babe?"

I shrugged. "I think I wanted to. I wanted to believe he could be...important to me. Our relationship was always easy, comfortable. We never fought, we never argued, we just existed together. When he asked me to marry him, I couldn't imagine living with him. Having him here or moving in with him felt like it would be more annoying than anything else. And after going to Hawaii and seeing Georgia and Eddie, and all those other couples, I knew I couldn't stay with him."

"I thought he broke up with you," Ian said.

I rolled my eyes. "Thanks. Yeah, he did. I chickened out when we got home. But I'd pulled back. He convinced himself I cheated on him while I was gone, and he said we always seemed like we weren't just friends and decided I must have slept with you."

"Did you tell him we didn't?"

I nodded. "Of course, but he didn't believe me. I'm sorry. I should have told you in case someone ever says something."

"I don't care what Willie thinks or says. I only care about you, Blake."

I drew in a breath, feeling like he meant it. We'd been friends forever, though. I knew he cared. He just didn't care like I hoped someone would care about me.

"I should go," he said, draining his water and putting the glass in my dishwasher. He knew I hated having dirty dishes in the sink.

I followed him to the door and held it open when he walked out.

"I'm sorry the night ended the way it did."

I nodded.

"Maybe we can try again sometime."

I smiled sadly at him. I would happily try again, but Ian

didn't go back to the same girl more than once. I'd missed my chance.

"I'll see you around, Ian."

He leaned forward and kissed my forehead. "Lock your door, Blake."

I nodded and closed it behind him. I turned off the lamp and checked on my mother then made sure the side door was locked. I put my glass in the dishwasher with Ian's and turned off the kitchen light, then headed to bed. Alone.

As always.

6

The following week went by quickly. We skipped girls' night Sunday because of Ms. Georgia's party, so I avoided answering questions about Ian. Finley texted me to see if everything was okay, and I assured her it was. She didn't push, and I didn't offer anything. It was like my night with Ian never happened.

Maybe it was all a dream. That was what it felt like. He didn't come in to Cracked while I was working, and I didn't see him in town. Usually I ran into him once or twice a week, but I didn't see him at all.

I had my shot at a night with Ian, and my mother ruined it. With zero remorse. The next day, she got up all happy and cheerful, smiling as she made breakfast. She had no idea what she interrupted or what she said to me. I wanted to hate her for it, but she was my mom.

Karissa told us her new app was live and asked us to all sign up. I'd never tried online dating, but I liked the idea of meeting a guy who reminded me of Westley from *The Princess Bride*. Hell, I just liked the idea of meeting a guy who would be there the next day. One who steamed my blood like Ian but stuck around like William.

Yeah, right. No guy like that was going to stick with someone like me. It wasn't an accident I didn't see Ian for a week. He went home and realized touching me was an accident. My challenge was going to be acting normal next time I saw him. Ugh. Normal left the building with his first kiss.

Damn him for making me think a guy like him could want a woman like me. Or that I deserved to have passion in my life that didn't fade. A few hours with Ian Jameson and I was done. Ruined. No other man would do. Dammit.

It was my turn to bring dessert to girls' night so I baked my better-than-sex chocolate cake. With moist, dense cake and sweet, rich cream cheese frosting, the cake was to die for. And in my experience, it really was better than sex. If it could talk to me, I'd seriously consider building a life with cake.

Finley and Karissa were approaching the door to Book Boyfriends Unlimited when I was. Finley groaned when she saw the cake through the container.

"Is that better-than-sex cake?"

I nodded. "It is. Since I'm not having any sex, I figured I could enjoy some cake."

Karissa snorted. "It's damn good cake, but I'd take the sex any day. It doesn't stick to my ass."

"Well…" Finley said with a smirk as she unlocked the door. "Sometimes it does."

"Ew," I blurted. "I don't need to think about you doing that."

"Doing what, Blakey? Anal sex is hot as fuck. There's nothing wrong with it," Finley said as we walked inside.

"Whoa," Laura said from right behind us. "I clearly missed something."

Karissa laughed. "I said I'd rather have sex than cake since it doesn't stick to my ass. Finley said sometimes it does, and sweet, innocent, un-fucked Blake got freaked out."

"I'm not sweet and innocent," I said with a scowl.

"But un-fucked applies?" Finley asked sweetly.

I rolled my eyes at her. "We all know I'm not getting any."

"And even when you were, it wasn't that good," Elise added, walking inside. "You didn't sleep with Ian last weekend?"

The others gave her a wide-eyed look that told me they all agreed not to ask me about Ian.

"Whoops," Elise said. "I mean, how was your week?"

I sighed. "No, I didn't sleep with Ian. He walked me home, and that was it."

"There's no way you and Ian left O'Kelley's together and didn't do something. I saw the way you two were dancing. And the way he kissed you," Karissa said.

I scoffed. "He kissed me because he thought William was trying to get back together with me or something. He was trying to get William to back off."

"Why did he think that?" Laura asked.

I shrugged. "Because William showed up at the party. I told him there's no way William wants to get back together."

"My brother is not the type to make out on the dance floor. With anyone. For any reason," Finley said with a toss of her chocolate hair.

I shrugged again, trying not to think too much about it. It might have been out of character for Ian, but nothing happened and nothing was going to happen. We kissed and he left when my mom showed up. End of story, end of opportunity.

"Has anyone gotten a match on Karissa's app?" I asked, hoping they would grab on to the subject change.

"Ooh, yeah, have you?" Karissa asked. "I've been advertising it, but it can take a little while for something like this to catch on. We definitely need more men."

"I mentioned it to Ian," Finley said casually.

My gaze snapped to hers, and she smirked. The tilt of her head said she wasn't done with the other conversation. My throat itched and my palms dampened. I didn't want to tell Finley how close I got to having sex with her brother. When we were younger, she told me how weird it was when any of our friends said Ian was hot. I couldn't imagine that changed just because we were in our thirties instead of teenagers.

"That's awesome," Karissa said. "I should ask him if I can put up a sign at Jameson Wooden Boats."

Finley nodded. "I'm sure he won't mind. He's been talking it up to the people he sees."

"I love your brother," Karissa said.

A knock on the door stopped our conversation. Finley got up to see who it was while I cut the cake and handed out plates to everyone. When Finley came back, Trinity was with her.

"Hey," I said to Trinity. "I'm so happy you decided to join us."

"Thanks for the invite. It's hard sitting around my apartment all week with no one to talk to," Trinity said.

"I'm the same way," Karissa said. "I try to take a walk on the waterfront every day and go out to eat a few times a week. It's so much better than being locked away and feeling like a hermit."

Trinity nodded. "That's a good idea."

"You guys should get together sometime, too," Laura said. "Since you're living and working in the same building. Go to each other's apartments to work or something."

Trinity and Karissa exchanged a look and shrugged. "We could do that."

"Have you gotten Karissa's new app yet?" Finley asked

Trinity. "It's a dating app based on the book boyfriends you wish were real."

"Yeah?" Trinity asked. "That sounds awesome."

"Thanks," Karissa said with a grin. "I'm trying to get as many people to sign up as possible."

Trinity nodded. "I could use all the help I can get. Most men take a look at my boobs and forget there's more to me than that. And if I can meet more guys like Ian, I'm all for it." She turned to me. "I'm sorry, again, for getting in between you guys. I had no idea you were starting something."

"We're not," I said firmly. "Ian isn't mine."

Trinity narrowed her eyes. "He looked like he was. Or wants to be."

I shook my head. "Ian doesn't do relationships. He's allergic to them. He's a one and done kind of guy, and we're done."

"So, you did sleep with him," Elise said with a wide grin. "I knew it."

"No, I didn't. I...we got interrupted. But I told him we weren't having sex. We just kissed," I said.

"We all saw you two kissing on the dance floor," Elise said. "We want to know what happened when you left O'Kelley's."

I shrugged. "More of the same. He walked me home, told me to invite him in, and we kissed for a few minutes on my couch. Then he left. I haven't seen him since."

"Ouch. Sorry, hun," Elise said.

"That sucks," Karissa echoed.

I shrugged, trying not to get upset. It made no sense that I wanted to cry over a missed chance with Ian but barely cared when things ended after five years with William.

Finley took a bite of cake and changed the subject from my non-existent dating life to all the ways cake was better than men and book boyfriends were better than real ones. I sat back and let the conversation happen around me. I grabbed a second piece of cake and knew no one would care. I wasn't going to be judged by my friends for how wide my hips were or how small my breasts were in comparison. They weren't going to tell me I should stop eating or try something healthier or exercise more. They loved me for exactly who I was. And I had to be okay with that because it was very possible I wasn't going to find the kind of love I read about in books. That kind of love was fun to dream about, but I'd never felt it in real life.

I HUNG around after the others left to help Finley clean up. She pulled out the small vacuum from the back to make sure no crumbs were left behind. We learned that the hard way.

I put the lid on my empty cake container and wiped down the table. Unused paper plates went back to the storage cabinet with the plastic silverware. I tied up the trash bag and took it outside, then grabbed the books Finley set aside for me. She always grabbed some of the new releases she thought I'd enjoy and put them aside for me to read.

I read the back cover of one with a beautiful sunset and a lighthouse off in the distance.

"That reminded me of our lighthouse," Finley said. "It sounds good."

I finished reading and nodded. "Yeah, it does. I need some sexy, happy stories right now."

Finley chewed on her nail for a second then caught my gaze. "You know I'm okay with you and Ian together, right?"

I huffed a laugh and shook my head. "You don't need to worry about it."

"I think I do."

I shook my head again. "Really, nothing happened. We

kissed, yeah, but…I know how Ian is. I'm not going to chase him or think he's in love with me or whatever. He got caught up in the moment. I'm new to him. But he doesn't go back. We both know that."

Finley sighed. "But you do, Blake."

I pressed my lips together and shrugged. "It doesn't matter. They were really, really good kisses, but that's all. I'm not going to put you in the middle of us. And if you see him, you can tell him I'm not going to be weird."

"Why would you be weird?" she asked.

I shrugged again. "I'm not. But if he's avoiding me, I don't want it to be because he's worried I'm going to be one of those girls who doesn't let go. I know it was a one-night, one-time only thing. It's done, and it's fine."

"Blake," Finley said.

I didn't want to look at her. She knew me too well. She would see how much I wanted to believe my words if I met her gaze. She would know I was full of shit but trying to be strong.

"Do you like my brother?" Finley asked softly.

I drew in a slow, unsteady breath. "I never did before, Finley. And this isn't going to be a thing. Sharing a room with him…"

"That was months ago. Did something happen?"

I shook my head. "No, of course not. I mean, I walked in on him in the bathroom once, but I left. And—"

"What do you mean you walked in on him? What was he doing?"

I swallowed, my throat dry and scratchy. "Um, he was… he…I think he just jerked off when I walked in."

"Did you see him? You know, his…It's my brother. Don't make me say it," Finley said with a sickened look.

I laughed. "I won't. And, um, yeah? He pulled his towel closed, but, um, yeah."

"Why didn't you tell me about this?"

I shook my head. "Why would I? I walked in on your brother and got dumped because William thought something happened."

"Wait, what? William found out? How did William know about that?"

I drew in a breath and twisted my hair behind my shoulder. "He doesn't know about that. He just convinced himself something happened with Ian and me since we shared a room. He broke up with me because of it."

"Shit, Blake. Why didn't you tell me all this? I'm your best friend."

I shrugged. "I felt…I didn't want to tell anyone. It was easier to tell everyone things ended because we weren't right for each other. I didn't want it to get back to Ian that William thought something happened. I didn't want him to think I told William anything."

Finley sucked in a breath and let it out slowly. Her gaze wandered as she processed everything. Finally, she shook her head and stood. "Ian won't care what William thinks or said. He does care about you, though. He'd do anything for you, Blake."

I nodded. "I know. I'm like another sister to him."

Finley shook her head but didn't argue. "I think you should tell him what happened with William."

I shook my head. "He knows. I don't think William ever said anything to anyone, but seeing us together…who knows. Either way, Ian and I are done."

Finley opened her mouth to argue again but I cut her off.

"Fin, I know you mean well. You want me to be happy as much as I want you to be happy, but curvy girls and sexy boat builders don't fit together. That's just my reality. I've always been okay with it. There's no reason for that to change."

"I think you're wrong, Blake. I think we're amazing women and we all deserve sexy men who will love our curves."

I smiled. "We are amazing, but we both know men who look like Ian usually judge women who look like us. We do deserve amazing men, and I hope we find them one day. I just don't think your gorgeous, perpetually single brother is going to be that guy for me."

She sighed. "You never know, Blake."

I just smiled at her. I did know. And I couldn't live in a dream world any longer.

ON MY WALK home I remembered I was going to talk to Karissa about the mural. I should have already asked her, but I convinced myself if I had a concept drawn up, it might be easier for her to agree.

I walked by Cracked and into the square. The lights strung up on the pergola and the streetlights that lined the square gave me enough light to see the wall.

Cracked was scrawled on the side in peeling paint. The old brick had been painted a few times, with the previous layers showing through. When I was little, the wall had a picture of what was supposed to be the shoreline. It was kind of abstract and I never understood it.

The last painting was done when I was in middle school, about twenty years ago. It was simple with the name and MacKellar Cove, New York written on the side. I liked the simplicity of it, but I agreed with Earl that it needed to be spruced up a bit.

I just wasn't entirely sure how to do it in a way that honored our small town and the woman who made the town feel like home to so many people.

I stared at the wall a little longer, then laid back on the grass. It was starting to get cool, but I welcomed the temperature. Talking about Ian heated me up, and that wasn't ever a good thing. It was easy to let my imagination get carried away, but my heart was dangerously close to following after dancing with him and kissing him. I didn't blame any of the women who ended up in his bed. Not after being on the receiving end of Ian Jameson's flirty side.

Laying there wasn't doing me any good. I stood and made my way through my sleepy little town alone. It was well past dark by the time I got home. My small house was quiet and dark and reminded me of walking in with Ian's arms wrapped around me.

Yep. He definitely ruined other men for me. Damn him.

7

IAN

I was a lucky son of a bitch. I pretty much always had been. A lot of things came easily to me. Girls, work, life. I had a great job and lived in one of the most beautiful places in the world.

But a week without Blake was seriously making me think I wasn't as lucky as I once thought I was. I was cranky and in general a pain in the ass. I was even annoyed with myself.

Which was why it wasn't a big surprise when my dad walked in my door mid-morning on Monday.

"Hey, son," he said in his trademark no-nonsense tone that set my teeth on edge.

I loved my dad. We'd always had a good relationship. Finley and our mom were close, and my dad and I were close. He was the person I talked to about starting Jameson Wooden Boats, and pretty much every other major decision of my life.

"Morning," I grumbled. I poured him a cup of coffee and handed it over. Black, like he'd taken it my entire life.

"Beautiful day, isn't it?"

I nodded, sipping my own cup. He liked small talk before

he tore me a new one. I wasn't sure if he was there to rip into me about my attitude lately or if it was something else, but I wasn't going to give him new ammunition.

"Is this Robert's boat?"

I nodded again and led the way to the beautiful creation that still didn't have a name. The guy was a dickwad, but he had great taste when it came to boats. His overall design was sleek and stunning, and with my added touches to make it a damn good boat, it was going to be a showpiece on the water.

"You've done a hell of a job. Is he the reason you've been an ass lately? Or is it a brunette that's got you all twisted up?"

I shook my head. "It's nothing."

"Blake Dewitt is not nothing, son. Especially not after you two were kissing all night at Georgia's party then left together."

"How do you know about that?" I blurted.

Dad chuckled, the light sound reverberating off the steel walls that surrounded us. "It's a small town, Ian. Everyone knows everything here."

I scowled at him, hating that all of MacKellar Cove likely knew my shame. Not only had I blown it with Blake, but it was public knowledge that even my dad heard about.

"I was just helping her out."

"That's not the way I heard it. And not the way I see it either. You've loved Blake for years. I'm guessing you saw that night as your one shot with her."

"She didn't want me, Dad. It was my one shot."

Dad shrugged. "Your mom asked me out three times before I said yes. I had other things going on. If she'd given up after one time, you and your sister wouldn't be here."

I'd heard the story many times before. Mom and Dad hit it off, and Mom was the confident one. She knew they had something special long before Dad would admit it, and she made sure he knew it, too.

But Blake and I weren't my parents. We had lives. We weren't in college. And things were complicated. Especially things like her mom.

"It's not that simple," I told my dad. I picked up the sander and moved toward the boat. I needed to get to work, and I didn't want to fight with my dad.

"Nothing is simple when it involves love, son. Your mom and I have had some real problems over the years, but no matter what, being with your mom has always been the most important thing to me. Is being with Blake the most important thing to you?"

His words struck a nerve, and I wanted to hit him. My own father. How could he even ask me that? If he knew I'd been in love with her for years, how could he ask me if being with her mattered?

"I think you have your answer, son. Now the only question is what you're going to do about it." He walked away whistling as though he was happy about what he'd done.

I wanted to hit something. If I knew what to do about Blake, I'd fucking do it. The problem was I had no clue what to do. She had more to deal with than I ever knew, and I couldn't insert myself in the middle of it.

I got to work and pushed all thoughts out of my head. I put on some music and let it fill the space around me. Devon, the kid I hired for the summer, wasn't there on Mondays, so I had the place to myself to crank the music and get shit done.

An hour later, when I admitted to myself I was hungry and needed to get some actual food in me instead of just coffee, I checked my phone. I groaned when I saw an alert from Karissa's stupid app. The last thing I wanted was to get to know some random woman. Finley made me sign up for an account, to help Karissa, but I didn't intend to actually use it.

Guess Karissa's app had other ideas.

I pulled it up to turn off the notifications when I saw the name of my match. CoveMouse. Mouse was the nickname I gave Blake years ago. No one else called her that, but it couldn't be a coincidence.

I pulled up her profile and read everything I could about her. She was looking for a friendship that could turn into something more. Sounded like Blake. She was an artist. Yep. And she loved her private space.

I sucked in a breath. There were a lot of things about my match that surprised me. Like she had a thing for action movies but preferred old classics and romantic comedies. She wasn't sure she believed in marriage. And the most surprising of all, she thought passion was reserved for one-night stands, not long term relationships.

It was possible it wasn't Blake, but I was almost positive it was. Which meant I needed to do a little more research. And I needed to go on a field trip. Hell, I was hungry anyway. Going to Cracked when I knew Blake would still be there was just a coincidence.

I cleaned up a little, making sure my hands were clean and I didn't have anything smeared on my face, then locked up and headed down the street. It was less than ten minutes from my shop to Cracked, but I made it there in half that time.

Before I went in, I peeked through the windows and spotted Blake. She was behind the counter sipping the water she kept filled up while she worked, after she switched from coffee. It was fairly quiet in there, which was good. I pulled up the app and tapped to send her a message. Simple and direct.

Hi, CoveMouse. Saw we were matched. It's my first time doing this. I could always use a friend if you're up for it. BTW, your profile pic is hot.

Her picture was a chili pepper. Funny enough, so was mine. I didn't remember setting that up. Maybe it was something the app did based on the answers to our questions.

I hit send and checked the window again. A second later, Blake pulled her phone out of her pocket. Her eyebrows tugged together, then she grinned and laughed. Her thumbs typed something, then she tucked her phone away again, just as my phone buzzed in my hand.

Thanks, Woody. Allen or Toy Story? Not sure which would be better. Your pic is hot, too. LOL.

I grinned and slid my phone back into my pocket, then headed into Cracked. She was smiling and flirting with me. We weren't done yet.

Blake looked up with a smile at the bell above the door. Her grin faltered when she saw it was me, but she recovered quickly. If I wasn't paying attention, I wouldn't have noticed, but I saw it. It hurt.

"Hey," she said after a second. "Um, you can sit wherever you want."

I nodded and headed for the counter. Her drink sat opposite the stool I picked, which meant she was taking care of that section.

She watched me with wide eyes, then forced a smile and grabbed the coffee pot. She poured me a cup and set the cream in front of me.

"The usual?" she asked.

I nodded.

She turned and put the order in, then carried the pot around the room. It wasn't long before she was back since there were only a handful of people there. She stopped in front of me and chewed on her straw.

"How are you?" I finally asked her.

"Great. I mean, good. I'm fine," she stammered.

I nodded. "Good. I just haven't seen you."

She nodded, avoiding my gaze. "I'm busy. You know how it is. Getting ready for summer."

I nodded and smiled behind my coffee cup. She was nervous. I kind of liked nervous Blake. It meant I threw her off, which she'd been doing to me for years.

"Have you thought about getting together?" I asked as I set my mug down. I watched her out of the corner of my eye so she wouldn't know it.

Her mouth opened and closed, then a blush raced up her cheeks. When I finally lifted my gaze, she drew in a breath that raised her perfect breasts and required me to shift in my seat.

"I, um, why?"

That was not what I expected her to say. "Why? Why not?"

She scoffed. "Have you run out of women to sleep with? I mean, I know I haven't been with anyone since William, but I really don't need a pity fuck, Ian."

I snickered, knowing it would piss her off. She huffed, but before she could say anything else, I said, "It would be more of a pity if you said no, Blake. And trust me when I tell you this isn't me trying to get off."

"Then what is it, Ian? You and I both know you're not one for relationships, and I am. So how would something between us work? Are you asking for a one-time thing?"

I shrugged. I wanted to ask her for forever, but Blake was as skittish as they came. She wasn't the kind of woman I could say that to. She didn't want to marry the guy she dated for five years, so getting her to agree to a date would be difficult.

"How about we get together sometime and see how it goes."

She narrowed her eyes at me. "Is this some kind of joke, Ian? Ask the fat girl out?"

I stood and walked around the counter, grabbing her hand. "Earl, we'll be right back," I called out, my gaze never leaving Blake's.

"No problem," Earl said back.

My mind raced as Blake fought me. I wasn't going to let her think I wanted her for any reason other than I wanted her. And I was pissed that she would not only say that about herself but think it about me.

I dragged her to the bathroom knowing it was the only place in Cracked where we could be alone.

"Ian," she hissed as my grip tightened on her wrist.

I ignored her and tugged her into the men's bathroom with me. I pushed the door closed and pressed her back to it, caging her in with my arms on either side of her face.

She looked from one hand slammed against the door to the other then up at me. "Ian?"

"I don't ever want to hear you say that again," I said, my voice low and rough. I was so fucking mad at her I could barely breathe let alone speak.

"Say what?" she asked quietly.

"That you're fat."

She scoffed. "Ian, don't. I know who I am. I like food, and I hate sweating. And I know men aren't dying to find out what's under this sexy apron I wear."

"I am," I growled.

She rolled her eyes. "Like I said, it's some kind of joke, right?"

I stepped closer to her, slowly moving into her personal space until I could feel every inch of her from her breasts to her knees.

She gasped when she felt my cock against her stomach. "Ian?"

"I can't fake that, Blake. This isn't a joke, it's not a game, it's not anything other than me wanting to be inside you so badly I'm losing my fucking mind."

"Ian," she breathed, her voice all raspy and sexy. I imagined it would sound the same when I sank into her, stretching her out and filling her up.

"Don't accuse me of fucking with you, Blake. I wouldn't do that to you, to any woman. That's not who I am, and it really pisses me off that you think that of me."

She shook her head, her gaze locked on mine. "I don't. I just don't know why you want me."

I eased back just enough to look down at her body, leaving my hips pressed to hers. I let all the heat I felt fill my eyes when I met hers again, and she gasped.

"Ian," she breathed once more, and I couldn't stop myself from closing the distance between us once more.

I grabbed her ponytail and tugged her head back. Her lips parted the second ours touched, allowing me to plunge my tongue into her mouth. She tasted like coffee and bacon. I growled and leaned my weight against her.

My other hand fell to her thigh and lifted her leg up over my hip. I ground against her, going dizzy at the heat pouring from her core. I throbbed in my shorts, aching to drop the barriers between us and finally know what it felt like to be sheathed inside Blake.

"Blake," I groaned as I dragged my lips down her neck. She tasted like syrup and smelled like pancakes. She gasped when I nibbled on her collarbone then sighed when I slid my tongue over the same flesh.

"Ian."

Some sense of where we were filtered into my head and I forced myself to pull back. Her plump lips were wet from our kisses. Her eyes still closed. She looked drunk, and I grinned. Hell fucking yeah.

"Not a pity and not a joke. But not here, either."

Her eyes finally opened, and she blinked away the foggy haze of desire. She licked her lips and smiled up at me. "Wow."

I chuckled. "Definitely." I took a step back and drew in a breath. "This isn't over, Blake."

She grinned wider and nodded. "I'm okay with that."

"Good," I said, leaning in to capture her lips once more. I didn't let the kiss linger, even though I wanted to. I stepped back again and closed my eyes for a second. I gave her a smirk and said, "You should go out first. I need to have a minute away from you before I can walk through the dining room."

She tilted her head in question then her gaze snapped to my dick. The greedy fucker twitched, trying to say hi again. She sucked in a ragged breath then fumbled with the doorknob and rushed out of the bathroom.

I chuckled and locked the door behind her. I could still smell her in the bathroom, so I ran cold water and splashed it on my face. Deep breaths only brought her scent back to me, but eventually I calmed down enough to walk out.

Jean smirked at me on my way back to my seat. My breakfast was sitting there, waiting for me. Blake on the other hand, was not.

She stayed away from me while I ate my breakfast. Her cheeks were pink the whole time, and every time she glanced my way, the pink got darker.

I smiled as I ate.

Jean filled my coffee and said, "You hurt her, you'll be wearing this."

I nodded sharply. "I'll kick my own ass first."

Jean stared at me for a minute then nodded. "I'll hold you to it."

I grinned at her, happy Blake had someone else looking out for her. One day that would be my job, if Blake would let me.

When I finished my breakfast, I sat on my stool and slowly drank my coffee. Blake was avoiding me again, but I could wait her out.

Jean cleared my plate and smiled. She knew exactly what I was doing and appeared to be on my side.

Finally, Blake walked over and tore off my receipt. She set it on the counter in front of me and turned like she was going to walk away again.

I grabbed her hand, holding her in place until she met my gaze.

"I'll see you soon, Blake."

Her lips twitched. She shook her head and grinned. "Okay."

I nodded and stood, letting her go. I paid my bill and walked back to my shop feeling like I could do just about anything.

8

BLAKE

I was sitting on the grass of the square Wednesday, eating my lunch, when someone lowered to the ground beside me. I was focused on my favorite design idea so far and didn't want to lose my train of thought, but I didn't have to even look to know it was Ian.

I finished my sketch and turned to him. "Hey."

"Hey," he said brightly. "Can I see?"

I nodded and handed over my sketchbook. I rarely let anyone see my work before it was done, but Ian was an artist and understood it was a process to come up with something beautiful from scratch.

"Ms. Georgia?" he asked.

I nodded. "Earl asked me to paint a new mural. He wants to honor her so people know her for years to come. Eddie's already approved it."

"Wow. That's awesome. What did Karissa say?"

I shifted uncomfortably. "Um, I haven't talked to her yet."

"Ah, babe. She's going to love the idea. You don't need to worry about her."

I smiled that he understood exactly what I was afraid of

without having to tell him. I shrugged. "I thought it would be easier to talk to her if I had an idea of what I wanted to paint. Show her how it would honor Georgia. I have all these ideas, but they felt like fragments. Nothing was big enough to fill the wall."

I watched as he flipped through my book, looking at the different ideas I'd drawn since Earl asked me about the mural. He stopped when he flipped back to the one drawing I did of him. The one I forgot was in there.

I reached for the book before he could look at it too closely, but he pulled it out of my reach. "Blake," he groaned. "This is us?"

I sat back and brushed the invisible grass from my shorts. "No. It's just two people."

"Having sex?"

"So?"

"Blake, is this what you want? To ride me like this, babe?"

My cheeks burned. I never showed anyone my sketches. Ever. And I drew that so long ago that I'd forgotten all about it. I'd done other sketches of Ian, and Ian and me together, but the one he saw was one I drew in Hawaii.

"It's not us," I insisted, even though it was obvious it was. The guy had his ripped abs and stormy eyes. It was the look he'd given me the night I walked in on him. I couldn't get it out of my mind and had to draw it so I never forgot it. And the woman, well, she was a slightly skinnier version of me. A few less rolls, better hair, and a perfect butt since I drew her from behind.

Ian leaned closer, bringing the book closer. I kept my gaze locked on the book, ready to snatch it from him until the man himself rubbed against my side. "I wish it was us. I've fantasized about this. Watching these perfect tits of yours bounce as you ride me, taking what you need from me. I want to see your head thrown back as you come, and find out how far down this adorable blush goes when you're so turned on you can't remember your name."

I sucked in a breath and slowly blew it out. My book was long forgotten as every thought in my head got stuck on Ian's words. He fantasized about that. About us.

"You…you've thought about us?" I breathed, barely able to get the words out.

He tilted my chin until our gazes collided. "Hell, yes, Blake."

"I…um…okay."

"You haven't?" he asked with a knowing smirk.

"Of course I have. But you're you. You can sleep with any woman in town, or out of town, or on the planet. Why would you fantasize about me?"

His grin widened and his gaze drifted down to the page open on his lap. He spoke without looking up again. "Because I don't want any of those other women. I want you, Blake. I told you the other day, and I'll tell you over and over until you get it. This is what I picture. You, blissful. Pleased. Relaxed."

I still didn't understand it, but I couldn't argue that I liked the picture he painted.

My gaze snapped to the mural and all of a sudden, I knew exactly what I needed to draw. I grabbed the book and flipped to a new page. "You need to go. Now."

"Blake," he said, disappointment in his voice.

I shook my head, not taking my eyes from my book. "It's not that, Ian. I just had a great idea. I need to draw it now before I lose it. I'm sorry. This is perfect."

He leaned closer, the heat from his body threatening to distract me from my task. Then he kissed my cheek and stood. "Good luck."

"Thanks," I said, barely noticing when he walked away. But I did feel him, and I knew it wouldn't be long before I saw him again. And maybe tried out a few of the fantasies I'd had about him. And learned some of his.

May was definitely heating up.

I WAS INSPIRED over the next couple days to not only come up with multiple mural ideas, but to create some new paintings. It turned out Ian was good for inspiring a lot of ideas.

Olive, the owner of Island Designs, was always willing to stock new prints of my paintings. Island Designs was a shop near Cracked that showcased crafts made by local artists. When I first moved back to MacKellar Cove, I got to know Olive as a customer. When she found out I enjoyed painting, she encouraged me to bring in some of my work. It sold well, and she asked for more. Over the last seven years, my artwork brought in enough money for me to buy my house and not have to stress all the time about money. That was huge when MacKellar Cove and the entire area practically shut down for half the year.

I wrapped up my new paintings to show Olive before I spent the money on prints that she wasn't interested in. She usually said yes, but I preferred to show her what I had before I counted on her approval. If Olive said yes, I would have a little confidence going into the weekend and the very necessary conversation I needed to have with Karissa.

Island Designs was busy when I walked in. Olive was always working and always sharing stories with her customers. She considered herself a MacKellar Cove historian. She knew the true history of the town and the unofficial, humorous past that the rest of us weren't sure actually happened. She didn't care, and she never bothered to tell anyone if the stories were real or fiction. To her, they were all true.

Olive nodded at me when I walked through and winked when she noticed the portfolio in my hand. I went to the back to wait for her to have a break.

I unpacked the paintings while I waited, but Olive joined me before long.

"What have you brought me?" she asked, rubbing her hands together. Olive's chunky brown braid had as much gray woven through it as brown. Her vibrant dress was almost blinding, but her bright smile was genuine and loving.

"I had a good week and came up with a few new paintings. I wanted to show them to you," I told her, gesturing to the canvases I brought.

Her hand went to the first one, a pink and purple sunset over the lake with the lighthouse in the foreground. It was safe, but a little different. Bolder and brighter. More of an abstract painting.

"I love these colors. Stunning. It still has your style, but you found some passion with this piece. What got into you, Sweets?"

My cheeks burned with the truth. I couldn't admit Ian had gotten into me, or into my mind. "Oh, um, I just found some new inspiration."

Olive gave me a skeptical look but didn't push. "Well, keep it. I like this new spark. Let me see what else you have."

Olive liked the next two paintings also, but when she got to the last one, she gasped. "Oh, wow, Blake. If I thought the others were good, this is sensational. I can feel the sensuality and the lust on the canvas." She looked up at me. "I didn't realize you were involved with someone."

I shook my head. "I'm not."

She narrowed her hazel eyes and studied me. "You're not? Because this isn't a painting by a woman without passion and romance in her life. This is a painting by a woman who knows what it's like to lose her mind."

She waggled her eyebrows at me and my cheeks gave me away.

"Ah, so you are the same woman, you just don't want to admit who it is that's bringing out this new, sexy side of you. Well, Blake, whatever it is, whoever it is, I like this new spark. You do beautiful work, but it's always safe. It draws in the casual person, the everyday person, but this will be something that commands the attention of someone special. This painting, these two figures on the square, intertwined in this way, this painting is going to light the fires for all the couples who come in here. Well done, Blake. Well done."

"Thank you," I said softly.

She set the painting down and smiled at me, her eyes as bright as her dress. "I can't wait to see what you come up with next, assuming you keep your latest inspiration. William is a nice man, but he's not the right man for you. I'm happy you found the one who is."

"Oh, no. It's not like that," I stammered. I didn't want anyone to think Ian and I had something that would last. And I certainly didn't want him to think I was telling people that.

"That's too bad, Sweets. You should really try to change his mind, though. He's good for you."

I smiled and didn't answer. I couldn't tell her anything. Not about Ian. Olive would tell everyone in town that we were together if she thought there was something going on. Nope. My mouth was staying shut.

I packed up my stuff and chatted with Olive. I thought about Trinity and said, "Oh! I met a new artist. She just moved here. She designs jewelry. I was wondering if you would be interested in taking a look at what she does."

Olive nodded. "Of course. You know I love helping local artists. Send her my way whenever she's available."

I hugged her. "Thank you, Olive. That means so much.

She moved here because of Ms. Georgia and thought about leaving, but I hope she stays. I've seen a few of her pieces and thought they were amazing."

"Well, if you think so, I'm sure I'll have no problem selling them. I look forward to meeting her." She walked out with me to the front and waited until we were at the door before she said, "And say hello to Ian, Sweets."

"I will," I said without thinking. I spun to look at her when I realized what I said, but Olive just smirked at me.

Dammit.

I DIDN'T WANT to take a chance that something got back to Ian before I told him that Olive knew about us. Not that there was an us, but after Georgia's party, I wasn't surprised people were talking.

The sound of the planer reached my ears before I made it to the door. It was closed against the cool afternoon breeze coming off the river. I pushed the squeaky door open and walked in. I slid it closed behind me and followed the sound to where I saw two boots sticking out from under a stunning boat.

I didn't want to startle Ian, but I felt like a creeper standing there. I chewed on my lip for a minute, debating what I should do, when the planer turned off.

"I didn't know you were coming by today," he said, pushing his way out from under the boat with a grin. "Then again, I'm already on my back and ready for you."

I scoffed, my cheeks heating at his flirtatious words. "I… Who did you think I was?"

He stood effortlessly, getting into my personal space. I ached to step back but I didn't, letting him get close.

"I knew exactly who was here the moment that door slid open, Blake."

"How did you know it was me?"

He raised an eyebrow. "Is that really what you came here to ask me?"

He was close. Dangerously close. The only other time I could remember being so close to him was when we danced and kissed. My pulse thundered in my ears, drowning out everything outside Ian and me. I saw the green flecks in his hazel eyes, a golden ring around his iris. I drew in a breath, and he brushed the hair back off my neck.

"Not that I don't love you showing up here, Blake, but was there a reason you came by?"

Sanity finally broke through my mind and I took a step back. "Sorry. You're right. Yeah, um, Olive. I went into Island Designs and she knows about us. I mean that we were kissing. At O'Kelley's. Not at my house. Well, I mean, I don't know if she knows about that, but I don't think so. I don't know how she would know. Hell, Olive makes up her own stories so maybe she guessed, but I don't know. She could—"

"Blake," he said, startling me out of my rambling. "You know how this town is. Everyone knows. Before we even walked out of there, everyone knew. And leaving together just made the tongues wag, babe."

"You're not mad?" I breathed.

He laughed and shook his head. "Why would I be mad? I knew exactly what was going to happen the first time I wrapped my arms around you." He pulled me close and nuzzled against my neck. "I have no right to be upset that the whole town is talking."

My head spun. I wanted to sink into him and forget about everything else, but something lingered. Something that told me I couldn't just let go and accept his words.

I pushed back from him. His eyes were closed, pure lust

written on his face. Lust for me. What the fuck? Ian and I were never like that. He slept with women, and I had relationships. We both knew it wouldn't work. But he looked at me like he wanted something to work.

"You've never been okay with PDA, Ian. Why aren't you pissed?"

He shrugged and pushed a hand through his hair. He raised his eyes to mine and said, "If we're going to convince Willie that you're really over, we have to let everyone else think we're together."

I nodded, a little frustrated. I could handle William. I had handled him. I thought Ian was wrong about William wanting me again, but regardless of that, I wasn't going to pretend to be with Ian because of it.

"William isn't interested in getting back together. Even if he was, I shouldn't have gotten carried away at Georgia's party. It wasn't fair to you to let things go that far. I'm not worried about William."

"What are you saying?" Ian asked.

I looked him straight in the eye and said, "I'm saying there's no reason for us to pretend we're together. You're off the hook."

He took a step closer. "And I told you the other day that I want you, Blake. It has nothing to do with Willie and everything to do with you. There's no one here right now, and I'm fighting every instinct not to throw you over my shoulder and carry you to my bed so I can have my way with you."

I gasped and took a step back. He kept saying things like that, but it was Ian. Ian who called me names growing up. Ian who dated skinny women forever. Ian who never got involved beyond a night or two.

We didn't match. He was fit, I was fat. He slept around, I got serious. He...looked at me like he couldn't imagine another minute without his lips against mine. And I sure as hell felt that way.

"What is this, Ian?"

He shrugged again. "This is me wanting you, Blake. That's all it is. Nothing complicated. Just me wanting you."

"When no one's around," I said softly.

He stepped into my personal space and forced me to look up at him. "I fucking kissed you at O'Kelley's, Blake. In front of the entire damn town. I walked out of there with you, knowing full well it would set off the rumor mill. I am not doing this now when no one is watching. But you better believe I'm not going to fuck you with an audience because you're all mine, Blake. However you'll let me have you, I'm not sharing you."

Well, damn. He sure knew how to tear down my defenses.

9

"Ian," I breathed, and that was all the invitation he needed. He closed the gap between us and scooped me up, tossing me over his shoulder and stalking toward the back of the shop where his apartment was.

I stayed perfectly still, afraid he'd drop me if I moved. I wasn't light, and even though Ian was strong, it was still very possible he'd drop me. His hand rested on my thigh, his fingertips teasing between my legs.

Oh, God. I was going to have sex with Ian Jameson. And I hadn't shaved in months.

We finally made it to his apartment, and he set me on my feet. He tilted my chin up with a fingertip. His hazel eyes blazed with heat, sending a matching fire through me. I wanted him. I wanted whatever he was willing to give me. Even if it was only one time, I wanted it.

"Tell me to stop, Blake," he whispered, his voice tight.

"I don't want you to stop," I answered.

Everything happened in a flash after that. I was pressed tight to his chest, his lips closing in on mine. His arm locked around my back, my arms trapped at my sides. His body filled the space mine did a second before, and then we were moving again.

He made me dizzy with his kiss. One second, he dove in deep, making my body pulse with desire. The next second, he backed off, making me hum with pleasure. Back and forth, he teased me until desire and pleasure became one and I was anticipating the pleasure as it raced down my spine and made me ache for him.

Then he pulled back and scorched me with a look that I felt all the way to my core. I nearly came just from the heat in his eyes. "Jesus, Blake, I want you so bad, but if you're not okay with this, stop me. You hear me? Any time you're done, I'll stop."

I chuckled. Like I'd ask him to stop.

He cupped my jaw and locked his gaze on mine. "I mean it, babe. Anything at all. You say stop or wait or no, and I'll back off. I promise you, Blake, I'm not going to do anything you don't want me to do."

I chewed my lip and nodded. I couldn't tell him I knew this was the last chance I'd get with him and that I'd probably do anything he wanted to do. William was never very adventurous, in bed or out. He rarely kissed me in public, and I told myself I liked it that way. But when Ian kissed me, I wanted the whole world to see it. I wanted to tell everyone that Ian Jameson thought I was beautiful and had his lips on mine.

Ian moved toward me slowly, drawing me in with each step. He breathed me in, tipping his head back as I went in for a kiss. He teased me, making me think he was going to kiss me, then pulling back at the last second.

Just when I thought maybe he wasn't going to follow through, he sealed his lips over mine and licked his way into my mouth. He tasted me like I was something new to be cherished and treasured. A soft moan, a subtle lick, a little nibble. All of it spun me around until I couldn't tell where I stopped and Ian started. We were one, connected, together.

His hands went from my cheeks down. Over my throat where one hand lingered and slid around to the back of my neck. His other hand drifted south, over my shoulder to run down my arm. He squeezed my fingers, then wrapped our hands behind my back. I was completely surrounded by him and absolutely fucking loved it.

He grew against my stomach, his erection pressing into me and making me squirm. I wanted to feel him again, to touch and taste and ride him. I wanted him in a way I'd never experienced before. Wild, crazed, and fierce, like if I didn't have him, I wouldn't survive the day.

We walked backward again, but he stopped and withdrew from our kiss. It took me a minute to blink my eyes open and focus on him. His face was twisted in a pained expression.

"What's wrong?" I asked, reading him the way I always had.

"I should have a bed for you. I shouldn't be spreading you out on my futon," he said, staring at the floor behind me.

I shook my head. Ian had that futon forever. I didn't want to know how many others he'd slept with on it. But it was Ian. He was the kind of guy who didn't even get attached to furniture. The futon would remind me that nothing and no one stuck with him.

"I don't care," I told him. "I don't need anything special."

He shook his head. "You deserve special, Blake."

I smirked. "I deserve another kiss."

He finally grinned and dove back in, kissing me with a new passion. I could barely keep up with him as he speared me with his tongue, taking everything from me. My sanity, my breath, and my desire. He had control of all of it, directing me where he needed me to be without words or thoughts.

The only thing that mattered was Ian.

I ached to touch him, to feel his skin under my fingertips. I slid my hand under his shirt and groaned at the feel of his smooth, firm flesh. I spread my hand wide so I could touch more of him, and he pulled back.

Without opening his eyes, he reached back and stripped his shirt off, baring his upper body to me.

I'd seen Ian in a bathing suit more times than I could count. I always knew he was attractive, but being able to touch and taste him, being so close to him, it was a whole new experience.

He still smelled like raw wood, but beneath that was all male. Musky and fresh at the same time. I pressed my nose to his chest and inhaled deeply, wanting to take every piece of the day with me.

I slid my hands up his chest, letting the soft hair tickle my fingers. I curled my fingers and drew my nails back down, smiling when he groaned.

I knew I wasn't really in charge, but it was a heady experience to take control for a minute. Things with William never changed, so neither of us was really in charge. I knew what he was going to do before he did it because he always did the same thing. We took our clothes off, got into bed, he touched me a little, then slid inside and thrust until he came. Half the time, I had to finish myself off, and the other half of the time I wasn't close enough to care.

But with Ian, I was already close and I was still fully dressed. Nothing with Ian was the same, and there was no doubt that he'd make sure I had enough orgasms to make up for at least some of the time I spent with William.

I leaned forward and licked Ian's nipple. He sighed softly and threaded his fingers through my hair. I closed my lips around it and took a small bite and his fingers clenched, tugging on my hair.

I glanced up and found him watching me. He gave me a crooked smile that spiraled through me. Who knew a smile could be so intoxicating? But from Ian, it was like a caress.

I turned away from him, feeling self-conscious, and kissed his chest again. I let my hands wander, touching his exposed skin and memorizing the feel of him. I thought about shoving him down onto the futon and crawling on top of him, or sitting on the edge and taking him into my mouth, but I wasn't sure he'd be up for either. Was this a make-out session, like the other times, or was this more?

He cupped my jaw and brought my lips back to his. He plunged his tongue between my lips again, sending all thoughts and fears far away. This was Ian. Even if we were only kissing, it was Ian. I knew him, and he wouldn't judge me for anything. He never had, and there was no reason for him to start now.

I finally worked up the nerve to press on his chest. He pulled back and took his hands off. "You okay?" he asked, his breath coming in pants and his entire body tight.

I nodded, looking up at him from under my lashes. "I want you on the futon. I want to sit on you. If that's okay."

His grin was part male pride and part panty-melting pleasure. Yeah, a smile was dangerous. A smile could take me from hot to oh-my-God in a flash.

He dropped to the futon and laid down. He reached for my hand and helped me lower onto him. We both moaned when I settled over him, nestling him between my thighs. His hands went to my hips and squeezed. His eyes were locked tight, hiding all his thoughts from me.

His fingers loosened, and he slid his hands up my sides, pulling me toward him. "Come here, Blake." His voice was raw and rough, husky, and sent a spiral of need through me.

I followed his order and braced myself on the futon, my hands going to either side of his head. He leaned up as I leaned down and kissed me until my hips moved all on their own. One of his hands eased back down and cupped my ass, guiding my uneven movements.

"Fuck, you feel good, Blake. I want to be inside you. I want to watch you ride me."

I wanted the same thing. I wanted to feel him stretch me. To have him slide in and fill me up. To have him erase the years I spent with William. William was a good guy, but I was beyond ready to move on.

"Ian," I moaned, feeling the pressure build in me.

Abruptly, he stopped, clenching tight on my hips and halting my movements.

I froze, wondering why he stopped. I blinked open my eyes to find him gritting his teeth. I worried I hurt him and started to move off him.

"Don't. Just give me a second."

"Did I hurt you? I knew I was too big—"

"Fuck, no, Blake," he growled, his eyes flipping open to lock on mine. "You're fucking perfect. Too perfect. You riding me, you calling my name, your smell, all of you, it's too much. I'm trying not to come in my pants right now. And there's no way in hell I'm going to do that when I have you right here. I want you, Blake. I've told you I want you."

"I want you, too, Ian," I whispered. "So much."

"Thank fuck," he growled. He flipped us effortlessly, like I weighed half what I did.

I sprawled on my back on the futon where seconds before he'd been. I looked up at the exposed metal structure of the roof and the fluorescent light hanging above us. Ian lifted my shirt, and all of a sudden the light seemed bigger and brighter. Getting naked in front of Ian was too much to think about. He'd see all of me.

"Um, can we turn off the light?" I asked.

"Hell, no," he said, kissing my stomach as my shirt lifted to the lower edge of my bra. "I want to see you, Blake."

"But I—"

"You're fucking gorgeous. I've been dreaming about this, Blake. Don't take it from me. I need to see you. All of you. I want to watch your face as you come and see your breasts flush that pretty pink color your cheeks get. I want to see my fingers and my cock disappear into your perfect pussy. I need all of you, Blake. Every beautiful inch of you."

I couldn't breathe. How the hell did he make me feel like I was the most beautiful woman he'd ever been with? I knew I wasn't. I'd seen more than a few the morning after. They came into Cracked and talked about their amazing night with him. Or he left O'Kelley's with them. Tall, skinny, perfect women that would have every man wagging his tongue. But Ian made them sound like second class compared to me.

Ian continued to kiss his way up my stomach until he reached the edge of my bra. It was white cotton and full coverage. Not at all sexy, but the way Ian looked at me was like I was decked out in satin and lace.

He smirked before he flicked his tongue over my nipple. The feel of the rough cotton being pressed to me sent a shiver through my entire body. Ian did it again, then closed his lips over my nipple and sucked, licking and teasing me through the cotton until it was see-through.

"I think white might be my new favorite color. I need to get you some more of these bras."

I choked on a laugh. He made it sound like there was going to be a next time.

Before I could think too hard on that, he switched to my other nipple and did the same thing.

He drew my shirt over my head and worked his way back down, kissing my throat and chest and stomach as he moved.

He undid the button on my jeans, then dragged the zipper down slowly, every click echoing in my head and telling me I was closer and closer to him touching me.

His gaze locked on mine once the zipper stopped. He leaned forward and pressed a kiss to my pubic bone, just above where my panties folded over beneath my belly roll. I wanted to pull my shirt down and cover myself up, but he already saw me. Kissed me. There was no more hiding.

His tongue darted out and slicked over my stomach, reverent almost, and I drew in a sharp breath.

"Lift for me," he said, his voice still rough, the jagged sound sparking my nerves.

I did as he asked and picked up my hips. He eased my jeans down my thighs, leaving my panties in place, and moved aside so he could pull them right off.

Without thinking, I grabbed the blanket next to me and pulled it over me. It smelled like Ian, and I pressed my nose to the fabric.

He yanked it out of my hands.

"Hey!" I said with a gasp.

"You're not going to hide yourself from me, Blake."

"I—" I had no defense. That was exactly what I was doing. I hated lying there, exposed, with his eyes on me.

Then he locked those eyes on mine and slid his shorts down, leaving his navy briefs on. The ones with a tent in the front.

I was speechless. Breathless. Mindless. A part of me still thought that maybe, just maybe, Ian was messing with me. That he was playing some elaborate joke on me. I'd known him most of my life, and never once had he looked at me the way he was. It had to be a lie. Otherwise, I would have noticed.

But I also knew Ian. He slept around a lot, but he wasn't cruel. I'd never heard of any of the women he slept with who were broken hearted after being with him. He was upfront, and while all of them were happy for a repeat, they all knew what they were getting into with Ian. It wasn't a relationship. It was sex.

And I had to keep reminding myself that's all I was getting from him. He hadn't said the words, but his reputation spoke for him. He knew it, and I knew it, so there was no need to come out and say it. Whatever happened with us was not the start of something.

"Dammit, Blake. I'm not going to get any work done the rest of the day."

"What? Why? I can go."

He laughed and shook his head. "Hell, no. You're the only thing I'm going to do the rest of today. You're all mine for tonight, Blake, so if you had plans, consider them canceled."

10

My breath hitched with his possessive words. No one had ever spoken to me the way Ian was. No one had ever made me feel the way he did. It was no wonder he had so many notches on his bedpost. He was a wizard in bed, and he hadn't even gotten me completely naked yet.

I shook my head. "I don't have any plans."

He smirked. "Good."

He stretched out next to me and ran his finger over my lips. A gentle touch that was barely there, just enough pressure for me to feel a breath. His fingertip slid down my neck and over the swells of my breasts, dipping in between. He went lower, circling my belly button and teasing the edge of my panties, before returning to my lips.

"I love your lips, Blake. The way you pout when you don't get your way, and the way you smile when you're happy. Kissing you is better than I ever thought it would be."

I smiled, unsure what to say. I felt so out of my league. I wanted to tell him I was a sure thing and that he didn't have to romance me into bed, but I wasn't willing to break whatever spell he was under. That was the only explanation. Or he was drunk, but he didn't drink when he was working.

He turned my face to his with a gentle touch and kissed me softly. His breath puffed on my cheeks, his lips brushing mine in feathery kisses. He parted his lips and licked mine, then kissed me with closed lips again. The whole time, I focused on the feel of his firm, thick lips against mine. The gentle breeze from the opened window chilled my skin.

Once he moved closer to me, the chill left my body. His chest grazed mine, his chest hair tickling my exposed skin. He looped an arm around me and rolled me to my back, resting his top half over me.

We laid like that, just kissing, for minutes. No pressure, no urgency, just enjoying each other. And when he slid his tongue between my lips and licked his way into my mouth, I drew in a breath, loving how he could take what could be innocent and made it deliciously dirty.

His erection pressed against my hip, his hand low on my belly. His forearm rested just above the band of my panties, where I could feel his heat.

Every shift of his body had my thighs aching, my core clenching, my entire body readying for him. But he stayed on his side, barely covering me. Close enough to torment me, but so far away from where I wanted him.

I groaned in frustration and shoved him off me. Before he could ask what was wrong, I climbed on top of him. His cock slid between my thighs, the thick length of him pressing against my entrance.

"I want you, Ian," I said, looking in his eyes. I needed to see the look on his face when I said it. I had to know he was on board.

"I'm not going to last long the first time, Blake. I'm warning you already. I'm about three seconds away from losing it right now."

"Then you better get naked and find a condom," I said. I stood, and stripped off my bra and panties. Before panic could set it that I was standing naked in front of one of the most attractive men in town, he shoved his briefs down and rolled to the side. He yanked the drawer of his nightstand open so hard the entire thing came out. A new box of condoms laid in the drawer, and I tried not to think about why he bought them or who he was with last.

He ripped the plastic off the box then tore it open, sending condoms flying. He grabbed the closest string and tore one off, ripping it with his teeth as he looked at me again.

"You're amazing," he said, groaning as he rolled the condom on. He stroked himself once, squeezing the tip and jerking with his movements.

His muscled corded with his efforts. Tendons stood out on his neck, and his cock twitched. I licked my lips, wishing I'd taken him into my mouth before he rolled the condom on. Next time. If there was a next time.

"Get your sexy ass back over here," he growled at me. "And stop looking at me like that. I need to get inside you before I lose it."

My gaze snapped to his, and I saw the same expression he had on his face in Hawaii. The same tight, unreadable look that I thought was desire then. Now, there was no question. Which made me wonder yet again who he was thinking about.

I moved to the edge of the futon and stepped over him. His hands came up to meet my body as I lowered down, spreading my thighs wide to try to fit over him. I was all hips, with breasts that were too small for my wide lower body. But with that wide lower body came thick thighs that barely fit around Ian's frame.

I jumped when one of his hands slid between us and touched me.

"I need to feel you, Blake. Can I touch you?"

I nodded, already shifting my hips to welcome his hand. His finger slid over my slick flesh. One finger eased into me, and we both groaned.

"Fuck me, Blake. You're tight, babe."

I nodded and chewed on my lip. "It's been a while."

"Since Willie? That's what you said, right?" he asked, his gaze snagging mine.

I nodded again, not wanting to ask about his last time.

"Thank you. I'm honored that you're letting me be your first since him."

As he talked, his finger stroked in and out of me in slow, deep strokes. William wasn't very big, and Ian's finger sank deeper than William's cock ever did. When Ian added a second finger, he stretched my body wider than William ever did. It was like everything was new again.

"You're so wet, Blake. I love the feel of you. So tight and ready for me."

"So ready," I murmured. Every tease of his fingers tightened my core. I wanted to ride him, to have him fill me up and make me come harder than I ever had before.

He withdrew his fingers and teased my clit for just a second, long enough to make my hips buck. "Ease back, babe."

He held himself still while guiding me down. I felt him at my entrance, and my body locked up.

"Relax, Blake. Let me in."

His thumb slid over my clit again, and he sank in an inch. I lifted a tiny bit and he stroked my clit again, sliding in another inch. Over and over until all of his inches filled me.

I sat on him, holding steady for a long moment. The only

other time I'd felt that good was when I used my vibrator. Silly me, I assumed real men weren't that big.

Ian definitely ruined me for other men.

Then we started to move. His hands guided me, lifting me up and encouraging me to slide back down. But it wasn't enough. I couldn't lift high enough to really get a good stroke going. He felt amazing, but I needed more.

Ian helped by shifting his hips in rhythm with mine. He groaned and helped me move, but it wasn't working.

"Get up," Ian said gruffly.

Disappointed that he wasn't enjoying it anymore than I was, I crawled off him. His hand slid between my spread thighs, and I almost fell.

"Lay down. On your back."

I followed his orders. He nudged my thighs apart with his knees and slid his hands up my thighs and lifted my ass. He slid in with one firm stroke, and I moaned.

He lifted my knees over his arms and spread me wide. His gaze stared straight down to where our bodies met with each powerful stroke of him into me.

"That's the sexiest thing I've ever seen," he groaned. Then he pulled out and dropped my ass to the futon again. "I'm going to come hard, but you need to come first."

I shook my head. "It's okay. I'm good."

He froze. "Please don't tell me Willie didn't take care of you."

I shrugged. "He was fine. And our sex life is none of your business."

Ian shook his head. "It is if your expectations are so low that you won't be pissed off if I fuck you and walk. You're going to scream my name today, Blake. And if you don't, I don't come."

"I'm not a screamer, Ian. I'm not— Holy shit!"

He licked me. Actually licked me. Between my legs. Where I hadn't shaved or waxed or done anything besides wash in far too long.

"Every woman is a screamer when it's good enough, Blake. You're going to scream my name today. And I'm going to stay down here until you do."

His hazel eyes were a deep forest green, full of lust and heat. I actually believed he meant what he said, but I wasn't all that experienced with receiving oral sex.

"I haven't shaved, though."

"I don't care," Ian protested, disappearing beneath my belly.

His tongue slid through my folds again. "Oh, God."

"Wrong name, Blake," he said gruffly against me. His voice rumbled through me, shaking me from my core.

His hands went under my ass again, lifting me and spreading my thighs at the same time. He licked me once more, but I didn't say anything that time. Not because I was ready for it, but because he didn't come up for air. His tongue slid from top to bottom then pulsed inside me.

Fingers, cock, and now tongue. This day was going down in history. I'd never had all three inside me on the same day.

He nipped my clit, and I gasped.

"Stop thinking, Blake. I want to hear my name."

"Ian," I groaned.

He bit me again. "Not like that."

"Oh, Ian," I moaned with a laugh.

He chuckled, the puff of his breath against my thigh as much of a tease as he was. "That's more like it, but without the laugh."

He ducked back down and spread me open with his fingers. I could feel his eyes on me, examining my most intimate part.

"What's wrong?" I asked, alarmed that he was just staring at me.

"Just looking at you. You have the prettiest pussy, Blake. And you smell so good. I could stay down here all night."

I started to laugh him off, but he slicked the flat of his tongue over me. Then he used the tip to part all my folds and lick me everywhere. He coaxed my clit out and slid a couple fingers inside me, and I was nearly lost.

My breath hitched and my heart skipped.

He reached up with his free hand and found my hand. He threaded his fingers through mine and squeezed, then rested our joined hands on my belly. It was intimate, like we were lovers instead of friends.

Then he picked up the pace. His fingers thrust faster, his tongue flicked over me like he was chasing the same thing I was. Blood roared in my ears, and my orgasm raced toward me.

Then he curled his fingers inside me, and I was done.

"Oh, God, Ian. Yes! Ian! Yes, yes, yes! Ian!" I shouted as I came.

I was lost in a sea of pleasure as the orgasm pulsed through me. The next thing I remembered was Ian sinking into me, our linked hands lifted above my head. He leaned over me, pressing his body to mine as he captured my other hand and linked those fingers together.

I finally managed to open my eyes and found him smirking at me. "I told you I'd get you to scream my name."

I huffed a laugh with him and shook my head. "I've never come like that," I confessed.

"Never?" he asked, his eyebrows drawing together.

I shook my head again, chewing on my lip.

"Ah, Blake. We have a lot of orgasms to make up for."

He withdrew then slammed back into me, hard enough that heat curled my toes and I moaned. "Oh, God."

"It's Ian, remember?" he asked with a grin.

I opened my eyes and smiled at him. "Trust me, I remember."

He leaned back, separating our chests. His hands held mine, both of us supporting his weight as he stroked in and out of me. Every thrust tightened the spool of desire in my gut until it was wound tight and ready to snap.

Then he snapped, throwing his head back and squeezing my fingers tight. I was mesmerized by him, a look of pure pleasure and joy on his face as he came. He whispered my name, like a prayer, then collapsed onto me, letting me absorb all his weight.

We laid like that for a few minutes, his face buried in my neck, his cock inside me, our hands still linked.

When he shifted, he kissed my neck and moved off me. "I shouldn't have crushed you like that. I'm sorry."

I shook my head and said, "I loved feeling you on me."

His gaze met mine and he grinned. "Me, too."

He leaned back in, kissing me softly. The orgasm that simmered just below the surface ignited, reminding me it was there.

Ian squeezed my hands and jumped up, pulling back from our kiss right before I moaned.

"I'll be right back," he said, heading to the bathroom.

I laid there for a minute, wondering what I was supposed to do. I'd only slept with guys I was dating, so we developed a rhythm after sex, whether it was stay and cuddle or leave right away. I had no clue what to do in Ian's bed.

I figured getting dressed was probably the right answer, so I got up and started to collect my clothes. I'd just picked up my panties when the bathroom door opened.

"What the hell are you doing?"

"Oh, um, I figured you'd want me to go."

"Is that what you want?" he asked.

I finally turned to look at him and had to suck in a breath. He was gorgeous. Dark blond hair covered his pecs and made a path down the center of his abs to circle the base of his cock, which was standing up still. Thick thighs and toned calves, both corded with muscles, gave him the sexy swagger he always had. Those hands that drove me crazy just minutes ago clenched into fists then released.

But it was his eyes that really did me in. His eyes told me he was hoping I said no, that I wanted to stay. His eyes said he wasn't done with me.

I slowly shook my head, and he was across the room and lifting me into his arms in half a second. He pressed his lips to mine as I laughed.

"Put those clothes down. You're not leaving until I've heard my name from these sexy lips at least ten times. And until we've tried a few more positions. I think I know how you can ride me."

"Ian," I moaned.

"And I still owe you that orgasm you were chasing."

"You don't owe me anything."

He eased back and looked in my eyes. He held my gaze for a minute. He brushed hair from my cheek and kissed me softly. "Maybe I don't owe you, but I'm not the kind of man who makes a woman take care of herself. You have me now. And you'll never go without an orgasm or six when I'm around."

I laughed with him, but I didn't say anything. I had him for the moment. Now was fleeting. Now could be over any minute. And I wasn't going to count on something lasting when I knew it wouldn't.

Ian would move on, and I'd be responsible for my own orgasms again. Except it would be worse next time because I would know what it was like to be with a man who enjoyed them as much as I did.

But I couldn't dwell on any of that. I had to take what I could get. And at the moment, what I could get was a sexy, smart, amazing man sliding his hand between my thighs. I was not in a position to say no to that.

IAN

$\mathcal{I}$'d never seen anything as beautiful as Blake coming apart. Watching her come was the best part of my day. The best part of my life.

In a million years, I never thought I'd be lucky enough to witness it, but I did. Not just once or twice, but eleven times. And yes, dammit, I was counting.

She was stretched out on my bed, the ugly-ass futon I'd slept on for years. I hated that I didn't have something better for her, but I definitely didn't plan on having Blake in my bed. I dreamed of it, but I wasn't crazy enough to plan for it.

The happy smile on her face told me she didn't care that we were on a futon and not in an expensive hotel room or something. I loved her all the more for rolling with it.

"I'm going to buy a bed," I said against her skin. I loved the way she smelled. A hint of lotion but mostly just her. Sweet with her own scent.

She shrugged. "Okay. I don't know why you're telling me that."

I kissed the side of her breast and nibbled my way up to

her collarbone. "So you know next time you'll be more comfortable."

"Next time?" she asked, like she was surprised.

I nodded. "Yeah. Unless you're done with me." I tried to keep my tone light, but every cell of my body tightened waiting for her response.

"No," she breathed, almost sighed. "Um, that would be good." She rolled away from me and stood on the other side of the futon. "I should go, though. It's getting late."

The sun had barely set, and it was a Friday night. I wanted to push for her to stay the night with me. Waking up in the same hotel room with her months ago had me aching to wake up with her in the same bed. She was up before me every day we were in Hawaii and I missed seeing her fresh out of bed. I wanted to see it, to feel it, to hold her and talk her into a day in bed.

But I couldn't push. She was still scared, and I'd never had a relationship. Not one I wanted to last longer than our next night together.

"Want me to walk you home?" I asked, rolling the other way and pulling on my jeans.

"No!"

I turned to look at her. Her cheeks pinked with her flush.

"Sorry, I mean, I'm good. But thank you."

"I don't mind," I told her.

She nodded. "I know. And I appreciate it. I just don't want more people to think we're together."

My brows knitted together. I rolled her words around in my head and tried not to be hurt by them, but it was impossible. She didn't want anyone to know about us. She was ashamed of me. While I wanted to tell the world and claim her as mine, she wanted to hide us from everyone.

"Does it matter what people think?"

She scoffed. "It always matters."

I really didn't know what she was talking about or why she cared. She never struck me as the type who cared, but maybe I didn't know her as well as I thought I did.

I walked her out through the shop to the door. She yanked it open without pausing, but I wasn't ready for her to run. Before she stepped outside, I slid my hand around her waist and pulled her back to me. She fell into my arms and looked up at me with wide, questioning eyes. I sank into the depths of her and had to think she could follow me. I needed her to go with me. To be there when I didn't know which way was up.

I kissed her hard, prying her lips apart. My hand went to her ass, grabbing a handful and pushing our bodies together. I needed to feel every inch of her once more, just in case she didn't come back again. The thought made me crazy, and I poured every bit of it into the kiss until she was hanging on me, letting me support her.

Only then did I pull back. I stared down at her beautiful, lust-filled face. Her eyes were closed, her lips plump and wet. Her cheeks were red, and the flush disappeared beneath her collar. I wanted to strip her again and kiss all the way down to where that flush disappeared.

Next time, I promised myself. Because I'd make sure there was a next time. Blake was mine, and I promised Georgia I'd tell her how I felt. Showing her worked, too.

She finally blinked her eyes open, sinking me again in the stunning depths of her endless brown eyes. I kissed her gently, telling her how precious she was to me without words. When I pulled back again, I finally let go of her, promising myself it wouldn't be the last time I had Blake in my arms.

"Thank you," she whispered, looking up at me. "I didn't come here for any of this, but thank you."

"Any time," I said honestly. I'd drop anything and everything for Blake. Any time she wanted me. Or needed me.

She flushed again and ducked her head. Then she looked up at me for a second and said, "Bye, Ian."

"See you soon, Blake."

She grinned and walked away. I watched until she turned the corner, smiling when she glanced back to see if I was still there.

I was as bad as a teenage girl with her first crush. I already wanted to text her. To tell her I missed her. But I couldn't. Blake was scared, and the last thing I needed to do was send her running.

So I did the next best thing, I messaged her in the app.

WOODY

Is your Friday night as boring as mine?

I knew she was walking home, so I didn't expect a response for a few minutes. I slid the door closed and finally went back inside, debating. I had work to finish on the boat, but I wasn't sure I could concentrate. Blake had filled my head, and I felt restless and amped up.

I went to my room and tugged on my shirt back on. I slid on a pair of flip flops and decided I needed to get out. Sitting around and thinking about Blake not being there would only make me crazy.

I was halfway to O'Kelley's when my phone dinged with a new message. I pulled it up and stopped when I read her message.

COVEMOUSE

I just got home. Had a really good day, though.

Hell fucking yeah. Me, too, babe.

WOODY

> I'm jealous. What happened that made your day so good?

I waited for her to text back and tell me she spent the afternoon with…well, me. I held my breath and blew it out in an exasperated sigh when I read her message.

COVEMOUSE

> I had a great meeting today. Sold some new pictures.

"Really?" I said out loud.

A guy walked by and laughed. "Yep, really."

I rolled my eyes at him and started walking again. I definitely needed a drink. I told myself it made sense she wouldn't tell some random guy about the great sex she just had, but I wanted to know she enjoyed it as much as I did.

WOODY

> Congratulations. I'd love to see your work one day.

COVEMOUSE

> Maybe one day. My new stuff was different. I was inspired by a friend.

WOODY

> A special friend?

COVEMOUSE

> Maybe. Sorry. I know this is a dating site. I'm not trying to be a tease.

I grinned like a crazy person.

WOODY

> No worries about me. We said we'd be friends.

COVEMOUSE

Thanks. I really appreciate it.

WOODY

Want to tell me about him?

COVEMOUSE

Maybe. Not yet, though. Don't want to jinx anything. He's not a relationship type, and I know it won't last.

I drew in a breath and debated answering her. My first thought was no one else was ever her, but I couldn't tell her that.

WOODY

You never know. He could have been waiting for the right one.

COVEMOUSE

LOL! Not this guy. And definitely not me. Guys like him don't end up with girls like me. Not in my experience.

I scowled at my phone and walked into O'Kelley's. There was no reason Blake and I couldn't be together, but if she didn't think it would happen, I had to work even harder.

COVEMOUSE

Anyway, I need to get some work done. I'm feeling inspired again. Talk soon.

WOODY

Yep.

I slid my phone into my pocket and sat at the bar. Hudson Grant set a bottle in front of me and nodded before walking to the other end of the bar. Hudson was a few years older than me. We played baseball together in high school, and he went to college on a scholarship. He blew out his knee sliding into second his junior year when the second baseman stuck his foot between Hudson and the bag. The other guy walked away with a few stitches. Hudson had to be carried off the field and never stepped foot on one again. He came back to MacKellar Cove and bought O'Kelley's from the longtime owners. He kept it the same, but added his own touches to turn it into a true local spot.

I scanned the room while Hudson served customers at the long, wooden bar. It was packed, which was typical for a Friday night. A few people nodded to me, but no one came over. I wasn't in the mood to talk, so it worked for me as I sipped my beer and stewed.

"Where is she?" Hudson asked when he walked back to me.

"Home," I answered automatically.

His dark eyebrows shot up. "Whoa. I didn't expect you to answer me."

I glared at him.

Hudson leaned on the bar. "Who is she? Maybe I should have started with that question."

I shook my head and drained my beer. Hudson saw me leave with plenty of women from his bar. I wasn't picky. I liked women, and they liked me. But I didn't get attached because they weren't Blake.

Now, I had Blake, I was attached, and she wasn't. It fucking sucked.

"Wait a minute. Are you hung up on Blake?" he asked, leaning back as he figured out what the rest of town already knew.

I glared at him again.

Hudson whistled low and shook his head. "When you two were in here, I wondered, but I figured she was just another one in line."

"Blake is the line," I growled.

"Wow. I never thought I'd see the day where Ian Jameson closes up his little black book."

I shook my head. "She doesn't want me. I can't close it up yet."

"What do you mean she doesn't want you? I saw the way you were together. She left with you."

"It's complicated," I said, not offering anything else.

"I've been told bartenders are really good listeners."

I snorted. "Too bad you own the place."

Hudson laughed and shook his head again. "Yeah. Maybe I should sell it."

I laughed with him and nodded when he set a new beer in front of me.

"She'll come around. You just need to give her a reason to see you as an option."

"She saw me," I murmured.

He rolled his eyes. "So you slept with her. I'm guessing you didn't tell her you want something more than sex, and now you're pissed because she thinks that's all there is between you."

I glared at him again.

"Women have two sides, man. One side sees a guy as someone she can have fun with. A guy to sleep with or hang out with or be friends with. She puts him in this off-limits category where she believes he's not someone to let in her heart. Then they have the other side, the side that looks for love. Even the ones who say they aren't looking are looking. But they don't look at friends and fuck buddies and guys who sleep with half the town. They look at guys who make them feel like they're special. Guys who romance them and spoil them and tell them how amazing they are. You're not that guy if you slept with her before you bought her dinner."

I scowled at him and took a pull from my beer. He leaned

back and waited for me to respond. "Don't you have other customers to piss off?"

He shrugged and glanced around to where his servers and the other bartender were taking care of everyone else. "Nope."

I drew in a sharp breath. "Let's say you're right. What the hell am I supposed to do?"

He grinned. "Treat her like a queen. Show her you're going to be there for her for something other than orgasms. You did give her orgasms, right?"

"Of course," I said gruffly. I wasn't usually one to kiss and tell, mostly because the entire damn town knew everything without me needing to confirm it, but if it helped me win Blake, I'd shout from the rooftops how many times she screamed my name.

"Good. Then at least she knows when you sleep together again she can count on you to make her feel good."

"I can't sleep with her again?" I blurted far louder than I intended.

"Sleep with who?" Eddie asked, sitting on the stool next to me.

"No one," I said the same time Hudson nodded at me and said, "Blake."

Eddie's eyebrows shot up the same way Hudson's did. "You and Blake?" He nodded to himself. "I like it. Georgia said she hoped you two got together. She saw something between you at our wedding."

I nodded but didn't speak. I never told anyone about the promise I made to Georgia. The woman saw everything, but I didn't want others to know I was chicken-shit when it came to telling Blake how I felt about her.

"I'm trying to tell him sleeping with her isn't the way to get her to be his," Hudson told Eddie. "He doesn't understand why he can't keep sleeping with her."

"What do you know anyway? You're single," I said with a grimace.

As soon as the words were out, I hated that I said them. Hudson froze for a second then tapped the bar in front of me and walked away without another word.

"Why did you say that?" Eddie asked.

"Because I'm an asshole," I replied.

"Yeah, you are. He doesn't deserve to be reminded of Hillary's passing," Eddie said.

I drew in a breath and got up. I slid my beer in front of Eddie. "Put your drinks on my tab. I'm going to talk to him and go."

Eddie nodded and took my beer. I went to find Hudson.

He was in the back room, staring at a case of beer. I knew he heard me walk in behind him, but he didn't turn around.

"I'm an asshole," I said. "And I'm sorry. It was a low blow. I'm just fucking scared and I hate it."

"Being in love isn't about being scared. Being in love is about knowing someone is there when you are," Hudson said.

"And you know more about love than I ever will. I can't even figure out how to get Blake to go out with me. She came over today because people are talking about us and she thought I was going to be mad. Because I have a reputation for not getting attached. She thinks I only want sex."

"I told you not to sleep with her," Hudson said, finally facing me. His arms were thick with muscles, his black tee stretched tight across them. He stood an inch or so taller than me, but he'd bulked up since he quit baseball and bought a bar. He easily had fifty pounds of muscle on me.

"I wish you'd told me that six hours ago. Then I might not be so fucked," I admitted.

Hudson shook his head. "You can change the way she sees you, it just won't be easy. You've always been a friend in her eyes. Now you're a fuck buddy. You've reduced your chances at her seeing you as someone she can count on, but it's not impossible to show her you can be."

I drew in a breath. "Thanks. I really am sorry about Hill. She was…"

"Everything," Hudson said. "She was perfect. And I don't think I'm ever going to find another woman like her."

I shrugged. "You never know. If I can get Blake to see me as something other than her friend and fuck buddy, maybe there's hope you'll find someone else."

He chuckled and shook his head. "You want Blake to want you. I'm happy on my own. I don't need another woman. I had my great love."

Shouting and a glass breaking sounded from the bar. I didn't think twice about following Hudson out and jumping in with him when he grabbed a wooden bat from behind the bar and got in between the two guys fighting.

One of them faced off with me, growling at me that I stood between him and the other asshole he was trading punches with.

"How about you calm down?" I said, not taking my eyes off him.

Hudson stood at my back, facing the other guy. His guy was clearly the aggressor. Hudson backed up into me when the guy he was opposing pushed forward to get to the guy I was watching. I didn't recognize them. They were younger than me, in their twenties, but clearly they knew each other.

"He had his hands on my girlfriend!" the guy behind me shouted.

My guy smirked. "She liked it."

"Dude," I said, shaking my head at him. "Don't make it worse."

He shrugged and smirked again. "If he doesn't know how to take care of his woman, I'll happily take over."

"I know how to take care of her," the other guy said. "You keep your fucking hands to yourself or I'll rip them off and shove them up your ass."

My guy snorted. "I'd kick your scrawny ass into next week if you tried."

"What's going on, gentlemen?" James Rucker asked, appearing next to Hudson and me. James was a MacKellar Cove police officer and a good friend of Hudson's.

The guy in front of me stood up and dropped his hands to his sides, looking submissive instead of cocky like he was seconds ago.

The other guy? Not so smart.

"That fucker touched my girlfriend. I'm going to kick his ass."

"Are you?" James asked.

"Hell, yeah, I am. He's going to regret ever touching her," the guy declared.

"Are you the one who started this? Who broke things?" James asked calmly.

"He started it when he put his hands on her."

James nodded, then calmly removed his cuffs and walked toward the guy. Immediately, he changed his tone.

"Whoa, whoa. What are those for?"

"Destruction of property and assault. We're going to take a ride," James said.

"Whoa, no. I didn't do all that."

James looked at my guy. "Your buddy here has a nice shiner. Someone hit him."

"Well, I did, but…"

"Then we need to take a ride. If he doesn't want to press charges, you can walk, but that's up to your friend."

My guy smirked. James glared at him and he wiped it away.

James cuffed the other guy and walked him outside, still

protesting his innocence. Hudson glared at my guy, but he walked away saying he wouldn't cause any more trouble.

"Thanks for having my back," Hudson said with a nod.

I nodded back. "Any time. Thanks for the advice."

He smirked. "I just hope you use it. Blake deserves it."

I nodded. I couldn't argue with that.

12

BLAKE

I couldn't remember the last time I painted so much. It's not that I didn't love it, but I struggled to come up with new things sometimes. But Ian sparked something in me that I couldn't walk away from.

It was well after midnight, and I was covered in paint. I had three new paintings done, paintings I wasn't sure I'd let anyone else see, and was working on another one. The colors and the passion and the sensuality of the pieces made me feel like a different person. Ian made me feel like a different person.

I finished the last stroke on the piece and stepped back. It was beautiful. Two people clearly having sex. Their faces weren't visible, and their features weren't clear, but in my mind, it was Ian and me.

The pieces I had would stay hidden in my closet, something I'd pull out and relive once Ian moved on to someone new. Maybe one day I'd meet someone else who made me feel the way he did, but for now, I was content knowing I could feel so alive.

I washed my supplies and had just changed out of my painting clothes into pajamas when the doorbell rang.

My heart leapt at the hope that it was Ian, but Ian was not the person who rang my doorbell in the middle of the night. As quickly as the hope blossomed, I pushed it away.

My mother leaned against the side of my house, asleep standing up. I shook my head and sighed, then helped her to the couch.

Just a typical Friday night.

I SPENT all day Saturday catching up on the things I didn't do during the week. Fun and thrilling things like laundry and dishes and cleaning my house. My mom left early Saturday morning without much of a thank you for letting her crash on my couch, again, but at least she was gone. I loved her, but I was sick of cleaning up her messes.

Saturday night rolled around and I still hadn't showered or gotten out of my pajamas. It was a really good night for a movie alone and a beer.

I'd just settled on the couch with my microwave dinner and beer when my phone dinged with a message.

Woody, my match from Book Boyfriends Wanted, sent me a new message. I was surprised when I got his first message. He sounded sweet and funny, and I wondered why a guy like him was on an online dating site. Karissa kept insisting most people used online dating these days. Since it'd been more than five years since I had a first date, I had to take her word for it.

WOODY

A friend told me women think of men as either someone they could see themselves falling in love with or not. Is that true?

I considered his question and wondered if there was an ulterior motive for asking.

COVEMOUSE

I thought you were okay with being friends.

WOODY

I am. Totally. But as far as I know, you're a woman, so you can help me out. Right?

I shrugged and thought about it. With William, we got to know each other through dating. We weren't friends first. We developed a relationship, but once we broke up, it was done.

The other guys I dated were similar. Even if I knew them before we got together, we weren't close. Ian was the first guy I'd ever crossed that line with.

COVEMOUSE

I think I'd mostly agree.

WOODY

Mostly?

COVEMOUSE

Well, friends can become lovers, but does it happen that often? Usually if you're that close, you don't want to ruin the friendship.

WOODY

Isn't love worth the risk?

I sighed. I wanted to believe it was, but I'd never experienced the kind of love that would be worth it.

COVEMOUSE

I don't know. I haven't had a friend I'd rather risk losing as a friend for a chance at love. Then again, love isn't something I'm confident in at all.

WOODY

You're a cynic? That surprises me.

COVEMOUSE

Not a cynic. A realist. I've seen people in love, the kind of love I used to dream about. I'm starting to think it's only an option for some people. Some of us are destined to have mediocre love lives and mediocre sex.

WOODY

That's the most depressing thing I've ever heard.

I laughed out loud.

COVEMOUSE

I know, but you asked what I thought.

WOODY

True. I shouldn't have asked if I didn't want your honest answer.

I wanted to tell him something that would give him hope. If there was a woman in his life he liked, I hoped it worked out for them, but I struggled with the idea of forever love. People fought and divorced and died. Nothing lasted to the end of time.

WOODY

So, if I have this friend that I like, and not just in a friend way, but in a I want to tell her I love her way, are you saying I shouldn't tell her because she probably doesn't feel the same way?

I drew in a breath. Part fear and part excitement raced through me. I didn't want him to tell me he liked me, but knowing there was no way he was talking about me hurt a little.

We agreed to be friends, but there was a part of me that hoped we could build something. He made me laugh, and if he was half as cute as he was funny, maybe one day we could actually meet.

Once things with Ian were over and I was ready to move on. If ever.

But he was in love with someone else. Someone real in his world. Someone who would be foolish not to love him back.

COVEMOUSE

She'd be a fool not to feel the same way about you.

WOODY

What makes you say that?

COVEMOUSE

You seem like a good guy. The kind of guy who would take her out and make sure she knew she was special to you. Even if you were friends, I think you're thinking about it the right way. You're not carrying her to your bed and making her scream. You're showing her you care.

I hit send before I regretted my words. I knew where things stood with Ian, but Woody wanted advice. He was looking to show the woman he loved that he wanted her. She needed to know it. And while Ian brought out more passion in me than anyone else I'd ever known, passion was Ian's specialty. He wasn't the kind of guy who would cook dinner or plan a date. He was a sexy, sweet, funny guy you could count on for a few orgasms and a few laughs. He was not the kind of guy you could count on for forever.

WOODY

What's wrong with carrying her to my bed? I do some of my best work there. 😉

COVEMOUSE

It'll mean more once she knows it's not just about sex for you. Sex is great, and great sex is amazing, trust me. But if you want something long term, sex is not the way to start.

WOODY

You sound like you're speaking from experience.

COVEMOUSE

Unfortunately.

WOODY

How do you know there wasn't more than sex with him?

COVEMOUSE

He's just not that kind of guy. I wish he was, but he isn't.

WOODY

Sorry, CoveMouse. Hopefully you'll find someone who is.

I sucked in a breath and nodded. I already knew most of the men in town, at least the single ones who were close to my age. I was losing hope that I'd find someone. But I was okay alone. I had my friends. I had my house. I had my work. And thanks to Ian, I had some amazing fantasies to keep me warm at night.

That was all I really needed.

SUNDAY AFTERNOON I headed over to Book Boyfriends Unlimited earlier than usual. I wanted to talk to Finley about the mural before Karissa showed up, and I was anxious about her finding out about Ian and me.

There were two customers inside when I walked in. Finley smiled and waved to me from where she was talking to them about the new release they were looking at.

"He's so sexy. I have a thing for alphas. Not the asshole ones, but the take charge and make you feel safe and loved ones. He's like that," Finley said.

"You make it sound like he's real," one of the women said. "Too bad there aren't men like him in the real world."

"I agree. Have you checked out the app Book Boyfriends Wanted? It's a new dating app. A friend on mine actually developed it because of exactly what you're saying." Finley pulled out her phone and showed them the app. "You answer a bunch of questions about the books you like to read and what draws you in, and then the app matches you with people who like the same books and have similar personalities."

"Are you kidding me?" the woman said, glancing back at her friend. "This is amazing. I'm getting it right now."

"Me, too," her friend said. "I'd love to meet a guy like the men in these books. Do they actually exist? Have you met anyone yet?"

Finley shrugged. "I've had a couple matches. A few guys I've been talking to. It's only been live a few weeks, so it's early. So far, I like it. What about you, Blake?" she called out to me.

I walked over and joined them. "I'm the same. I'm not really looking for a relationship right now, but I wanted to support our friend. I've matched with a couple, but only one that I chat with regularly. There aren't any pictures so you're getting to know people without knowing anything other than what they say."

"Which is interesting," Finley said, "because you could

know these people in real life but have no idea it's the same person. I like it because it opens you up to new people."

I nodded in agreement. I wondered who Woody was, but it didn't really matter. He was a nice guy who was becoming a friend. That was all I really needed, and knowing he didn't know who I was allowed me to be more honest with him than I would have been with most other people.

"I'm so happy we came in here today. Between the new books and the app, I feel like it's going to be a great week."

Finley led the women to the register and chatted with them while they checked out. I went to our seat in the back and claimed a chair while I waited for her to join me.

She said goodbye to the customers and was standing in front of me when the door closed. "How's it going?"

I nodded. "Good. But I wanted to talk to you."

"About my brother?"

"What? No. Why?"

Finley shrugged and looked away. "I just figured you were here to talk about Ian. What's going on?"

I shook my head. I did want to talk to her about him, but if she already knew then maybe I didn't have to. "I, um, I have mural ideas. I was going to show them to Karissa tonight, but I wanted to see what you thought first."

She opened and closed her fists quickly and said, "Gimme, gimme, gimme."

I chuckled and handed over the drawings I did. I printed out copies for Karissa to keep in case she wanted to think about it for a few days. I hoped she loved my ideas, but I was nervous.

"Wow," Finley breathed when she looked at the first one. It featured Ms. Georgia, but it also had Earl and the logo, along with tables and nondescript people. It gave a feel of the restaurant, but it wasn't all that central to Ms. Georgia. It was one of my earlier attempts.

Finley looked at the next one with MacKellar Cove as the central piece. Others had the river, the square, or other parts of town, all with Ms. Georgia as a part of the drawing.

The last one, which I strategically put last, was of Ms. Georgia waving you over. Her smile was bright and welcoming. Her eyes glistened with joy. Behind her was a table with Eddie and Karissa. Earl was in the kitchen, a pancake flipping in the air. The water moved behind them as though the back doors were open and the river was a part of Cracked. The colors were vibrant and fun. The entire picture felt like Ms. Georgia.

Finley's eyes welled and she shook her head. "Oh, shit, Blake. This is the one. That's Ms. Georgia. I can see her. I can even hear her saying, 'Come on in. We always have room for you.' Karissa is going to love this."

"Are you sure?" I asked, chewing my nail. "I don't want it to upset her."

Finley shook her head. "She's going to love it."

I took the stack of pictures back from Finley and nodded. "Thanks, Fin. I appreciate your help."

She grinned and wiped the tears from beneath her lashes. "Any time." She took a deep breath then met my gaze. "So, what's happening with my brother?"

The direct question shouldn't have surprised me, but it did. Finley made it sound before like she was okay with Ian and I getting together, but I wasn't sure if that was still the case.

"I don't know."

"Does that mean something is going on with you guys?"

I sucked in a breath and blew it out slowly. "You know how Ian is. I mean, he's an awesome guy, but he's not the kind of guy who's going to stick. We...I went over there Friday to talk to him, and we ended up..."

"In bed?" she asked, her eyebrows jumping up in surprise. "Wow."

"I know, I'm not his type. But—"

"Whoa, wait, what? Did he say that?"

I shook my head. "No, but I've seen the women he's left O'Kelley's with over the years. They don't look like me."

"So?"

"So, I'm just not his type. And he's not mine, really. He's too good-looking for me, and he's not a forever kind of guy. This guy I was matched with? He's a forever kind of guy. He's in love with his friend, and he asked me how he should tell her. He's nice and funny and he's the kind of guy I should be going after. Not Ian who'll never commit to one woman long enough to fall for her like Woody."

"Woody?" Finley asked, her attention snapping to me.

I rolled my eyes and held up my phone. "The guy from the app."

Her lips pinched. "Oh."

"I like Ian. I don't know if you want to hear about it, but I like him. He's always been a good guy, and…how much do you want to know?"

She shrugged. "You can say whatever you want. I'm your best friend. Just because you're talking about my brother doesn't mean I can't be objective."

"Finley, I've never felt like I did when we were together. I mean, he does this thing with his tongue and—"

"Wait a minute," Finley said with a wide grin. "Are we talking oral sex? Like Willie never did?"

I groaned. "You can't start calling him Willie, too."

She snorted. "I always did, behind your back. You know I never loved him. Not for you. He's too stiff, and not in a good way."

I couldn't help my laugh. "I shouldn't laugh at that. He's a good guy, and he was good to me."

Finley shrugged. "He was, but it sounds like in just one day someone else might be better." She drew in a breath and shuddered. "Okay, tell me fast because I really don't want to think about my brother's mouth between your legs the next time I see him."

I snorted. "It was so good, Fin. He said he loved it, and oh, my God, I can't even remember how many times I screamed his name. And the sex? I've never had sex like that. Where we couldn't get enough of each other. It was like everyone talked about in Hawaii. Remember?"

She nodded, a dreamy look in her eyes.

"I didn't think it existed, but it does. But I know it won't last. It's Ian, and he'll move on soon. I'll still be friends with him, but I'm not getting attached. I promise. Nothing needs to change. Okay?"

Finley pressed her lips together and nodded. She gave me a smile that looked more than a little forced, but before I could push her, Karissa and Laura walked in.

"Hey, Rissa, Blake and I got you two new subscribers today. Super cute girls who were complaining that the men in books aren't real," Finley said.

I wasn't sure if she didn't want the others to know I'd slept with Ian or if she just wanted to talk about something else, but I forced a smile and went with the new topic of conversation. After all, we weren't there to dissect my love life. We were there to eat cake and talk about book boyfriends. At least I knew with them it would all work out in the end.

13

*E*lise brought strawberry cheesecake and set it on the table in front of us. She was the last to arrive, but we were still catching up on the week so she hadn't missed anything.

"That smells like heaven," Karissa said. "Where are the forks?"

"No plate for you tonight?" Finley teased her.

Karissa shook her head. "I've been working on updates for the app all weekend and I've barely eaten anything. I'm running on coffee and sugar at this point."

"You need real food," Laura told her.

Karissa growled at her. Actually growled.

We all leaned away.

"Um, Ris?" Finley said.

She sighed. "I'm sorry. I'm just ready for this to roll out to more people. Right now it's doing really well, but it's not an easy thing to create these apps. Especially one like this."

"Are you okay?" I asked her.

She nodded and sat back. "Yeah, just tired. Sorry, Laur. I

know I need to eat better and sleep more and do all the things my mom always made me do. When I was this deep into apps before, she always showed up with home-cooked meals for the freezer and demanded I take a break. It's…hard. You know?"

The rest of us nodded. I reached for Karissa's hand. Finley took my other one, and Laura grabbed Karissa's. Elise and Trinity held on, too. The six of us sat there for a minute, smiling at each other.

"Mom would have loved this," Karissa said. "She loved all of you like her own daughters. And I'm sure she loved you, too, Trinity."

We all laughed.

"I loved her," Trinity said. "She was one of those people who was only in my life for a short time, but her impact will last forever."

"Speaking of an impact that lasts forever, Blake has something to ask you," Finley said.

"Fin," I hissed.

Karissa turned to me. "What is it?"

"I—" I huffed and glared at Finley. "I was going to talk to you after. When everyone was gone."

Karissa shifted in her seat. "Um, okay. It's up to you."

"Just tell her now," Finley said. She picked up my folder and handed it to Karissa. "Rip the band-aid off."

Karissa looked up at me expectantly. "Blake?"

I drew a breath and blew it out slowly. "Earl asked me to do a new mural on the side of Cracked. He wanted something with your mom, something so people would know her. Even people who'd never met her."

Karissa's eyes teared up. She pressed her lips together and looked up at the ceiling. Her throat worked to swallow stiffly. Finally, she took a breath and met my gaze. "Are you going to do it?"

I hesitated then nodded. "If you're okay with it. But you have to approve it."

"Eddie's—"

"Earl talked to him before he talked to me," I said.

Karissa blew out a laugh. "Chicken. Figures he'd ask Eddie and leave you to talk to me."

I breathed a laugh. "Yeah. I should have asked you before, but I wanted to have some ideas to show you. You can take all of those home and think about it. If you say no, it's done. Earl said the same thing."

Karissa shook her head. "No, it's fine. Mom was a staple in there. She loved the place. It's really amazing that Earl wants to honor her like that, and that you're going to be the one to do it. I like that."

"Thank you, Rissa," I said softly, emotion choking my words.

"Do I get to pick which one you do?"

I nodded. "If you'd like to, absolutely. Earl has final say, and he has his favorites, but I'm sure he'll go with whatever you want."

Karissa nodded and opened the folder. She smiled at her mom's face and ran a finger over her smile. I held my breath as she slowly flipped through one after the other pictures. After each one, she handed it to Laura, and they were passed around the room. I had the first one in my lap when Karissa gasped.

"That's her," she breathed. "Oh, God, Blake. You captured her right there. How she looked before she was sick. She always waved people in, showing them to a table and pairing people up so no one went without a seat. And, oh, Blake. Is that me and Eddie?"

I nodded.

"And Earl. You guys should all be in there, too. The river.

Blake, this is it. This is the one. I love them all, but this is the one," she gushed.

I smiled at her and accepted the praise from the others as Karissa's favorite, and mine, was passed around. Everyone agreed that it looked just like Georgia and had to be the picture on the side of Cracked.

It was also Earl's favorite so I had no doubt he'd approve it.

"Thank you for doing this, Blake," Karissa said. "It really means a lot to me."

I shrugged. "It was Earl's idea. I'm just the cheapest painter he knows."

Karissa laughed with me but shook her head. "You're the best painter he knows. Can I keep this?"

I nodded. "Of course. I have the original painting, though. If you'd rather have that."

"You don't mind?"

I shook my head. "Of course not. I'd be honored if you had it."

"Thanks, babe. You're going to do her justice. I just know it," Karissa said with a bright smile, one that matched her mom's.

I was honored she trusted me so much. I just hoped I could do her justice. That I could bring Ms. Georgia to life the same way she brought everyone around her to life every day.

I sat back and let the conversation happen around me. A lot of thoughts ran through my mind, from Ms. Georgia to Ian to Karissa and the rest of us. It took Ms. Georgia a long time to find Eddie again. She had two great loves, but did that mean someone else missed out? Was love finite, or did it get refreshed?

That was the question Finley asked when I jumped back into listening to the conversation.

"I have to believe we can all have as much love as we want," Elise said. "If not, then what's the point?"

"All those people at Georgia's wedding made me think love might actually exist," Finley confessed. "When I opened Book Boyfriends Unlimited, I wanted to believe in love, but a part of me thought the only way I'd ever experience it was between the covers of a book. After meeting all of them and seeing love played out in so many ways, I have to think it's out there."

"But none of us have seen it," I argued.

"I loved someone once. I thought I was going to spend my life with Xavier," Karissa said quietly.

"But that's my point. Love is flawed. I want to believe in it, but I've never seen it. All those people, they were on vacation. They were in the middle of paradise. We have no idea what it's like when they're home," I said.

Laura leaned forward and shook her head. "They're all like that all the time. When I lived in Winterville, it blew my mind. I was jealous of it, which isn't fair, but it's the truth. Peyton would talk about them all and she was baffled, but she became one of them."

"But things almost ended with her and Wyatt," I added.

Laura nodded. "Almost, but that's what love is. Not giving up. Sticking by the person you love no matter what. Always putting them above you. Dying for them if you have to."

"And that's why you love Romeo and Juliet," Finley teased. "Hopefully you don't have to die to find love. But Blake's more cynical. She's Buttercup, you guys. It's not just her favorite book, she is Buttercup. *The Princess Bride* speaks to her."

"I'm not Buttercup," I argued.

"You are, though," Karissa said. "I'd be willing to bet someone could walk right up to you and tell you he loved you, and you'd just laugh and say he was joking or lying. You don't believe in it."

I shook my head. "Weren't we just talking about how love is finite? What are the chances some random guy is going to walk up to me and tell me he loves me?"

Finley shrugged. "Maybe he isn't random. Maybe he's someone you already know, but you don't think he'd ever actually feel that way about you. Maybe you're too busy looking for the flaws to see that everything and everyone is flawed, but those flaws are what makes love and life beautiful."

"When did you become such a romantic?" Laura asked Finley.

Finley smiled and reached across me to grab Karissa's hand. "When I went to Hawaii and witnessed love joining two people forever."

Karissa drew in a breath and nodded. "We should all be so lucky."

"We will be," Elise said. "I can feel it."

EARL WANTED me to start on the mural right away, but I needed the tips from working at Cracked, so we agreed I'd split my time and work the morning shift every day and spend my afternoons on whatever I needed to do. I wanted to do something on the mural every day, but with three jobs now, it was tough to work out what my schedule needed to look like.

I spent the first week outlining my drawing using the bricks on the building as my guide. Earl had the building pressure washed and all the paint cleaned off, so it was ready as soon as I was ready.

I wasn't ready.

I stared up at the wall and what would become Ms. Georgia's face and couldn't get started. I seriously considered walking away for another day when my phone dinged.

I smiled when I saw the message was from Woody. We'd been chatting regularly, and while I wasn't close to ready to tell him who I was, I enjoyed having a friend I could say just about anything to. Especially a male friend who wouldn't judge me and could give me advice on men.

If I ever wanted to ask.

WOODY

I hate wondering what someone is thinking. Like right now, I really want to know what she's thinking, but she feels so out of reach.

I smiled. Woody told me about the woman he's in love with. I was a little jealous, but we were friends so I was also happy for him. I wasn't jealous that he loved someone else, more that I didn't have someone who loved me like he loved her.

COVEMOUSE

You should ask her.

WOODY

LOL. She's too skittish for that. She'd run. Every time I tell her I like her, she disappears for a while.

COVEMOUSE

Sometimes we can't handle things like that. It's hard to believe people when you've always been let down.

WOODY

So, what do I do?

COVEMOUSE

Keep trying.

WOODY

Thanks. I guess that's all I can do.

I took a deep breath and blew it out slowly.

COVEMOUSE

My mom is a train wreck. I've been taking care of her for years. I don't know how to help her without losing her. My dad has never been in my life. I have an amazing group of friends, but they've known me forever. For me, letting someone in is painful. I'm always waiting for them to disappoint me because it's what I've always had. If your girl is anything like me, she needs a lot of reassurance that you're not going anywhere.

WOODY

I love you! You're so smart, and I know you're right. Thanks. Truly. Thank you.

I smiled and tucked my phone away. My heart jumped at his words, but I knew he didn't mean them the way I wanted them to be said. The woman he loved was lucky. She had an amazing guy just waiting to love her. I wanted that. I talked a big game and told myself, and my friends, I didn't know if love existed, but the truth was I wanted it to. I saw it in other people, and I really wanted to think it could happen to me.

But telling myself it couldn't or wouldn't was easier than having hope crushed every time I let it blossom.

I looked up at the wall again and smiled. Georgia was always smiling down on us. I knew that without a doubt. And I had the wonderful honor of bringing her to life so she could smile down on hundreds, if not thousands, of others. I was ready to make it happen.

I hooked up my harness and climbed up onto the scaffold. I'd decided to paint Ms. Georgia first then work on the rest of the mural. I let myself get lost in the day, slowly bringing part of her face to life. I was so focused on what I was doing, I barely noticed the outside world until the sun dipped low and shadows grew on Ms. Georgia.

"You hungry?" I heard from below me. I peeked over the edge of the scaffolding and smiled. Ian was standing on the sidewalk across from me holding up a bag of food from Cracked.

"Always," I said back.

"Then get your cute butt down here and have some dinner with me," he said.

My cheeks warmed at his words, but just like with Woody, I knew he didn't mean them the way I wanted to take them.

My hands were a mess, and I could only imagine how much worse the rest of me was. My stomach said not to care and I climbed down. I tugged on the straps of my harness to get it free, but the one strap was stuck.

"Need some help?" Ian asked, his husky voice sending a shiver down my spine.

"Um, yeah. I guess wearing it for so long without loosening it, I pulled something too tight."

He ran a finger along the strap between my breasts and looped his finger under the D-ring nestled right there. He tugged, pulling me to him. "I'm really happy my shop doesn't overlook the square. I wouldn't get anything done if I could see you all day. Strapped up in this thing so your breasts stand out and your ass is highlighted. I'm going to have fantasies about you wearing only this."

I narrowed my eyes and laughed. "I think that would chafe."

He smiled at me. "I'd rub you down with lotion and make it all better."

I laughed again, wondering what in the hell was happening. I tried acting like nothing had changed with Ian, but in my mind, everything had changed. He'd been inside me. He'd kissed me and touched me and made me scream his name. I'd never screamed during sex before, but with Ian, I couldn't help myself.

But it was Ian. My friend. My best friend's brother. A guy who moved on after one night. And it'd been eleven days since we slept together.

"As much fun as I'm sure that would be, I'd rather not suffer through the chafing first. And I'm starving."

I tugged at the harness again, and he slid his hand down my side then between my thighs. My breath hitched at the feel of him there. Heat pooled in my belly, and need sparked to life in my veins. Every night since we were together I'd thought about the way he touched me. And every night I'd been disappointed that I couldn't come close to making myself feel the way he did.

I was sexually frustrated in a way I'd never been in my life. I spent five years with William and was indifferent to sex the whole time. One time with Ian and I was dying for another night with him. A night I knew would never happen.

"Spread your thighs for me, Blake," Ian said, the low rumble of his voice only making the whole situation more unbearable.

I did as he asked and clenched them right back together when his hand brushed the inside of my thigh, an inch from where I ached to have him touch me.

He chuckled. "I can't get the strap loose if my hand is trapped between your legs."

I took a breath and spread my legs again. I counted to ten

and closed my eyes, praying he was fast. I wouldn't be able to hold back a moan if his fingers lingered too long.

"There," he said triumphantly.

The straps fell away from my thighs, and the entire harness draped, allowing me to loop it over my head and free myself from it. "Thanks."

Ian nodded but stayed close to me, close enough that I could still feel his heat as I folded up my harness and stuffed it into my bag.

"Come and eat, babe," he said when I zipped up the bag. He grabbed the bag from me and took my hand with his other one.

How many times had Ian held my hand and I never thought anything of it? How many times had he called me 'babe' and it didn't faze me? How many times had he bought me dinner or something and we ate together?

What should have been normal was now tainted. Nothing between us felt natural. Not for me. I kept remembering the way his hands felt holding my breasts. The way his tongue felt inside me. The way *he* felt inside me.

"Sit," he said forcefully when we reached the pair of chairs with our food and his sweatshirt. "You've been out here for hours. You must be starving."

I nodded. "I am. I didn't realize how late it had gotten."

"Good thing I came along, huh?"

I smiled at him. "Always."

He held my gaze for a long minute, both of us lost in each other. I wanted to lean forward and kiss him again, but we weren't in his shop. We weren't in private. And he wasn't mine to kiss in public. He was my friend. Nothing more.

"So, what did you bring?"

He shook his head slightly, leaning back. He looked away and focused on the bag in his lap. "Everything. Broccoli and cheddar omelet, potatoes, french toast, bacon, and milkshakes."

My eyes widened. "Milkshakes?"

He nodded and pulled one out of the bag. "Chocolate. Of course. I know what you like, Blake."

Now why did that sound so dirty? And why did I think he actually meant it that way?

14

IAN

I tried so hard not to go straight to sex with her, but it was almost impossible. After holding back for so many years, being able to say things to her about how beautiful she was and let her know I thought she was amazing was really hard.

See? Dirty, dirty. Just like I wanted my girl.

Her eyes dilated when I told her I knew what she liked. I couldn't get exactly what she liked out of my head since she left my bed. I was hard every time I walked into my room because it still smelled like her, and I was more than ready to have her back in my bed.

"Well, I have been drinking chocolate milkshakes since I figured out what chocolate was," she said, again dismissing the point.

I leaned in closer. "That's not what I meant, and you know it, Blake." The scarlet blush on her cheeks was enough of an acknowledgement for me. I nodded to the wall. "It looks good."

She scoffed. "It's a little bit of brown on a brick wall."

I shrugged. "Yeah, but I can see it. I think it's good that

you're starting with Ms. Georgia. She's the whole point, and everything revolves around her."

She met my gaze with her own surprised one. "That was my thought, too."

I grinned. "I do know you, Blake. A little better than I did a few weeks ago, but that doesn't change the fact that I know who you are."

She smiled and ducked her chin. Blake didn't like talking about herself. She never had. She wasn't the kind of person who bragged about what she did, even when she had every right to. I always wondered why, but after learning about her situation with her mom, I couldn't help but think it was another thing Nadine had taken from her.

"Eat," I said gently, nodding toward her food. She'd only taken one bite, and I knew she had to be starving.

"Maybe I'll lose some weight working on this painting. Forgetting to eat and being on my feet and working all day might be good for the size of my ass," she said with an eye roll.

I growled at her. "What did I tell you about saying things like that?"

She looked up at me, her mouth full and her eyes confused. She didn't remember.

"That if you kept it up I was going to have to silence you. Your curves are hot, babe. You shouldn't want to change anything."

She shrugged and chewed slowly.

"You're thinking about it, aren't you, Blake?" I asked, dropping my voice so my words barely lingered between us. "About all the ways I can silence you. And all the ways I can make you scream again."

She sucked in a ragged breath, her breasts rising and stretching out her tee. The faint line of her nipples stood out.

"You're turned on, aren't you, babe? You want me as much as I want you."

"Why?" she breathed.

"We're not fucking doing this again, Blake. I told you I want you. Why do you keep asking me for a reason? You're gorgeous and being inside you was like…everything, Blake. I want to fuck you. I want to make love to you. I want to lick you until you can't breathe and all you can do is beg me for more. I want you, Blake. Why does there have to be another reason?"

Her pulse fluttered in her neck, but there was something in her eyes that said she didn't like my answer. Something that told me I was wrong, again, to make it all about sex. She told me not to. She told me to tell her how I felt. And still, I kept her at a distance. I didn't trust her to love me back.

"What are you doing tonight?" she asked after a minute.

"Well, I got as far as buying you dinner, but I wasn't going to hope for anything more than that."

She smiled. "Want to come over? We don't have to have sex or anything. I mean, we're still friends, right? We can just hang out?"

"Always, babe. What do you need to do before you go?" I asked, hating that she put a barrier between us. I knew I wasn't supposed to sleep with her again, but I didn't want us to go back to being just friends either.

She looked up at the mural, excitement and joy in her eyes. "I need to pack up the paints and get everything inside. The scaffolding stays up, but all my supplies are going in the office."

I nodded. "I'll start on that while you finish eating. Anything special I need to do with the brushes?"

"I'll clean them. If you want to get them inside, I have a bucket to wash them."

"Got it. Relax and enjoy your dinner. I'll do what I can."

She smiled up at me as I got up and jogged away. I needed a few minutes away from her. To clear my head. I didn't want to be just friends with Blake, but if that was all she wanted, I'd have no choice but to take it. No matter what, I wanted her in my life, so I was going to let her make the next move. And if she didn't, I had my answer.

I cleaned up her supplies and told myself I'd spent years keeping my hands to myself and I could do it for another night. I brought her dinner with the intention of seeing her, not screwing her, so keeping my hands to myself should have been easy for a few hours. Forever wasn't going to be as simple, but once she found someone else, I would back away. I'd done it when she was with Willie. I wanted her to be happy, and if that meant she wasn't with me, I'd deal with it.

And hate every fucking second of it.

"Dammit," I swore into the utility sink.

"Whoa," she said from right behind me. "Don't kill my brushes. What's wrong? I have more if something happened."

I shook my head. "They're fine."

"Are you okay?" she asked, parroting the question I asked her so many times. I always hoped she'd open up to me whenever I asked that question, but just like her, I closed up.

"I'm good. Almost finished here." I forced a smile for her and stepped back when she nudged me out of the way.

I set the cans where she told me they went and stayed out of her way while she finished cleaning the brushes, then walked out with her.

She was quiet as we went through the streets of our town. I could see the wheels spinning in her head, but I let them spin since my own were spiraling out of control.

"Ian!" someone shouted from behind us. A woman.

I turned and just barely caught Beth before she leaped into my arms. I stumbled but grinned at her happy laugh.

"Where are you going?" she asked when she pulled back.

Her legs were wrapped around my waist, her large breasts touching my chest even as she positioned away from me.

We'd been in the exact same position when we slept together. It had been over a year ago, but Beth was fun. She was great in bed. But she wasn't Blake. She didn't even compare to Blake.

I nodded toward Blake and tried to set Beth down with my hands on her hips. She refused to unwrap her strong legs as I said, "Blake and I are hanging out."

Beth pouted and stuck out her bottom lip. She was one of those women who used her sexuality to get what she wanted. "You should come hang out with me. I haven't seen you in forever."

I tried again to push her off, but she still didn't budge. "Not tonight, Beth. Maybe another time."

"It's fine," Blake said with a forced smile. "I don't mind."

"See?" Beth said. "She doesn't care. Come hang out with me. We're drinking shots. Maybe if you're really good, I'll let you do one off me." She looked down to her breasts, cleavage on full display.

Yep, I'd taken more than a couple shot glasses from between her tits. And a few shots from her belly button. And licked her neck once or twice. Beth was fun. But I didn't want meaningless sex. What I wanted was walking away from me at a fast pace.

"Blake!" I called out.

She just waved and kept walking.

"Don't worry about her," Beth said. "I'm single again, and we can hook up."

I looked at Beth and clenched my jaw. She wasn't dumb and she wasn't a bad person. But when I looked at her, I could see the pain in her eyes.

"You should go see Ricky."

She blanched and pulled away from me.

"I heard he's a mess without you, and I think you feel the same, Beth. Don't throw away what you had on a night with me or some other guy who isn't worthy of you. Fix things with the guy you love."

She sucked in a breath and finally unwound her legs. Her eyes were glassy as she turned them away from me. "I…"

"Try, Beth. You'll be happier."

She looked up at me again and nodded. "Thanks, Ian. And I'm sorry."

I shrugged. "I can still catch her."

Beth looked down the street after Blake then back at me. "I think she'll be good for you. I hope it works out."

I nodded, hating how see-through I was to everyone but Blake. "Me, too."

I waited until Beth turned around before I took off after Blake. She'd turned off the street already, which meant she was almost home. Getting through a locked door was harder than walking in with her.

I couldn't see her when I approached her house, and I almost gave up. But it was Blake. And if I was going to find out if there could be anything between us, I had to keep trying.

I rang her doorbell and waited. I wanted to pound on the door, but she was in charge. I had to remember that.

I rang the bell again, and she finally opened the door. She'd changed into pajama pants and a tank top, one that fit tight over her breasts and highlighted her nipples. Jesus, the woman was going to fucking kill me.

"Where's Beth?" she asked.

I shook my head. "She didn't want me. She just wanted to erase Ricky."

Her eyebrows jumped up for a second. Her lips pursed together. She nodded once. "I see. Well, there are plenty of other options for you."

"What did I say?"

She forced a smile. "Nothing, Ian. I'm tired. I'm going to bed."

"Blake, talk to me. What did I say?"

She started to close the door without another word, but I stuck my foot in. It hurt like a son of a bitch when the heavy door hit my foot, but I wasn't going to move it until she let me in.

"Please, Ian. I'm exhausted. I don't have time to be one of your women. I don't have the energy."

"What are you talking about?" I asked.

She sighed. "You collect women, Ian. I'd be willing to bet you've been with at least one or two women since we slept together. I know who you are, and I'm not going to ask you to change, but I don't have the energy to fight with you about it tonight. Or to have sex with you knowing the only reason you aren't with Beth is because she changed her mind."

I clenched my jaw so tight it cracked. I was fucking pissed off. She had no idea, and the only way to clue her in was to tell her the truth. Fuck me.

"Beth changed her mind because I *told* her to go see Ricky. Because I'd rather be here with you than with her. So, first of all, let's get that straight. I'm not the kind of guy who thinks about one woman while I'm inside another. That's a shitty thing to do. And I haven't been with anyone else since you. I haven't been with anyone else since Hawaii because you're the one I want, Blake. I don't know what it's going to take for me to get that through your head, but you're the one whose doorstep I'm on, begging to come inside. You're the one I think about when I wrap my hand around myself. You're the one I was thinking about when you walked in on me in Hawaii. And the only reason I didn't ask you to join me then was because you were in a relationship. I've tried to give you a chance to get over Willie, but I'm fucking done waiting,

Blake. I want you. I want you in my bed. I want you in my life. And if you don't feel the same, put me out of my misery and tell me now."

Breath heaved in and out of me, dragging my chest up and down. Blake just stared at me. Her mouth fell open sometime during my rant. Her gaze was locked on me. But I had no idea what any of it meant.

Then she opened the door and jumped at me. I groaned as I caught her, sliding my hands over her ass and stepping inside. I kicked her door closed behind us and walked straight to the couch, kissing her the entire time.

I sat down with her on my lap and ran my hands over her body. I loved touching her. Her curves drove me crazy, and being able to feel them through her tiny little tank top made it even harder to keep my control. I swiped my thumbs over her taut nipples and earned a moan for it. I tugged her hair to twist her head where I wanted it and she sighed into my mouth.

Kissing Blake was a full body experience. She got into it as much as I did, her hands running down my chest, then sliding back up and fisting in my hair. I groaned and pulled her closer, needing to feel every inch of her pressed against me.

She moaned again and slid her hips back, grinding her center on me. I felt her heat pulsing through me, and every cell in my body ached to fill her.

I slid the tiny straps of her tank top down her arms to where they caught at her elbows. I tugged her top down, exposing her breasts, and dragged my tongue down her neck until I could lick one nipple. She held my head in place, rocking gently over me while I enjoyed the feel of her.

My thumb brushed bare skin at her waistband and dipped under her shirt. Her skin was soft and smooth and warm. I drew her nipple into my mouth, fitting almost her entire breast inside, and spread my fingers on her back so she couldn't move.

She whimpered and pushed against me. "Ian," she cried.

I ignored her and switched to her other nipple. I nipped the side of her breast on my way and flicked the tip of my tongue over her peaked nipple. She gasped and leaned back, letting me support her weight as I had my way with her.

"Ian," she moaned softly.

My cock throbbed. The way she said my name made it impossible to resist touching her. I wanted to feel her. To make her as crazy as she made me.

"So beautiful," I murmured against her flesh.

She snorted.

I nipped her.

"Ow!"

"You're beautiful, Blake. The most beautiful woman I've ever seen."

She shook her head. "Beth and every other woman you've slept with—"

"Don't you dare tell me you aren't as sexy as all of them combined," I growled at her. "I won't let you speak that way about yourself. You have all of them beat by a mile, Blake."

She rolled her eyes quickly, as though she thought I wouldn't notice.

I bit her again.

"Stop doing that!"

"Stop acting like you're not gorgeous, babe. I'm here with you because I want to be. Because I think you're amazing. Because you're the only one I want to be with. I know all you see are what you think are flaws, but I see a strong, sexy, smart woman who drives me crazy and makes me forget everything outside of us."

"How do you do that?" she breathed.

"Do what?"

"Make me forget that I'm not perfect? You did it when we were at your place, too. I don't feel like I'm...the same Blake when I'm with you. I feel like I'm someone else. Someone different."

I shook my head. "You're still the same Blake. You're just letting yourself see the woman I see instead of the woman you always see. See yourself through my eyes, Blake."

I slid my gaze down her body and let all the ways she turned me on show on my face. Giving her that peek inside my head was terrifying, but it was damn worth it when goosebumps rose over her bare flesh and a red flush slid from her throat to her nipples. Her perfect breasts rose and fell quickly with her rapid breaths. Her fingers tightened in my hair, tugging on the short strands, but I didn't care. All I cared about was the look in her eyes. The one that said she understood how much I wanted her and wasn't going to run from it.

Until she pulled back, slipping away from me and making me doubt everything.

15

I watched her, my breath frozen in my lungs, as she withdrew from me. I wanted to reach for her, to drag her back to me, but I wasn't going to force her to be with me.

I released my hands from her back and let her slip away. She sank to the floor in front of me and looked up, and my brain finally kicked in with a loud *fuck, yeah*.

Her hands went for my shorts and fumbled with the button. I sucked in a breath, aching for her touch. She finally released the button and drew down the zipper, then reached into my briefs and wrapped her hand around my dick.

"Jesus," I breathed, jerking at her touch.

She stroked me slowly, squeezing at the tip and dragging her hand back down to my base. I lifted my hips and pushed my shorts and briefs down to my ankles, dying to see her hand on me.

Her short nails were speckled with brown paint. Her small hand barely wrapped all the way around me. I licked my lips as she brought her hand to the tip, then groaned when she smeared my precum with her thumb. She looked up at me and held my gaze as she lowered her lips to me.

"Blake," I groaned. "Fuck, Blake."

She licked her lips a second before she parted them. I watched as my cock disappeared into her warm, wet mouth. She sucked hard then circled my tip with her tongue. Then took me in until I hit the back of her throat, then withdrew and did it again.

I threaded my fingers through her hair and pulled her brown locks back from her face so I could watch her. In and out, my dick slid, and the woman was a master. With every stroke of her mouth, she licked and sucked and even dragged her teeth. I wanted to explode in her mouth, but I wanted, no needed, to feel her pulse around me with her own orgasm before I did.

"Blake, babe. You need to stop. I'm almost there."

She shook her head.

"Blake," I groaned.

"Let me taste you," she murmured around my shaft. "Please, Ian."

She renewed her efforts, bobbing her head faster and faster until I couldn't hold back. I pumped my hips and fucked her mouth. Nothing had ever felt as good as Blake. Nothing.

"Blake," I moaned. "Fuck, Blake. Yes, baby. Suck me. Hard. Take all of me. Ah, fuck, babe. God, I fucking love your mouth. Aargh!"

Her nails dug into my thighs as I came in her mouth. I stopped breathing and blacked out for a second, knowing it was as close to heaven as I'd get on earth. Blake. All Blake.

I released the hold I had on her hair and looked down at her. She was watching me. Jesus, the look in her eyes had my dick twitching all over again.

She pulled back slowly and swallowed, then sat back on

her heels. I couldn't handle her being so far away. I reached for her, lifting her onto my lap and holding her close. I buried my face in her neck and breathed her in, memorizing her smell and her feel. Blake. My Blake.

"That was amazing," I finally said against her neck.

She shivered and kissed my cheek. "Thank you."

I laughed. "I should be the one thanking you. Please don't tell me where you learned to do that. I might have to knock Willie on his fucking ass next time I see him. Or kiss him for being enough of a dumbass to let you go."

She shook her head. "We weren't right for each other."

"No," I said, pulling back to meet her eyes. "You weren't. Not at all."

She smiled softly at me, and I couldn't resist kissing her. The salty taste of my come was still on her tongue, and it made me ready for her again.

I toyed with her nipples, pinching one and grazing the other. She jerked and twitched and moaned the entire time. I chased her with kisses, bringing her lips back to mine every time she pulled back for a moan.

With my shorts on the floor, the only thing separating us was her thin pajama pants and panties. The heat from her body wrapped around mine. I needed her. Again.

"You're wearing far too many clothes," I told her with a grin. "I think it might be time to take some of them off."

She shook her head. "I don't have any condoms."

I smiled. "Well, we need to change that, but for now, I have one."

She didn't look as happy as I thought she would be. She took a breath, then gave me a forced smile. "You need to tell me what kind you like. I know there are a lot."

I tipped her chin up and kissed her nose. "I don't care as long as I get to use them with you."

She smiled, but that look was still in her eyes. Like she didn't quite believe me. Or wasn't sure I meant what I said.

I reached around her to grab my wallet and retrieved the condom I stashed in there earlier. I wasn't hopeful, but I was always going to be prepared. Especially when it came to Blake.

She stood while I rolled on the condom, her eyes on me.

"I don't know why that's so hot."

I smiled up at her and reached for her. Slowly, I drew her pants and panties down her hips, inch by inch exposing her. The dark mass of curls at the vee between her thighs. Her thick thighs and calves, then she stepped out of the pants.

I kicked mine away with hers, leaving us both bottomless. I reached back and pulled my shirt off, then tugged hers down so we were completely naked. And I just stared at her.

She crossed her legs, hiding herself from me. She wrapped one hand over her waist and the other across her chest. She hid every inch from me.

I looked up at her. "I want you, Blake. I want to see all of you. To watch you lose your mind. To know I'm the one who's doing it to you."

She dragged in a breath and her muscles eased slightly.

"See yourself through my eyes, Blake. See yourself the way I do. Let me see you."

She chewed on her lip as I watched her. Her legs spread first. Her thighs brushed each other, like they always did. I loved that she was so lush, so curvy. When she let me between them, I knew it was because she wanted me there. She welcomed me in.

I brushed my knuckles over her thighs. She twitched and spread her thighs more. From my seat, I could almost see her clit. I slid my hands higher and urged her thighs farther apart.

"You didn't shave," I said softly.

"I'm sorry. I didn't think this would happen again."

I looked up at her and grinned. "I'd rather have you like this. Just how you were meant to be. How you're comfortable."

"Well, William—"

"I'm Ian," I growled. "Don't say another man's name when you're standing naked in front of me."

She grinned, then giggled.

"Why are you laughing?"

"Because you sound like you're jealous." She laughed again.

"I have every right to be jealous. He had you for five years and didn't please you. I'm not going to make the same mistake. I'm going to make sure every ounce of pleasure is wrung out of you every chance you'll let me, Blake. Until you're done with me."

"You'll be done with me before I'm done with you," she said quietly.

"Not likely, babe," I admitted, kissing her thigh as I said the words.

I was sure she'd have a question or a retort, so before she said anything, I thrust two fingers into her.

She screamed at the intrusion, then moaned and spread her thighs. "More," she begged. "Please, Ian."

I fucked her with my hand as I sat back on the couch and watched her come apart. The hands covering her body lifted her breasts and teased her nipples, plucking them and pinching them as I finger-fucked her.

She bucked and moaned and let go. "Ian, I'm going to fall."

"No, you're not. Stand there and come for me. I want to watch you. I want to see your come run down your thighs. To watch your body twitch right before you lose all control. Focus on standing, Blake. Stay on your feet and come for me."

With my other hand, I exposed her clit and pinched it. Harder and harder, I thrust into her with my fingers, pinching and teasing her clit with the other until she did exactly what I said and she came with a long, loud scream.

"Ian! Oh, God. Ian! Yes, yes. Ian. I'm coming, Ian. Coming!"

I waited until her knees buckled, then caught her and lowered her to the couch on top of me. I wanted to sink into her, but I wanted to look in her eyes when I did. I needed to see her, to know she was with me when I filled her.

She huffed her breath and twitched as she came down. She finally took a deep breath and pushed away from me. "You have magical hands."

I skimmed my hands down her back and kissed her softly. When our gazes met again, the words I ached to say to her almost fell out. It had been years since I knew I loved her, but I never thought I'd have the chance to tell her. Sitting there, wrapped around each other on her couch, seconds after her orgasms, I almost said it. I wanted to. The moment was perfect, and she was happy.

But something whispered in my head that she wasn't ready. Maybe I wasn't ready either. What we had was fun. It was easy. It was amazing sex, and a connection I'd never felt with anyone else, but there was a lot more to love than that. And if I jumped the gun with Blake, I could lose her forever. Not just as my lover, but as my friend.

"Thank you," she said after a long minute.

I swallowed my words and kissed her again. I let myself fall into the kiss, getting sucked into everything Blake. The feel of her thighs around mine. The sensation of her taut nipples against my chest. The taste of her lips on mine. Everything with her was new and special and amazing, even if we'd been there before.

She shifted her hips and tried to line us up. When I

notched inside her, I pushed up, and she pulled away from our kiss with a happy sigh.

"God, I just…you feel so good inside me," she said. "Big. And thick. And amazing."

I smirked. I couldn't help it. What guy didn't love hearing he had a bigger dick than the last guy a woman slept with?

"Shut up," she said with a light slap.

"I didn't say anything," I argued.

"Your face did," she said back with a pouty look on her face.

I thrust hard into her and erased that look. Her lips parted and her eyes rolled back in her head. That was better.

"God, you feel so good."

"Need you, Blake. So good," I murmured, holding her close.

Sitting on her couch, she had more leverage than on my futon, and she was able to lift her hips and slide down. I met her stroke for stroke, barely holding back the need to flip her and drive into her.

"Don't…stop," she gasped. "Please, Ian. So close."

"Harder?" I asked, gritting my teeth.

"Yes, oh, please, yes."

I pushed her off my lap, and she cried out. "No, don't stop. Please."

"Lay down," I commanded her, standing with her.

She laid down quickly, spreading her thighs to welcome me in. I nearly lost it when she did that. No hesitation, no reluctance, no fear.

I slammed into her hard, and she moaned. "Oh, yes."

I did it again, drawing her leg up and setting it over the back of her couch, spreading her thighs so I could sink in deeper.

"Yes, Ian. Oh, my God. Yes. I'm so close."

I pumped into her harder and harder. Every cell in my body ached to come. My balls drew up tight. My spine tingled. My vision dimmed around the edges. But above all of it was Blake. Blake spread out below me and begging me to make her come.

I pushed myself up and changed the angle. My calf cramped from the position I was in, barely reaching the floor. But I didn't care. It was Blake.

"Ian," she whimpered. "Please."

I pushed down every last shred of need and set my mind to making her scream. I shifted again and she gasped.

"Oh, yes, right there. Don't stop."

"My name. Say it, Blake."

"Ian! Fuck me, Ian. Harder, Ian. More, Ian. I love…Yes!"

Her channel locked down on me. One more thrust and I followed her, letting her body draw me in and take what she needed from me.

I collapsed onto her, both of us breathing heavily. Our sweaty bodies cooled as our breathing slowed, but I didn't want to get up. I wanted to stay wrapped around Blake forever.

She pushed at my shoulders, and I finally moved off her. "Sorry. I didn't think about how heavy I was on top of you."

She shook her head. "You aren't. I just need to pee."

I nodded and stood so she could go down the hall. I tossed the condom in the trash and pulled my shorts and briefs back on. When Blake came back, she had a bathrobe on.

"What is this for?" I asked her.

"My clothes were out here."

"So?"

She laughed. "I'm not going to walk around naked."

"You totally should. Make all the other women in town jealous. Wait, no. On second thought, don't, because then all the men in town will see you, and I want to keep you all to myself."

She rolled her eyes, but she didn't say anything. Smart woman.

"Thank you for dinner. And…um…"

"Dessert?" I said with a smirk.

A laugh burst from her. "Yeah, that, too."

"And now you're throwing me out?"

She hesitated for a second then nodded. "I am. I have to be up early to go to work."

"One day I'll get to spend a whole night with you."

She smiled. "You don't do sleepovers. You never have."

I pulled my shirt on and stepped into her personal space. I waited until she looked up at me to say, "I would with you, Blake."

She smiled again, then pushed me toward the door. "Not tonight, Romeo."

"As you wish," I said automatically.

She gasped, and I remembered The Princess Bride was her favorite book. Mine, too, if I was being honest. But it was also likely the reason we'd been paired together in Karissa's app. Which she still didn't know, and I couldn't tell her.

"Good night, Blake," I said, kissing her until she was breathless, and hopefully forgot about my slip.

She stood at the door watching me until I was in front of her neighbor's house. When her door closed, I tried to tell myself it wasn't with finality.

TRUE LOVE WAS a dumbass name for the boat, but that was what Robert wanted it to say. It was probably because the boat was the only thing he really loved. It was a chance for him to show the world how much money he had, and how much of an ass he was. Of course, he didn't see the second part. He just saw the chance to brag.

I was finally almost done with the boat, though, and that was good news for me. I had more customers than I could handle, and making a custom boat like True Love, with weekly changes and delays because of it, wore me the hell out. Of course, I also charged Robert extra for the changes, which he argued about, but it was in the contract he signed, so he had no way to get around paying it.

I was daydreaming about ways I could celebrate with Blake when the door opened. For about half a second, I hoped it was her, but the footsteps weren't hers. They were familiar, though.

Finley whistled before she walked around the end of the boat. "Nice work, big brother. This is a fancy one."

"With a fancy price tag and a pain in the ass owner to go with it."

"Ouch," she said. "Is that why you haven't told me you and Blake were paired on Book Boyfriends Wanted? Because you've been too focused on the boat?"

My smile faded, and I turned away from her to focus on the boat. "I don't know what you're talking about."

I could feel her roll her eyes. "Don't give me that. She told me you were matched."

"Blake knows?" I gasped.

Finley smirked and shook her head. "She doesn't know it's you, no. But she mentioned she was paired with a guy named Woody. I set up your profile. Did you really think I didn't know your name?"

"Shit," I breathed. "What are you going to do?"

Finley crossed her arms and studied me. We'd gotten along fairly well since we became adults. As kids, though? She was my pesky little sister, and I hated her. All the times I picked on her came back to me, and I started to sweat.

"There are so many options. I could make you clean my store. Or clean my apartment. I could ask you to build me my own boat. Or maybe I could just tell you I'll kill you if you hurt my best friend."

I took a step back. "Yeah, right. What are you really going to do?"

She stepped forward and patted my chest. "I think I'm going to hope it all works out. Because Blake deserves a good relationship. She should have someone in her life who loves her."

"I…"

Finley smiled at me. "Blake's been my sister in my heart forever."

"She doesn't love me," I blurted.

Finley laughed. "She doesn't trust you, Ian. There's a difference. If she thinks she can trust you, she'll be open to loving you. Right now, she thinks you're just fooling around."

"She told you about us?"

Finley nodded. "We all saw you two leave together. And after that, yeah. She mentioned you were together. If you really are just sleeping together, don't lead her on. She's not the kind of woman who can handle a fling."

"I'm not," I said adamantly.

"Good. Then make sure she knows she can trust you not to break her heart. If she knows that, I think she'll give it to you."

"I don't want her to give it to me because I'm safe, Fin," I said harshly. "I don't want her settling for me."

She smiled again. "There's nothing safe about you, Ian. Not for Blake. She never told me, but I think she was going to break up with William because of you. I think she liked you long before all this. She stayed with William for five years because he was safe. If she lets herself fall for you, it'll scare the shit out of her."

Finley started to walk away, but I needed to know one more thing.

"Do you know about her mom?" I asked before I thought better of it.

Finley turned and walked back to me slowly. "What about her mom?"

"About her drinking?" I said softly.

"Blake told you?"

I shook my head. "She showed up after Georgia's party when I was there."

"Blake doesn't talk about it. Ever. She hides it from everyone, but I think everyone knows. It's why I always invited her over on the weekends when we were kids. Even now, I try to get her to stay with me sometimes, but she never does."

"She shouldn't have to deal with that," I said.

Finley shook her head. "No, she shouldn't, but it's Blake. Blake loves her mom as much as she hates her, and for her, the two emotions overlap. That's why safe works for her. Safe means she doesn't love, and that means she doesn't hate. But it also means she's not really happy. I think you make her happy, Ian. But if you screw it up, I'll kill you myself."

Finley walked away with that parting shot.

"Thanks, sis!"

She waved over the edge of the boat, and I had to admit, I did feel better.

16

BLAKE

The next couple weeks flew by in a blur. I spent my mornings at Cracked serving breakfast to the locals and the few early tourists. MacKellar Cove was starting to get busy as June settled in and summer drew closer. By July, all the local hotels would be packed with tourists getting away from their life and enjoying the beauty and serenity of the place I called home.

My afternoons were just as busy painting Ms. Georgia and the rest of the mural. Day-by-day she came to life before my eyes. Her smile welcomed me after my lunch break, and I wanted to do her justice. I owed it to her to make her truly sparkle.

To my surprise, many of my evenings included Ian. I didn't expect him to keep coming back. Every time he showed up on my doorstep with dinner or beer or a joke, I considered it a gift.

When I wasn't with Ian, or working, I was getting to know Woody. He continued to tell me about his friend he was in love with, and a part of me grew more and more jealous. I couldn't understand why this woman didn't see what she had. A wonderful man loved her and she kept him at a distance, where I was falling in love with a guy I knew wouldn't be around long. Too bad we couldn't swap places.

Earl wanted the mural finished in time for the July 4th Festival, so I had to pick up my pace a bit. The days were getting longer, so I decided to work late a couple days during the week and get up early on Saturday mornings. The procrastinator in me said I'd get it done, but I couldn't count on perfect weather or everything falling into place.

Even though I was exhausted, Finley talked me into meeting her, Karissa, and Trinity at O'Kelley's Friday night. I hadn't spent nearly enough time with my friends lately, so I agreed. I dressed up in a pair of purple shorts and a light, loose geometric top that made my boobs look bigger and my waist look smaller. I left my hair down, but dried it to give it a little extra fluff, and added mascara and lipgloss. I tied on my favorite sandals, ones with straps that criss-crossed up my calves and made me feel sexy.

A part of me hoped Ian would be there, but I had no clue. I never knew when he was going to show up at my house or what he was doing. We hung out and slept together, but it was clear he wasn't interested in building a relationship. Not when I had more conversations with a stranger than I had with the man I shared my body with a few times a week.

As I walked through MacKellar Cove toward O'Kelley's, I told myself it didn't matter if Ian was there or not. I was going to see my friends, and if he happened to be there, that was fine. But if not, I wasn't going to stress about it.

When I arrived, Trinity was sitting at a table by herself with a pitcher of beer and six glasses. She waved to me and smiled. She fit right in with our group, which was nice. I knew Ms. Georgia wouldn't steer her wrong.

"Hey! I was so excited when Finley said you were coming out tonight," Trinity said in greeting.

I nodded. "I've missed too much lately."

"With good reason. It sounds like things are going well with Ian."

I shrugged. "I don't know. I guess. Maybe."

"Um, that doesn't sound good," Trinity said. Her mass of curls shifted as she tilted her head. I wish I had hair like hers. Beautiful, rich, and curly. My mousy brown locks were poker straight and dull. But everything about Trinity said *look at me*. Her curvy figure was that perfect hourglass we all wished for. She wore a low-cut gray top with one of her colorful necklaces nestled between her breasts. The top was tied over her shoulders with tiny straps that said she was either wearing a strapless bra or none at all. I didn't have the guts for either, even though my boobs were much smaller. Trinity was the kind of woman I envied for her confidence, but it was well earned. And it made it easier to like her because she wasn't bitchy or snarky. I really liked her.

Which was one of the reasons I told her about my relationship with Ian. "It's just tough. I almost wish we'd never gotten involved. And not because it isn't great, but because I…don't just want it to be sex."

"How do you know it's only sex?" Trinity asked.

I smiled. "Because it's Ian. He's amazing, but he doesn't get involved."

"I get that. You mentioned it before. But how do you know this isn't different for him? You've said you know one day he'll stop showing up, but he hasn't yet. It's been, what, a month?"

I nodded. "Six weeks."

"Maybe the reason he hasn't had a relationship in the past was because he wasn't in one with you."

I shook my head. "I've known Ian forever. He's just not someone who likes to be involved with one woman for long. I mean, you're right that I've never known him to be with the same person as long as we've been together, but we don't talk about things. We either hang out like friends, or have sex. We don't go on dates. He doesn't invite me over to his place. We just act like normal."

"Except you sleep together sometimes," Trinity said with a smirk.

"Yeah, except that," I agreed.

Karissa and Finley sat down as I was speaking. Karissa immediately poured herself a beer and downed half of it.

"Wow," Trinity said. "Rough day?"

Karissa nodded. "Yep. Tell me about something. Take my mind off it. What were you guys just talking about?"

"Blake and Ian," Trinity said without hesitation.

I glanced at Finley. We talked weeks ago about Ian and me, but I still worried she didn't like the idea of us together. She smiled at me. "How are things going?"

I shrugged. "Good. Fine. Nothing to complain about."

"She thinks they're just having sex, not actually building a relationship because Ian has never been with anyone else this long so she's waiting for him to just stop showing up at her house," Trinity said instead.

Finley's brows drew together. "Haven't you seen each other this week?"

I nodded. "We have. I see him three or four times a week, but I just…it's not going to last."

"You don't want it to?" Finley asked.

I shook my head. "No, that's not what I'm saying. I just know it won't."

"Buttercup strikes again," Karissa said.

I glared at her.

Karissa raised an eyebrow and smirked at me. "You have a cute guy spending time with you, and instead of making an effort to build something, you're sitting back and complaining that it's not going to last. Why would it last? We all know Ian hasn't ever stuck, but he's sticking with you. The two of you have been together over a month. And you admitted last week that he's always the one who shows up. He's the one who comes to you. You sit back and let him instead of making any effort yourself." Karissa leaned forward. Her eyes went soft. "You have a guy who's doing all the right things, and instead of meeting him halfway, you're waiting for him to walk away. If it happens, it's going to be because of you, Blake. Not him."

"But I..."

"Blake," Trinity said, "I think she's right. I don't know either of you as well as Karissa, but listening to you talk about him tells me you care about him. And the way you all talk about Ian, I don't think this is a simple thing for him."

I wanted to believe them, but Finley wasn't saying anything. I wanted to ask her, but I wasn't sure I could handle her confirming what I already knew was true. That eventually Ian would stop showing up.

"Thanks, guys. I'll see," I said quietly, forcing a smile for them.

Thankfully, they changed the subject and moved on to something other than my love life. I participated where I could, but mostly I sat back and listened. I felt off-kilter. One side of me wanted to believe everything Karissa and Trinity were saying. That Ian could be waiting for me to show him I wanted something more. I'd never been the aggressor in any relationship I'd had. I'd never been the one to ask for a date or to push for anything. Even with Ian, I let him take the lead from the first time he kissed me. I always considered myself lucky if a guy was interested in me.

But Ian told me over and over how much he wanted me. If that wasn't just empty words, then maybe they were right.

But if that was the case, why didn't Finley say something? Why did she just sit back? Did she know something? If she did, would she let me walk into something knowing I'd get hurt?

I had a hard time believing that, too.

That was why dating William was so easy. There was none of this emotional, confusing stuff. It was all safe. I cared about him, but not enough to be heartbroken when things ended. Or to be upset when plans changed and he couldn't come to something. William was safe. William was easy. William was…

Boring as fuck.

Being with Ian was everything being with William wasn't. I just had to decide if the risks were worth it.

ON OUR WAY out of O'Kelley's, Finley pulled me aside.

"If my brother hurts you, I'll kill him. You know that, right?"

I chuckled. "He's your brother."

"And you're my sister," she said fiercely.

I smiled and hugged her. "I'd ask what you'd do to me if I hurt him, but we know that won't ever happen."

She pulled back and avoided my gaze for a second. I almost asked her what the face was for, but then she said, "Give him a chance, Blake. I love my brother, but he's an idiot."

I nodded, wondering what she was talking about. *Give him a chance* rang in my head my entire walk home. Ian wasn't at O'Kelley's, and my phone had zero texts from him. I wanted to give him a chance, but the idea scared me. Terrified me. I felt like I was giving him a chance. A bunch of them. But he wasn't asking for more than sex from me. I was okay with that, to a point, but I was getting attached. I was starting to fall for him.

Oh, hell. Who was I kidding? I already fell for Ian. But I wasn't ready to admit that to anyone. Because saying it made it real, and if it was real, it would hurt that much worse when it ended. And it was definitely going to end.

I debated sending Ian a text once I was home and changed into my pajamas, but it was late and I didn't want to bother him if he was sleeping. He was almost finished with *True Love* and said he hoped to hand it off early next week, so I wasn't going to risk waking him up and throwing off his schedule. And I was getting up early to work on the mural, so I needed my own sleep.

I'd just finished setting up my coffee maker for the morning and was turning off the lights when my doorbell rang. I screamed and jumped, clapping my hand over my chest to stop my heart from pounding its way out.

I went to the door and peeked through the peephole. I couldn't see the person on the other side of the door, but she leaned against the post like it was the only thing between her and the ground, and I knew it was my mom again.

I closed my eyes and drew in a deep breath, then opened the door to let her in.

"I'm going to be sick," she said as she turned to me.

"Bathroom's this way," I told her in a soothing tone, wrapping my arm around her shoulders.

She made it inside and leaned against my couch. I stopped to close and lock the door, and when I turned around again, she was holding on to the edge of my couch. I shouted, "Wait!" but it was too late.

My mother vomited all over my couch.

I almost cried. Or screamed. Or threw up myself. I wanted to throw her out on her ass right there.

When she was done, she stood up and looked at me. "You look like crap, Blake. You really need to get more sleep."

All I could do was stand there. I was so shocked and angry that I couldn't do anything besides look at her.

"What? Why do you look like that?"

I didn't answer her because I knew if I opened my mouth I was going to yell at her.

She turned back to the couch and turned up her nose. "Gross, Blake. I can't sleep there. I'm exhausted. I'm going to sleep in your room tonight. You really need to get me a bed. I have an extra one for you. Why don't you have a bed for me?"

Her voice faded as she walked down the hallway to my bedroom. I clenched and unclenched my fists. My pulse roared in my ears and anger filled my veins.

She was the parent, but I was the one constantly cleaning up after her. I stared at my ruined couch until tears blurred my vision. I couldn't do it. I couldn't continue taking care of her. I was tired, and I was sick of it.

I let the tears fall for a minute, then I drew in a deep breath, and immediately regretted it. I turned on the lights and tried to figure out if I could salvage my couch. It wasn't new, but it was mine. It was one of the first things I bought when I moved into my house. It was comfortable and perfect, and I loved it.

I grabbed my cleaning supplies and a trash can and got to work. I scrubbed for hours, hoping the smell would eventually go away. Since my couch was dark gray, I couldn't use bleach, but I used everything else I could think of.

When the sun peeked through my front windows, I accepted that I couldn't do anything else. The couch needed to go, and I wasn't going to get any work done. I needed a shower, a few hours of sleep, and a day off.

I didn't even try to be respectful when I went into my bathroom and turned on the lights. I got in the shower and washed off the day, and night. I ached to cry, but I wasn't going to give her the satisfaction.

She stumbled into the bathroom while I was still in the shower. "What the hell, Blake? I was asleep."

"In my bed, Mom. Because you threw up all over my couch."

"I never throw up, Blake."

I snorted. "Yeah, well, tell that to my couch."

She sighed like I was being a petulant child. I closed my eyes and counted to ten.

"I should go. I'm awake anyway. I'll get out of your way."

"That would be nice," I said, not bothering to hide my anger.

I could feel her there for another minute. Eventually her footsteps carried her away from me. Only when I knew I was completely alone did I turn off the shower and get out. I pulled on a tank top and panties and fell into my bed, exhausted and angry and hurt.

It was still before noon when I woke up. My stomach hurt from the anxiety, and I was hungry. I pulled on a pair of shorts and changed into a comfortable MacKellar Cove tee I'd had since high school. I went to make my coffee and fix breakfast, but the smell hit me.

MacKellar Cove was the type of town where you could leave your front door unlocked and not worry about anyone stealing anything. The people were friendly and good neighbors and always watched out for each other. That was the only reason I knew I could open all the windows in my house and leave. I couldn't be in there, and until I could get rid of the couch, I had to air it out.

I poured my coffee into a travel mug and left. I needed to walk, to get away from my mother. I sipped my coffee as I walked through town, not caring or paying attention to where I was.

Until I found myself in front of Jameson Wooden Boats.

17

I should have turned around and left, but instead my feet carried me right to the door. I pulled on the handle and was surprised when the door opened.

I walked inside quietly, even though I knew Ian was awake. He didn't open the door until he was up. Unless Devon was there.

The soft murmur of two voices finally reached my ears. I followed them until I walked around the end of the boat. Ian and Devon were huddled together looking at something.

"I think that'll work," Ian finally said. "Good plan."

"Thanks," Devon said, beaming. He seemed like a good kid, but he was young. He still had a year of college to go, and even though he was talented, there was no reason to think he'd come back to MacKellar Cove. "Um, boss?" Devon said, nodding to me when he saw me.

Ian turned and smiled slowly. "Hey. I wasn't expecting you this morning."

I nodded. "Do you have a boat I can borrow?" I asked, not bothering with pleasantries.

Ian nodded slowly and reached for me. I let him cup my elbow and pull me away from Devon. "Are you okay?"

I wanted to lie to him, but I found myself shaking my head. "I really want to go fishing."

"Okay. Not a problem. Let me grab the keys. Stay here."

I nodded and crossed my arms. He held my gaze for a second, as though he thought I was going to run the second he left, then he turned and jogged off. He said something to Devon, then was back in a few minutes dangling keys from his fingers.

"Let's go."

I shook my head. "You're busy. I didn't want to mess up your day."

He smiled and wrapped an arm around my waist. "I'm good. Devon has everything under control. I could use a few hours of fishing."

I resisted, but the idea of having him out there with me was more appealing than going by myself.

Growing up on the Saint Lawrence River meant learning to fish and swim and dive from a very young age. I wasn't a huge fan of diving, but fishing had become a retreat for me. A chance to escape. Jump in a boat and go out on the water. The river wasn't wide enough where we lived to really get away, but it didn't take much to feel like we were isolated.

I sat on the soft leather seat of Ian's prized boat and let the rumble of the engine and the slap of the wind fill me. He drove out past the bigger islands close to the Cove and continued north to where the river narrowed again. There weren't many islands in that part of the Thousand Islands, but the water was shallow in places and the fish liked to hang out there. Ian and I had been fishing in the area with Finley since she and I were in high school.

Ian handed over one of the fishing poles and opened the tackle box. He waited for me to pick one of the lures and attach it to my line before he chose his and closed the box. We stood side-by-side at the back of the boat, casting into the shallow water and watching the bobbers.

We sat down to wait and watch, the aisle between us feeling wider than the river around us. I felt alone.

Then Ian reached across the aisle and grabbed my hand. He didn't say anything, just threaded his fingers through mine and held on.

I sat there, staring at the line and trying not to cry, but I held out long enough.

My shoulders shook with my silent sob, and Ian tugged me across the aisle and onto his lap. I curled up with him and let him hold me while I cried. He didn't say anything. One hand glided up and down my back and the other held me close to him. And I just let out all the emotions that wracked me since my mother showed up at my door hours earlier.

I didn't know how long we sat there, and I really didn't care. When I finally calmed down enough to look at him, his brows were drawn together, his hazel eyes concerned. He wiped the tears from my cheeks and brought my hand to his lips.

"Are you okay?"

I shook my head.

He pulled me against him again and tucked my head under his chin, holding me close. I felt safe and loved and like nothing bad could happen as long as I was with Ian.

"You can talk to me if you want, but if you just want to sit here, I'm okay with that, too."

"I don't want to talk yet."

He nodded. "Okay."

We sat there, him cradling me and me staring at the water. Our bobbers both dipped below the surface, but neither of us moved to check the lines.

The sun climbed higher into the sky, and I finally figured

I should give his legs a break. I climbed off him and moved back to the seat I started in. "I'm sorry," I said.

His brows narrowed again. "For what?"

I gestured to his tear-stained shirt. "For crying all over you."

He shook his head. "I don't care about the shirt. I only care about you. Are you okay?"

I drew in a shaky breath and shrugged. "Not really, I guess."

"Do you want me to take you back? You can talk to Fin or one of the girls?"

I shook my head. "No. I don't want to see any of them."

"But you wanted to see me?" he asked, clearly surprised.

"I…" I had no answer. I ended up at his place because he always made me feel good. Like I was more to him.

"Thank you," he said after a second. "For trusting me enough to come to me. I'm always here for you, Blake. No matter what you need."

I laughed mirthlessly. "Like moving my couch?"

He nodded. "Anything, babe. Everything. Whatever you need."

I nodded, getting choked up for a different reason.

He pulled me onto his lap again and kissed me softly. "Talk to me, Blake. What happened?"

I drew in a breath and let his touch surround me. "My mom. Except this time she thought my couch was the toilet."

His grip tightened. "Shit."

I nodded. "Yeah. I tried to clean it, but it still smells. I need a new couch. My house reeks. I left all the windows open, but my house is going to smell for a while."

"We'll get it out today," he said.

I shook my head. "I have to call and schedule a special pick up."

"I'll carry it to a dumpster if I have to. You're not going to live with that in your home. And you can stay with me if you need to. If the smell is too bad."

I shook my head. "I'm sure I can stay with Fin and Rissa if I need to. Hopefully it's not that bad, though."

He nodded once. "Whatever you want, babe."

I sighed. "I want her to stop drinking. Maybe that makes me childish, but I'm done with this."

"It doesn't make you childish. If she can't handle it, she should stop. She's not being fair to you. And you shouldn't have to deal with it."

I shrugged. "She's my mom. There's no one else to deal with her."

He hugged me tighter and breathed in my hair. "I'm sorry, Blake. I wish I could do something."

I shook my head. "You are, Ian. Just being with you makes me feel better."

He smiled and brushed my wild hair from my lips. "Good."

He kissed me softly, barely a kiss. A part of me wanted to lose myself in him, but it wasn't fair to Ian. If I did, I'd be using him to forget about my mom. I didn't want things to be that way between us.

He pulled back and held me. I wondered if he was thinking the same thing. We'd been friends for years, but I'd never gone to him when I was upset about anything. Maybe Karissa and Trinity were right and I needed to open up to him. Trust him. Let him in.

We stayed on the water for a few hours. We threw our fishing lines in the water, but we didn't really try. By the time Ian drove us back to Jameson Wooden Boats, I was starving.

"Want to grab dinner?" I asked him.

He looked surprised at my question. When he shook his head, I was more than a little disappointed.

"How about I cook for us?" he said.

"You don't have to do that," I argued.

He shook his head again. "I didn't say I had to. I just figured it would be nice if we didn't have to go out. You can relax and not worry about seeing other people."

My shoulders sagged. He was right. The idea of being out and having to pretend I was okay was exhausting without even thinking about it. A night in sounded perfect.

"You're right. But I feel bad asking you to do everything."

He smiled and winked at me. "I offered, babe. You hang out here for a while. I'm going to run out and get a few things I need to make dinner, but I won't be long."

"I can go with you."

He kissed me then. A full body kiss where I felt him all the way to my toes. His hands wrapped around me and held me tight. His tongue snaked into my mouth and caressed my tongue in passionate strokes. His chest rose and fell with mine, our breath mingling as he made me forget all about what sent me to his doorstep to start with.

"Stay here," he said softly. "I won't be long. And when I get back, you can help me cook if you want. Or you can chill and watch Netflix or something."

I nodded, falling just a little deeper in love with him. He knew exactly what I needed. Had anyone else ever seen me that well? Had anyone else ever cared to?

The only TV was in Ian's bedroom, so I went in there and stretched out on his futon. I propped my head up and flipped through the options until I came to a movie that sounded cute. A movie about a girl falling for her best friend's older brother.

I could definitely relate to her.

My eyelids drooped as I watched the movie. It was funny and cute, but I was exhausted. I tried to stay awake, but I couldn't do it.

The next thing I knew, Ian was kissing me. I moaned against his lips and whispered his name.

"Are you ready to eat?" he asked.

"You? Hell, yes," I said with a smile.

He chuckled, but it wasn't a dream like I thought.

I blinked open my eyes and found him sitting next to me grinning. "I just said that out loud, didn't I?"

He smirked. "Maybe I can be your dessert."

I pushed at him, and he just laughed.

"Come on, Sleeping Beauty. You need some food."

"I don't know if I have the energy to cook right now," I whined.

"No need," he said, pulling me to my feet. "I already cooked. You were passed out pretty hard, but I didn't want to let you sleep all night without eating something."

"You already cooked?"

He nodded. "I did. Come and eat."

I let him lead me out to his kitchen area and stopped short when I saw the candlelit table and smelled the amazing food he had on it.

"Ian," I said questioningly.

"I thought the overhead lights might be too much when you just woke up," he said, shuffling his feet and avoiding my gaze.

I walked up to him and stood in front of him until he looked at me. "Thank you for this. I've never had a candlelit dinner."

He smiled. "Neither have I. It sounds like we're both overdue."

He held out my chair as I sat, then guided it in. He had my favorite beer and made grilled filet, mac and cheese, and green beans. There was a cheesecake from Cove Bakery on the counter.

"You did all this for me?" I breathed.

He nodded. "I'd do anything for you, Blake. You deserve to be treated like this every day."

"Ian," I said quietly.

He held my gaze for a long minute. His hazel eyes blazed with something that looked frighteningly like love, but Ian Jameson didn't do love. Ian Jameson also didn't do candlelit dinners and romance, but I was enjoying both at the moment.

We talked about the summer and all the events coming up as we ate. The July 4th Festival really kicked things off for MacKellar Cove. It was three weeks away, and the whole town was getting ready for it.

"What's your favorite part of the Festival?" he asked me.

I shrugged. The last five years I went to the Festival with William. He didn't like most of it, which meant I hadn't enjoyed it in far too long. A part of me couldn't even remember everything that happened.

"My favorite is the fireworks dance," Ian said when I didn't answer. "I'm really hoping I have a date for it."

I laughed. "Usually you prefer to be single for things like that."

He shook his head. "Not anymore, Blake. I want you with me. If you're interested."

I nodded. "It sounds like fun. I've missed a lot over the last few years."

"Stick with me," he said with a grin. "I'll make sure you don't miss any of the fun."

I smiled at him and knew it was true. Ian wasn't the life of the party kind of guy, but he always knew where the fun was and never missed out on it. I definitely needed more of that in my life. More of Ian.

Once we finished dinner and cleaned up, I said I needed to go home and deal with my couch.

"Why don't you stay?" he asked.

I shook my head. "No. I'm not going to ask you that."

"Blake, I want you here. I want you to stay."

My heart jumped at his words. His tone, his eyes, everything said he meant it. But I couldn't get the Ian Jameson I'd known forever out of my mind. The guy who never spent the night. The guy who never stuck around. The guy who never got attached.

"Blake," he said roughly, swallowing then stepping toward me. "Babe, you're different for me. I know you're afraid because of my past, but I don't want you to be. I haven't been worthy of you, and I'm still not, but I want you to know I'm not holding back what I want with you. I'm not going to let you think this is another fling for me. Because it's not, Blake. You're not. I…I care about you. A lot. And you staying here isn't because it's convenient or because your couch smells. It's because I want to wake up with you in my arms. I want to go to sleep with your hair in my face. I want to feel your body against mine all night long. We don't have to have sex. We don't have to do anything. I just want to be with you, Blake."

"Ian," I breathed. "I don't…"

His hopeful smile fell, and he took a step back. "Oh. I see."

I chuckled and moved into his space, waiting until he met my gaze. "I was going to say I don't know what to say. I feel all the same things, Ian. I just never thought I'd have the chance to tell you. But that no sex thing is definitely something I need to argue with you about."

His grin went from joyous to pure sin in a flash. He scooped me up and kissed me, his tongue thrusting between my lips as he carried us toward his bed.

And when he kicked the door closed and stripped us both naked, Ian didn't hold anything back. Just like he promised.

He loved me all night until we both fell asleep with the night sky watching over us.

No matter what I told myself, I couldn't convince any part of me that I wasn't head over heels for Ian Jameson. But for the first time in my life, the idea didn't make me jump up and run for cover.

18

IAN

Waking up with Blake in my arms was the best kind of torture. I'd never been much of a morning person, but I was up with the sun watching her sleep despite my severe lack of sleep. It was well worth it to spend the night showing her how much I loved her and to be able to watch her as she slept.

When she finally stirred, her backside brushed against me first. She froze for a second and her eyes popped open. Then a beautiful smile curled her lips and her eyes slid closed again. She stretched and pressed her backside against me again, and I couldn't hold back my needy groan.

I slid my hand tighter around her belly and drifted to cup her breast. A breath shuddered through her when I brushed my thumb over her nipple.

"Ian," she breathed.

I fucking loved the way she said my name. That breathy, sexy tone that said she was as gone as I was was quickly becoming as addicting as the woman I didn't ever want to let out of my bed.

I kissed her shoulder and ran my tongue down her back. I

nipped at the dimples right above both her cheeks and urged her to her back so I could have her for breakfast.

She was already wet and ready when I took my first swipe of her. She moaned and bucked her hips against my face. My girl needed to come first thing in the morning. I liked that.

I licked and sucked her until her moans filled the air around us. Then I pushed two fingers into her and she shattered for me, screaming my name as she came hard.

I was wrong. That was my favorite way she said my name. But the breathy one was a close second. Because both were only for me. No one else was going to hear her say my name like that.

I kissed my way back up her body, letting her settle down before I reached for a condom and slid into her. She gasped, then sighed and wrapped her legs around my hips.

"We need to do that more often," she said with a blissful smile.

"Do what?" I groaned, finding it hard to carry on a conversation when I was balls deep in the woman I loved.

"Have sleepovers. Especially if they're like this." She moaned long and low and spread her thighs so I could sink deeper.

I moaned with her and gritted my teeth. "Definitely more sleepovers," I agreed with her. "All like this."

She smiled up at me and reached for me. She drew me down to her and kissed me, her soft tongue gliding alongside mine. I slid in and out of her, each stroke bringing me closer to the finish line, but I wasn't in a hurry to get there.

I always thought people who said something was about the journey, not the destination were crazy. Why would you go somewhere if you didn't want to be there as quickly as possible and spend as much time there as you could? But making love to Blake was exactly that. It was the journey. It was the slide inside her. It was the smell of our bodies. It was the taste of her come and the feel of her losing her mind. It was the extended bliss and heightened awareness that came from being with Blake. She was the journey. She was my journey. And being in it was better than any destination could possibly be.

I didn't hold back with Blake and kissed her like I'd always dreamed of. I let her feel everything I was feeling, everything I'd always felt. When she twitched under me and came with a scream, I couldn't stop my own orgasm from chasing hers and sending us into oblivion together.

I collapsed onto her, but quickly moved to roll off her. She tightened her grip on me and wouldn't let me move. I didn't fight her. I held her as she held me, both of us locked together as our bodies cooled.

Her grip finally eased and I rolled to the side, turning her with me so we were facing each other. I kissed her, not pushing for more than a simple kiss, but even that had my heart pounding in my chest. It was Blake. Everything was Blake.

I got rid of the condom then went right back to bed and pulled her close. We both drifted off again, but I woke to her trying to sneak out of bed. "Where are you going?"

She winced. "Sorry. I was trying not to wake you up."

"I'd rather you did. Is everything okay?"

She turned back and nodded. "I'm just hungry. I was going to go. You've been amazing. And I need to take care of the couch today. And I should get some work done."

"Blake," I said firmly. "Is that all it is?"

The flicker in her eyes said it wasn't, but she smiled and nodded. "Yeah, of course."

I jumped out of bed and had to hide my grin when her gaze slid down to my cock. It jumped, and her eyes widened. God, I wanted to drag her back to bed and have my way with her for a few more hours, or lifetimes, but I was starving, too. Making love to the woman of my dreams all night definitely wore me out.

"Let's go to Cracked for breakfast, then I'll help you paint today," I suggested.

She shook her head. "I can't ask you to do that."

"You keep saying that, Blake, but you're not asking. I want to spend the day with you. I want to be with you. And if you're working, I want to be there. Even if it's just to sit in the square and watch you work. I can bring you supplies and make sure you take breaks and feed you."

"Ian," she said softly in that tone she used when she was close to giving in.

I stepped closer to her and slowly slid my arm around her waist and pulled her to me. "Blake," I said in the same tone she used.

She laughed and put her hands on my chest. "You might need to put some clothes on."

I shrugged. "Or I could just drag you back to my bed and take all yours off again," I teased.

Her face went serious, and she tried to twist away from me. "I can't. I'm sorry."

"I was joking," I said.

She sighed. "I know. But it just reminds me that I ended up here yesterday because of my mother. And I was supposed to work yesterday. And if I had, I'd be able to stay here with you. It's just one more thing she ruined."

I pulled her back in and held her until I felt her rage slip away.

"I'm sorry," she said softly.

"You never have to apologize to me. For anything. You have every right to be pissed off at your mother. But don't think you working today has ruined anything. I like watching you work, and I want to spend time with you however I can get it. Give me a minute to get dressed, and we'll go."

She drew in a breath and nodded. "I need to go home to change. And if you're still willing, we can try to do something with my couch. Maybe I should just go now."

I shook my head. "I'll only be a second, Blake. Don't go anywhere."

I waited until she nodded before I turned away from her and grabbed clothes. I was dressed in under thirty seconds, and had her hand back in mine and we headed to her house.

We walked in companionable silence, neither of us feeling the need to fill the quiet. I enjoyed the feel of her hand in mine, and the smiles on the faces of people we passed when they saw us together. One of the best and worst things about growing up in MacKellar Cove was knowing everyone in town. And holding hands with one of the servers at the one of the most popular restaurants turned some heads. Especially since I didn't have a reputation for holding on to a woman.

We were almost to Blake's when we walked past friends of my parents. They lived on her street, and she said hello and tried to let go of my hand. I held on tighter and made it clear we were together.

"Well, hello you two," Mrs. McGraw said.

"Good morning. How are you doing today?" I asked.

Mrs. McGraw smiled and let her gaze drift to where our hands were linked. "We're doing well. It's a beautiful day for a walk, isn't it?"

I nodded and brought Blake's hand up to my lips for a kiss. "It is. We were just talking about how we're going to spend the day. Blake is working on her mural, but she wanted to change first and she didn't bring clean clothes when she came over yesterday."

Mrs. McGraw's wide grin was worth the bright red stain on Blake's cheeks.

"Tell your parents we said hello," Mr. McGraw said, tugging Mrs. McGraw away before she could pry.

"I will," I told them cheerfully, then kept walking with Blake.

"What the hell was that?" she hissed.

I shrugged. "Being neighborly."

"Why did you tell your parents' best friends that I spent the night at your place?"

"Because you did," I said simply, pulling her to a stop. "Do you not want anyone to know about us?"

"I…No. It's not that. I figured you wouldn't want anyone to know."

I leaned in and kissed her. In broad daylight in view of whoever was out or looking out their windows. I wanted to shout to the world that Blake slept in my bed overnight. That she woke up in my arms. That I was the one making her scream all night.

Well, maybe I'd keep the last part to myself, but the rest, I definitely wanted to tell the world.

"Ian," she whispered in that breathy tone when I finally pulled back.

I leaned in and kissed her again, unable to resist her pull. "We better get to your house or I'm going to embarrass myself right here on the street."

She smiled and threw her arms around my neck, teasing me with a shimmy of her hips. My cock rose to the occasion and pressed against her belly.

"You're dangerous."

She grinned. "Yeah, well, you just told my neighbors we had sex. I figured I can tell the rest of them."

I grabbed her ass and hauled her closer, thrusting my tongue deep into her mouth and grinding my dick against her. I didn't care that we were in public or that anyone could look out and see me mauling her. I only cared about the way Blake moaned into my mouth and the shift of her hips to line us up.

"Ian," she moaned. "We need to go inside. Now."

Reluctantly, I let go of her and grabbed her hand again. We half-ran, half-walked the rest of the way to her house. She unlocked her front door and pulled me in for a kiss, then stopped short.

"What the hell? I closed the windows. Wait." She breathed deep. "It doesn't smell." She turned to where her couch used to be and gasped. "Where's my couch?"

"You said you wanted it gone. When I went out last night, I had Ramsey help me get rid of it. I didn't want you to have to worry about it. I was going to tell you when I got home, but you were sleeping and by the time I woke you up, I'd forgotten."

Tears slid silently down her cheeks. Fuck. I thought I was doing the right thing. Maybe she wanted the couch? I wasn't sure I could get it back. Or that she'd want it back. It was bad.

"Blake, I'm sorry. You said—"

"Thank you," she said softly, reaching up to stroke my cheek. "I…thank you. I hated asking you to take care of it, but I never thought you'd do it without me really bugging you. William…it was almost impossible to get him to help me out with stuff like this. I would have dealt with it for a week or more, especially if he was working or something. But you just took care of it."

I shrugged, wanting to kill Willie again for not being better to her and wanting to thank him for being a dumbass. It meant the bar was low where Blake was concerned, but she deserved the world.

"You deserve better than that. You should have called me. Even when you were with him. You know I'll do anything for you, Blake. Whether we're together or not, I'm always going to be here for you."

She stepped into my arms and rested her head on my chest. "Thank you, Ian. I can't tell you how much I appreciate it."

I kissed the top of her head and smiled when her stomach growled again. "Go change so I can feed you, beautiful. Do you need anything for the mural?"

She shook her head and walked away. "I'll just be a minute."

I nodded and winked at her. Her cheeks pinked and she pressed her lips into a happy grin.

It was getting harder not to tell her how I felt. Saying *I love you* felt so easy. I'd never even been tempted with other women, but with Blake, it was almost a compulsion. Like if I didn't tell her, I wouldn't be able to survive.

She came back a minute later wearing a pair of skin-tight black shorts and a loose white tee that fell to mid-thigh. Her tee had splatters of paint all over it, giving it a true artist's feel. Her hair was tied back in a ponytail with a scarf wrapped around her head. The small black purse she normally carried was draped across her body, separating her breasts and highlighting both of them.

My mouth watered at the sight of her. This was the woman I fell for. The messy, disheveled, sexy woman who didn't think twice about the way she looked. She was herself, unapologetically Blake. She never looked hotter to me than when she let go of all her worries about what everyone else thought and was herself.

I crossed the now wide-open room to her and tugged her against me. She gasped as I leaned down to kiss her, and I took full advantage, plunging my tongue into her mouth and taking what I wanted from her.

She kissed me right back, bringing her hands immediately up around my neck and toying with the hair at my nape. I tilted my head and thrust my tongue deeper into her mouth, earning a moan from her that went straight to my cock.

I slid one hand down her back and squeezed her ass. She wiggled against me and lifted her leg, letting me slide between her delicious thighs.

"Oh, God," she moaned, pulling back from our kiss. "I thought we were going to breakfast."

I stepped back, letting the thick air of desire fill the space between us. "We are." I headed to the door, not looking back until I turned the knob. "Are you coming?"

Her eyes widened. "Well, I thought I was, but I guess not."

I smirked. "Making you wait will only make you more ravenous later. I can't wait to watch you lose control completely."

"You think I haven't already?"

I shook my head. "I know you've been holding back on me. But the next time I get you naked, you won't."

"What makes you so sure?" she asked, finally joining me at the door.

I opened it and stood back for her to walk through. When she passed by me, I smacked her ass. She gasped and jumped. "Because if you're half as crazy by the time we're home as I am right now, you won't be able to hold back. You'll be begging me to let you come, to make you come. To fuck you hard, then stretch you out with slow, deep strokes. To kiss you until you can't breathe, then put my mouth to good use elsewhere on your body."

"Ian," she whispered in that damn tone.

"I fucking love when you say my name like that," I told her. "It makes me so fucking hard."

"We don't need to go get breakfast yet," she tried.

I shook my head. "We do. Because the next time I get you

in a bed, I'm not letting you out for a while. I've gotten addicted to you, Blake. And I'm not sure I can sleep without you next to me again."

"But I have to work in the morning," she said softly.

I shrugged. "So? I promise I'll let you get some sleep. After a dozen orgasms or so."

"A dozen?"

"Two dozen?"

She laughed. "You're insane."

"And you're amazing, Blake. Now, let's go so we can eat and you can work. I have big plans for our afternoon. Involving you, me, a bed, and zero clothes. Sound good?"

"Yes," she whispered, and that one word was almost as good as my name. Almost.

19

I watched Blake work from the grass on the square. She was so focused and so beautiful. She glanced back at me a few times, but it wasn't long before she forgot about me entirely and lost herself in her work.

I laid back on the grass and watched my woman do her thing. She was adorable when she shifted her hip and tapped her lip with the end of paintbrush. I was smiling up at her back when Ramsey dropped to the ground next to me.

"Your girl's got some serious talent," he said.

I nodded. "Hell, yeah, she does."

"Does she know you're gawking at her?"

I shoved him but laughed. It wouldn't have been the first time I'd stared at Blake when she wasn't aware of my existence. "Yes, asshole. I came here with her."

His dark eyebrows shot up and he grinned. "Well, well. Good for you."

I rolled my eyes.

"Still together since last night?"

I nodded and tried not to grin, but dammit, I was happy as shit.

"Good for you, dude. Glad to hear someone's love life is going well." Ramsey shook his head and glanced toward the water.

"Where is Melody today?" I asked.

Ramsey shrugged. "No clue. She didn't come home last night."

"What? Is she okay?"

Ramsey shrugged. "I think so. She told me she was going out last night and not to wait up for her. She sent me a text that she was staying with her sister."

"Willow never liked you," I said.

"Tell me about it."

He was quiet for a minute, and I found myself asking the question I'd wanted to ask him for a while. "Do you think you guys can fix it?"

He didn't answer right away, and I wondered if he actually heard me. I was going to just let it go, but then he shifted and laid on the grass with me.

"I love her. I think that's the biggest thing. For me at least. I can't imagine my life without her in it. I don't want to. But I also can't live with her the way things were before. Losing the baby and almost losing her was too hard. I almost didn't survive it."

I nodded. I barely saw Ramsey during that time. When I did, he was a shell. He was obviously depressed and just plain miserable. I tried to get him out once in a while, but he never took me up on it. It was almost a year before he started to rejoin society. Things were good between him and Melody for a while, but that definitely wasn't the case anymore.

"How do you keep going?" I asked him, truly wondering. I wasn't foolish enough to think relationships were easy. Just a few weeks with Blake told me anything long term with her was going to be a regular challenge. Especially convincing her I meant it when I told her I thought she was beautiful or I wanted her. I couldn't even imagine how tough it was going to be to convince her I loved her.

He smiled and slapped me on the shoulder. "Love, man. Maybe that's cheesy or whatever, but I love her. She's it for me. If she really wants a kid, I'll probably give in. I'll hate every fucking second and be scared for the rest of my life, but I'll have her, so I'll deal."

I drew in a breath and looked at Blake again. She was still painting, lost in her own world as the rest of the town existed around her. My chest hurt when I thought about losing Blake. Watching her walk away and never come back. I didn't think I could handle it. We'd only been together a few weeks, but not being with her was beyond my comprehension.

"Things are going well?" Ramsey asked, nodding to Blake.

I nodded. "Yeah, they are. She's got a lot going on with work, but I'm trying to be there when she's not working."

"Or when she is," he said with a laugh.

I chuckled. "True. Thanks again for helping me move the couch."

He nodded and held my gaze for a minute. "You going to tell me what happened to the couch?"

I thought about it. When I asked him to meet me at her house, I knew he'd want to know. I also knew if I told him I couldn't talk about it, he wouldn't push. He didn't ask as we tried not to vomit all over the vomit-scented couch, but I wasn't surprised he asked after the fact.

"One of the many things Blake has going on."

Ramsey nodded and didn't ask anything else about it.

We sat and watched the town for a while, letting the quiet between us be comfortable. After a few minutes, Ramsey slapped my leg and stood.

"I need to go. If I stay here any longer, I'm going to fall asleep. I'll see you soon."

I nodded and waved as he walked away. The slump in his shoulders bugged me, but until things were back on track with Melody, that slump was going to hang around.

I was paying attention to Ramsey so much that I didn't notice Blake until she was standing right in front of me. I jumped to my feet.

"Hey. Are you done?"

She shook her head. "Not yet. You don't have to hang out here all day. You can go with Ramsey or whatever."

I smiled and kissed her softly. "I don't want to go anywhere else."

She smiled back. Her gaze followed Ramsey, then her smile slipped. "How are things with him and Melody?"

"Not great," I admitted. Finley and Melody never really got along, but I wasn't sure how Blake felt about her. "She wants to try for kids again."

Blake sucked in a breath. "Wow. I'm not friends with them, but even I could see how hard that was. I don't think I'd have enough courage to try again if I were them. Of course, that means I'd have to try in the first place."

I was more than a little surprised. "You don't want kids?"

She shrugged. "Not really. Maybe one day, but I'd have to find someone…" She pressed her lips together.

"Someone what?" I prompted.

She smiled and looked up at me. "The right someone. I haven't really ever let myself think about it. With William, a part of me always knew we weren't going to be together forever. I cared about him, and I wanted to love him, but things with him were easy. He never asked questions about me not letting him stay over because he didn't want to. He didn't push to be more involved in my life, and I didn't push to be involved in his. We just existed together for years, and I'm not looking for something else. Especially not something like what I had with him."

"What are you looking for?" I asked, my breath stuck in my throat. I wanted her to smile at me and say she was looking for me. That what we had was what she always wanted. But instead, she shrugged.

"I don't know. I guess someone who'll surprise me. Who'll make me want new things. Who'll love me." She looked at me as though she forgot I was there and grinned. "I know you don't get it, but there's a big part of me that still holds out hope that love exists, and that maybe it could be out there for me."

"Why do you think I don't get that?" I asked.

She chuckled. "Because that's not who you are, Ian. Don't worry. I have no delusions that I'm going to trap you in anything long term. I'm having fun, but I promise I will let you go when we're done. I'm not going to lock you in with a fake pregnancy or something."

"Or a real one," I teased, knowing I had to say something or I'd throw up.

Blake laughed and shuddered. "God, I hope not."

I smiled with her, but inside, I wanted to scream. I told her over and over how much I wanted her. That I wasn't going anywhere. But she was still convinced we were on a clock. She was waiting for it run out of time.

Blake laughed again, then patted my chest. "Okay, I need to get back to work. If you've got something to do, don't worry about hanging around here all day."

I nodded but couldn't say anything. She didn't lean in and kiss me or touch me or anything before she walked off, checking the street before she crossed and climbed her scaffolding again.

I sat back down and tried to figure out what the hell I was going to do. And to think, I was feeling sorry for Ramsey. At least he could go home and tell the woman he loved how he felt. I couldn't do that. I couldn't say the words.

I stayed there the rest of the day and when Blake was done, she had to run home and shower before girls' night. I wanted to see her, but I was thankful for the reprieve. I wasn't sure I could spend another night with her without telling her how I felt.

I spent the next few days working my ass off to finish *True Love*. When Robert showed up first thing Wednesday morning, I realized I hadn't spoken to Blake since Sunday.

"Well, hell," Robert said when he let himself into my shop. "She's a beauty."

I nodded because she was. The boat was stunning with a small cabin and enough seating for at least six up top. Robert wanted something that had an expensive feel, so in addition to the seating and the cabin, the boat had a sleek narrow design and a custom paint job that covered up the stunning teak I used for his boat. I couldn't understand why he wanted a wooden boat if he was going to hide the fact that it was wooden, but the customer was always right.

"So, it's just like we talked about. The cabin has a bed in the back and a galley kitchen. There's a table down there. And of course, up top you can seat six. I think it's perfect for you."

Robert gave me a look that promised he'd find something wrong. He nitpicked at the pinstripe color on the seats even though he'd chosen it. He pointed out the narrow opening to the cabin. He even said the paint on the boat was a shade off.

He'd specifically picked out everything, down to the exact design even though I told him the entrance to the cabin was narrow because of the design of the boat, but he insisted on it. Boy was I happy to be done with him.

I listened to him complain for almost thirty minutes, but when he handed over the balance he owed and I traded him for the keys and helped him hook up the trailer, I finally smiled.

The first thing I wanted to do was call Blake. Take her out. Celebrate. See her. Love her.

I told myself to back off, but backing off wouldn't get me anywhere. Not with Blake. She had to know I was there and I wasn't going anywhere.

I finally sent her a text asking what she was up to later.

Couch shopping.

Want company?

LOL! Why would you want to go shopping with me?

Because I haven't seen you. I was hoping to take you out tonight.

Sorry. I really need a new couch and it's my only night off this week.

Where are you going?

Local. If I need to run to the city, I'll go this weekend.

I have a truck. If you find something, we can take it home. Let me come.

Okay.

Dinner before or after?

Definitely before.

See you at 6?

I'll be ready.

I smiled and finally took a deep breath. She didn't blow me off. Couch shopping wasn't what I had in mind, but maybe if she found one she liked, we could break it in.

I had plenty of work to do the rest of the day, but my mind lingered on Blake the entire time. I didn't like going longer than a day without seeing her. Even when she was with Willie, I always made it a point of seeing her. Showing up at breakfast once in a while or running into her around town. Not that I was stalking her, but I felt like I could breathe better when Blake was in my life.

I was at her house just before six, but I didn't have a chance to get out of my truck before she was rushing out her door.

"I was going to come get you," I said once she climbed into my truck. She wore a pair of jeans and a black tee. Her hair was tied up in a loose ponytail, showing off her neck. I leaned over and kissed her, lingering on her neck for just a minute until she squirmed.

"That feels good," she said in a throaty voice.

"Then come back here so I can do it again."

She giggled when I leaned in and pushed me away. "You're bad. But come on. The place I really want to check out closes at seven."

"We probably should go there before we eat then."

She nodded. "Yeah, I think so. Are you okay with that?"

I put the truck in gear and backed out of her driveway. "Of course. Whatever you want to do."

I turned south toward the first store Blake wanted to see. Small town living meant most people closed up shop early. Blake had two more places on her list to check out, but she seemed hopeful the first place would be the jackpot.

We pulled into the parking lot and headed inside. I followed Blake around the store, smiling when she ran her hands over some fabrics and rubbed her fingers together to erase the feel. I finally asked what she was looking for, and she sighed.

"I don't know. That's part of the problem. I've had that

couch for years, and I loved it. I hadn't planned to get something new for a while, so doing this is stressing me out."

"Do you want something like what you had?" I asked, hoping to help her narrow it down.

She nodded then shrugged. "Maybe. I loved that couch, but I loved it because I bought it with my own money. It wasn't something I got from someone, it was a brand-new couch I bought for myself."

"Well, you're buying another one. You can love this one just as much."

She nodded and went searching some more. We wandered for the better part of an hour before she gave up and decided to try somewhere else.

The second store was just as much of a bust as the first. She was clearly getting frustrated, and I figured dinner was more important than finding a couch. We stopped at a sub shop, even though she tried to talk me into going to one more store. I could hear her stomach growling and knew it was for the best.

"I really don't like you sometimes," she grumbled.

I grinned and pushed her sub toward her mouth. "Eat. You'll like me better when you're not so hangry."

She tried to scowl at me, but she did eat. I was silent for a few minutes, letting the food sink in. When she finally sighed and closed her eyes, I knew she was feeling better.

"Sorry."

I grinned. "No need. You feeling better?"

She shrugged. "The whole thing just makes me mad. I don't want to be couch shopping because I want my old couch. I shouldn't be spending my money on a couch when I had a perfectly fine one until my mother decided to ruin it. I'm just pissed off, you know?"

I nodded because there was nothing I could say. I felt the same way she did. It wasn't fair, and it wasn't right. She had every right to be mad at her mom, and Nadine should be the one forking out the cash for Blake's new couch, not Blake. But I had to be the supportive friend who wanted to listen, not the guy who had to fix all her problems.

Yeah, I listened sometimes.

"I really liked that couch."

I nodded. I did, too. I'd spent many nights sitting on that couch watching movies with her, and recently, making out with her. I had a lot of memories of Blake on that couch. She fell asleep on my shoulder once, and I held her for hours. When she woke up, she was disoriented and so sexy I almost told her to leave Willie right then and there and be mine.

"I can't keep letting her do this."

"What are you going to do?" I asked, hoping it was okay for me to ask.

She shrugged and finished her sub. "I don't know. I just know it's gone on long enough."

I nodded in agreement.

Blake was too tired to check out the last place. She wouldn't have had much time there anyway, so she opted to skip it. I offered to go with her over the weekend to shop, and she said she'd like that.

I held her hand on the way to her house. It was really starting to feel like we were building something. I almost called her my girlfriend at the couch store, and by the time we pulled up in front of her house, I convinced myself she might not have been upset if I did.

Then we got out of the truck and noticed she had a visitor.

20

BLAKE

"Mom? What are you doing here?" I asked. She wasn't leaning against the post, but that didn't mean she wasn't drunk. She didn't usually get wasted during the week, but there were no guarantees on that either. She usually didn't throw up on my couch, so I was out of promises when it came to my mother.

"I wanted to talk to you. Hi, Ian. How are you?"

"I'm good, Ms. Dewitt. How are you?"

She smiled at him and noticed his arm around my waist. I'd gotten so used to Ian touching me that I didn't even realize he was until my mom did. I thought about stepping away from him, but his touch brought me comfort. He wasn't shying away from my mom or the messy parts of my life. He was standing strong beside me.

"I'm doing better than the last time we saw each other. I'm sorry for the way I spoke to you. I was out of line."

He nodded and I wondered what happened between them. "Respectfully, I'm not the one you owe an apology to."

She held his gaze for a second than nodded and met mine. "He's right, and that's why I'm here."

What they just said to each other finally clicked in my head. Ian was calling her out for hitting on him and telling me I should sleep with him the first night he came over. I'd almost forgotten that humiliation. Almost.

"Mom, you don't have to say anything."

"Why don't you listen anyway," Ian suggested. "I'll make you two some tea. Or I could go if you'd rather."

He raised his eyebrows at me, giving me the chance to decide. If I wanted him there, he was willing to stay. If not, he would go.

I smiled at him. "Thank you, but we've got it from here. I really appreciate your help tonight."

He nodded and kissed my forehead. "Good night, Ms. Dewitt."

"Good night, Ian."

We both stared after him until he backed out of my driveway and drove off. Only once the rumble of his truck faded did I turn back to my mother and invite her in.

"That would be nice."

I unlocked the door and almost laughed when I realized the last time my mother walked into my house under her own power was when I first moved in. I closed the door behind us and turned back to find her chewing her nail and staring at my empty living room.

"I thought that was a dream," she said quietly. "Then someone asked me why you were getting rid of your couch. They saw Ian and Ramsey taking it out of here."

I shrugged. "I tried to clean it, but I couldn't get the smell out."

"I'll buy you a new couch," my mom said.

I shook my head. I wasn't interested in her empty promises or her weak apologies. I'd heard enough of both over the years. "What do you want, Mom?"

She looked around, unsure of herself. Her brown hair, the

same shade as mine but with auburn highlights, looked brighter than usual. Her dress was neat and modest, almost to her calves. The bright blue color and figure hugging shape of the dress showed off her slim figure. For a woman who could retire in the next decade, easily, she could have passed for my sister instead of fifty-four.

"Can we sit?" she asked finally.

I scoffed. "Where?"

"How about your kitchen?"

I sighed and held out my hand for her to go ahead of me. She smiled and went straight to the cabinet where I kept the tea.

"Ian mentioned tea, and now I want some. Do you mind?"

I shook my head.

Mom busied herself with the tea, filling the kettle and grabbing two mugs. She selected two bags and waited for the water to boil.

Once the tea was brewing, she finally faced me, carrying the mugs to the table where I sat. "I always thought Ian was a nice boy."

I snorted. She made it clear the night she hit on him and told me I should sleep with him.

"I know. I was horrible that night. I'm trying here, Blake."

"Yeah, but I don't know what you're trying to do, Mom. You show up on my doorstep almost every weekend, drunk as hell and unable to stand. Now, you ruin my couch and show up during the week. What do you want?"

"I want to apologize. I'm sorry, Blake."

I drew in a breath. I'd wanted her to say those words for years, but I wasn't sure if she said them soon enough.

"I know I have a lot to apologize for. Years and years of taking advantage of you. Of you cleaning up after me and taking care of me when I should have been taking care of you. I hate to admit it, but until I realized I threw up on your couch, I didn't know how bad my drinking was."

"Really?" I asked, struggling to believe it. "Do you really expect me to believe that?"

She looked up at me. Her hazel eyes looked closer to amber when she was emotional, but dark and almost vacant when she was drunk. Amber eyes stared back at me, pleading with me to believe her.

"I wanted to let loose. I wanted to enjoy life. I didn't know I was an alcoholic, though. I thought I could handle it. I stopped drinking at times—"

"Yeah, when you lost yourself in a man," I said.

She stopped talking, her mouth open in shock. "You know, Blake, you're being a bitch."

I laughed. "Oh, yeah? Well, I just spent my only night off this week shopping for a couch because you're an alcoholic and I have nowhere to sit to watch television."

She ducked her chin and closed her eyes. "I'm sorry, Blake. I really am. And I owe you more than just an apology, but I deserve a little respect from you."

"Mom, I'm sorry, but I lost pretty much all my respect for you a long time ago. When I was living with you, I used to pray you'd get involved with someone so I wouldn't have to clean up after you all weekend. But that always meant listening to you having sex all weekend. Tell me what part of that was good for someone at twenty-two? Don't even get me started on how that was when I was only sixteen. And fifteen years later, tell me why I should still be patient with you."

"Alcoholism is a disease," she argued.

I shook my head. "I know that, Mom. And I get it. It's not something you can control. It's something you have to fight. But I'm still pissed off. I'm still hurt. You just told me you didn't think you were an alcoholic because you could give up drinking for the men you were involved with. But you couldn't give up drinking for me. Your only child. I wasn't important enough. So forgive me for not throwing a party and congratulating you on getting sober or recognizing you have a problem or whatever it is you came here to tell me when I've never been important enough before."

I glared at her, my chest heaving with anger and disappointment and frustration. She didn't look at me, just stared at her tea cup, until a single tear ran down her cheek. She didn't make a move to wipe it away, just let it slide down slowly.

There was a part of me that wanted to apologize. To tell her I didn't mean it and that I was sorry. To take it all back. But that wouldn't do either of us any good. She needed to know how hurt I was, and she needed to know I wasn't going to be her whipping post any longer.

"You're right, Blake. And I don't blame you." She got up and rinsed her tea down the drain. When she turned back to me, more tears were in her eyes. "I won't keep you any longer. I just wanted to tell you I'm trying to get better. I know I have a problem, and I'm getting help. It isn't fair to ask you for more help, so I won't. But I'm trying, Blake. I hope we can start to repair our relationship. I'd really like that."

I couldn't reply, and she didn't wait for me to.

She walked to the entrance to my kitchen and stopped. "Let me know how much your couch is when you find one you like. I'll pay for it, Blake. It's the least I can do."

I nodded, and she walked away. I sat at my table until the front door opened and closed, and until my tea grew cold. Then I got up and put the mugs in the dishwasher and went to bed.

I WOKE up to a text from Ian asking how things went with my mom. It was from sometime late the night before. I thought about replying, but I didn't want to wake him up.

I got dressed and went to work, letting myself get lost in the daily rush. When my shift was over, I grabbed lunch then climbed the scaffolding to work on the mural. I had a little over a week left to finish, and I was loving it, but even that didn't bring me the same joy it usually did.

By the time I was done, I was drained. I cleaned up and went home, needing food and my bed. But first, a shower.

I was in my pajamas and staring into my fridge when my phone dinged with a text.

How are you?

I smiled.

Doing okay. Still processing.

Are you hungry?

Yeah, but in for the night. Exhausted.

I have pizza.

I might love you.

LOL. I know the feeling, babe. I'm at your door.

I laughed and closed the fridge. Ian was indeed outside my door holding a large pizza that smelled like heaven.

"Hey," he said softly, stealing a kiss on his way by. "I brought you some beer, too."

"Thank you," I said, feeling more touched than I should.

Ian headed straight for the kitchen and set the pizza down on the counter. He put the beer in my fridge and pulled one out for me, opening it before handing it over. He went to the cabinet and grabbed plates, knowing where everything was without me having to say anything.

I sat at the table, watching him in my kitchen the same way I watched my mother the night before. Instead of resenting his presence like I did hers, I was happy he was there. She knew her way around my kitchen also, but in a clunky way since it was similar to hers and set up the same. Ian didn't hesitate or think about where things were, he just knew. He'd been there. He'd spent time with me. He'd paid attention. He was there for me in a way my mother never had been.

All of a sudden, everything I'd been trying to bury for twenty-four hours bubbled to the surface. A man I was sleeping with took better care of me than my own mother. She showed up with flat apologies, and he showed up with pizza. She threw up on my couch, and he took me shopping for a new one, after he got rid of the old one so I didn't have to. Nothing was the way it should be.

A sob ripped from my chest and echoed into the kitchen. Ian spun around, his face a mask of fear and concern. He was in front of me, on his knees on the floor, in less than a second.

"Blake, what's wrong, honey? Are you okay?"

I shook my head and cried. I couldn't say anything, just sobbed, trying to suck in a deep breath that wouldn't inflate my lungs.

Ian just sat there, rubbing my back and tugging me into his arms. After a minute, he pulled me off the chair onto his lap and rocked with me until my tears slowed and I could finally breathe again.

Ian kissed the side of my head and held me tighter. He didn't say anything, just let me sit there.

When I pushed away from Ian, he let me go. He waited

until I stood, then climbed to his feet right next to me. He tilted my chin up and kissed me gently. He meant the kiss to be comforting, soft. With everything I was feeling, it was a lifeline. A connection to someone. It was everything in that moment, and I needed him.

I thrust my tongue into his mouth, prying his lips apart. It didn't take him long to stop fighting me and give in. And when he did, he stole my breath.

He pushed me back until I hit the edge of the counter. All my breath rushed out, and Ian was right there, filling me up with himself instead. He angled his head and took over our kiss, plunging his tongue in and out of my mouth until I moaned and clawed at him for more.

Without a word, Ian picked me up. He set me on the edge of the counter and settled between my thighs. He was hard against the heat of my core, and I couldn't wait to feel him inside me. I tugged at his shirt until he reached back and yanked it off, tossing it behind himself before he dove back in and kissed me again.

I felt like I couldn't get close enough to him. Like I couldn't get enough of him. I pulled him closer with every second we kissed and groaned in frustration that I couldn't just climb inside Ian and have him keep me safe.

He slid his hand up under my shirt and pulled the cups of my bra down. His thumbs brushed over my nipples, and I moaned. He pulled away from our kiss and replaced his thumbs with his lips. I held him in place and leaned back, letting him love my body.

He tasted and teased my nipples until I couldn't settle for just that. I needed him inside me, and I told him so.

He didn't say anything, just pulled back enough to lift me and kissed me as he carried me through my house to my bedroom. He slapped the lights on and stripped my clothes off, then took care of his own clothes.

I stared at him, marveling for the millionth time that a man like him had any interest in me. He was hard where I was soft. His muscles bunched with each of his movements where my rolls flopped. But the look in our eyes was the same. Need. Desire. Passion. All the things I'd been missing from my life before Ian.

He pressed my thighs wide and ran a finger over me. I shuddered at his touch and gasped when he thrust his finger into me. Ian groaned, but he didn't speak. His gaze ran over my body, lingering on my face every time he pushed into me. I held his gaze, needing to see him as I came apart on his hand. His strokes went faster and deeper, and when he slid his thumb over my clit, I couldn't hold back and came apart for him, screaming his name as I did.

He didn't let me come down before he was pushing me over another higher edge. Over and over again, he pushed until all I could do was beg him to fuck me. I needed it. I needed him.

He sheathed himself while I watched. I couldn't move or even speak. He wore me out, but I wasn't done. I had to have him.

He held my gaze as he pushed inside me. Fire sparked in his eyes, and he closed them once he was all the way in. I slid my thigh up his hip and smiled when he rubbed his hand over my skin. Every time I was with Ian was like a full body experience. He touched me everywhere at once and made it feel like he surrounded me.

I was ready for fast and hard, but Ian's strokes were slow and deep. I groaned in frustration, but he didn't change. He just held me and watched me. His eyes were lit with passion, but something else was there. Something deeper. I reached up and touched his face, and he sighed like that was what he needed. He tilted his head to trap my hand between his cheek and shoulder, and held it there for a minute.

We weren't having sex. We weren't fucking. We were making love. I wanted quick and passionate and effortless, but just like everything else Ian had done, he was showing me he cared. And just like everything else, he was proving to me I'd never truly been cared for. Not like he did. Ian went above and beyond with everything. Whether it was spending the day with me or having sex or showing up with pizza when he knew I had a bad day, Ian showed me what it truly meant to have someone in your life you could count on.

All that emotion I buried when he kissed me came back to the surface. Ian wasn't mine forever. I knew that the same way I knew I'd never be able to recover from being with him. Ian wasn't the kind of guy who got attached, but he was definitely the kind of guy who left broken hearts in his wake. There was no way every woman he'd ever been with hadn't fallen for him. Not if he was half as attentive and sweet with them.

As for me, if I believed in finding love for myself, I would admit being with Ian was what love should feel like. Comforting, passionate, and like everything was going to be okay simply because you weren't alone.

Ian's deep strokes tipped me over the edge suddenly, without warning that I was going to fall. He followed me over, trembling inside and all around me as he came. And when he lowered his weight onto me, I wondered how I was ever going to move on from Ian Jameson.

Ian and I shared cold pizza in bed. We turned on the TV and got lost in the show. We barely spoke, but when he settled under my covers with his arm around me, both of us naked, I didn't protest.

It wasn't long before his breathing deepened and his arm grew heavier over me. I laid there, staring at the blackened room. I never imagined being with a guy like Ian. Sure, I always thought he was gorgeous, but letting myself get attached to him was only going to lead to pain for me. He wasn't going to stick around forever. I wanted to think maybe I could be different, but forever never worked out for me. My father left long before I was born. My mother was more worried about herself than me. Every boyfriend I'd ever had said we just weren't right for each other. That they didn't feel like I was invested.

It all boiled down to me. I was the common thread. I was the thing that led to all of them not wanting me in their lives. It wouldn't be long before Ian told me the same thing as the rest of them.

I was restless all night, trying to figure out what I was

going to do. I was getting too attached to Ian, I knew that, and if I stayed with him even longer, it was only going to get worse when we ended.

The next morning, I was up and gone before Ian woke up. I spent the day in a daze, exhausted from not sleeping and lost in my own thoughts. When I made it home that night, I crashed into bed and slept until my alarm went off the next morning.

I spent the rest of the week avoiding Ian and thinking about my mom. I wanted to help her, if I could, but I wasn't sure how. And Ian…I wasn't sure how I was going to let go of what we had, but I knew I had to do it.

I waited Friday and Saturday night for my mom to show up on my doorstep, but she didn't. No ringing doorbell. No pounding on the door. No messages that said she needed to come in. Nothing.

Sunday morning, I picked up two coffees and went to see her. She was surprised and a little skeptical when she opened the door and saw me.

"Blake. Hi. What are you doing here? I mean, how are you? Come in." She stepped back and let me in. Her smile was tentative as she led me to the kitchen and gestured for me to sit.

"I brought you a coffee."

She took it and smiled again. "Thank you. I appreciate it."

I sipped mine and picked at the paper. "You didn't show up this weekend."

She nodded. "I told you I'm done drinking, Blake. I meant it."

I drew in a breath and tried to figure out how I was going to say the things I wanted to say. I sipped my coffee to delay the conversation.

"I spent last night watching TV," she said, filling the

silence. "I wanted to go out. It was hard. But I know it's the right choice. I have to do this for me this time."

"Definitely not for me," I blurted. "I'm sorry. That wasn't fair."

"Actually, I think it was. Everything you said the other day was true. I haven't been the mom you need. The mom you deserve. I wish I'd been able to see what I was doing to you, but I couldn't. Or maybe I didn't want to."

"It's been fifteen years, Mom."

She nodded. "I know. And like I said, when I would stop, I convinced myself it was because I didn't have a problem. But when each relationship would end, I'd jump right back into it. Drinking made me feel good. I had friends. People liked me. It was fun. I was fun."

"You don't have to drink to be fun," I countered.

She smiled sadly. "I know that now, but it wasn't easy for me to accept. I spent most of my life caring for you. Raising you. I don't blame you, and I wouldn't change any of it, but being a single parent isn't easy. I was isolated."

"You didn't have to be. Finley's parents wanted to get to know you."

"I know. I let being a single mom become an excuse for not getting to know other people. The people my age were having fun and getting drunk when I had a toddler at home. They were getting married when I was sending you off to school. I missed out on that part of my life. I let that define me, and I pushed everyone away because I didn't think I was good enough for them."

"Why?"

She shrugged. "I thought the only way to show I could handle everything was to do it myself. When you got older, I felt like I'd done it. I'd raised you and I could relax just a little. The first time I went out drinking, people talked to me. I discovered this other side of MacKellar Cove full of people

I didn't know. I liked it. I didn't feel like a failure around them. I felt like I was one of them."

"So you just kept drinking? Because you had friends? Because you could forget how much you hated being a mom when you were with your friends?"

She shook her head. "No. It wasn't like that. I never hated you, Blake, and I never regretted having you. I loved you, but you were becoming an adult. You didn't need me anymore. I missed it. But none of it was your fault." She paused and sighed. "I don't want you to think I blame you. Every drink I ever had was my fault. No one forced me to drink. No one. I did it. Every single time, I did it."

"But you did it because of me."

She leaned across the table and rested her hand on mine. "No, Blake. No. I did it because of me. I did it because I needed someone else to make me feel good. People who made me feel like I was someone who mattered."

"You mattered to me," I said softly.

She drew in a shocked breath and nodded slowly. "You mattered to me. You still do. That's why I'm done. Because I know I'm destroying every chance I have at a relationship with you. I want us to get to know each other again. But I won't push you. If you're not ready, I understand. This is all new, and I haven't been there for you in years."

I took a breath and tried to believe her words. I wanted to believe her. She was my mom, and she was the only one I'd ever have. She made mistakes, but we all made mistakes. I couldn't hold it against her forever.

"I can't go back and forth with you, Mom. Maybe that's not fair, but if you tell me you're going to do this and then change your mind, I don't know if I can stand by and watch."

She nodded. "I understand. And I don't blame you. But I made a promise to myself the same as I made a promise to you. If I do all this for you, it won't stick. It has to be for me, too."

"I hope you do it then. For both of us," I told her.

She looked up at me with a smile. "Thank you, Blake. For reaching out. I'm really happy you came here."

I nodded. "Me, too, Mom."

We finished our coffees and Mom walked me to the door. She stopped before she opened it and chewed on her lip.

"What is it?"

She scrunched up her face and shook her head. "It's nothing."

"Just tell me. I know there's something you want to say."

She tilted her head to the side and asked, "Are you in love with Ian Jameson?"

I laughed. "No, of course not. Why would you ask me that?"

She shrugged. "You're more like me than you think, Blake. You've always worried about what people think of you. I don't think Ian is good for you. I would love it if he was, but he's not the kind of guy who will be there for you when you need someone."

"You don't know Ian, Mom, but it doesn't really matter. We're just having fun."

She nodded slowly. "I've had fun with a lot of men, Blake, and when they end things, it doesn't hurt any less." She hugged me. "Just be careful."

I nodded, feeling numb and confused. She released me, and I walked outside into the bright sunshine. It followed me home, confusing my mind and messing with me. I wanted to crawl under my covers and hide from the world, but the sun was shining and it was a beautiful day. I was going to see my friends. Everything was good.

Except it wasn't. Because my mom echoed the same thing

I'd been thinking since the first night I kissed Ian. Things were going to end with him. It was only a matter of time.

July 4th was less than a week away. The mural was finished, and Earl loved it. Eddie and Karissa were fans also, raving about the welcoming feel Georgia gave to Cracked.

It had been almost two weeks since I saw Ian. He sent me a few texts every day, but we hadn't seen each other. I didn't know what to say to him. I had never broken up with someone before.

But that wasn't really what I was doing. Our relationship had run its course. We were done, and that wasn't something that would change by hanging on longer.

I'd spoken to my mom every day since I left her house, and she was doing well. The weekends were the hardest for her, but she found other things to do so she didn't think about going out. So far, it was working and she hadn't been out yet.

I was walking home and thinking about my mom when Ian appeared next to me. "Hey," he said, sliding his arm around my waist.

"Hey," I answered. I hadn't prepared what I would do when I saw him again, and being surprised was never good for me.

"I've missed you. Is everything okay?"

I nodded. "Yeah, good. Just busy. With the festival next weekend, everything is crazier."

"The mural looks great," he said with a smile.

I returned his grin, but his didn't reach his eyes. He was wary and trying to act like nothing was wrong when we both knew everything was wrong.

"Thanks. Earl, Eddie, and Karissa loved it."

He nodded. "They should. It looks just like Ms. Georgia. Like she's watching over all of us and inviting us in. You're amazing."

I smiled and stopped at my door. He looked at me, waiting for me to say something to either invite him in or send him away. I wasn't that cold.

"Want to come in for a minute?"

He nodded and let me walk ahead. I went straight to the couch without thinking, then tried to veer toward the kitchen before he noticed.

"You got a new couch? When did you go?"

"Oh, yeah. I was off Tuesday and decided to go to Syracuse and found it. They just delivered it Friday afternoon."

"I would have gone with you," he said. "You could have asked me."

I sighed. He wasn't going to make this easy on me. "What are we, Ian?"

"What?"

I met his gaze. "What are we? Are we a couple? Are we friends with benefits? Are we just sleeping together? What are we?"

He shrugged. "I…What do you want us to be?"

I sighed and fought back the pain brewing in my chest. "We've been friends for a long time. I know you, and I know how you are with women. It's only a matter of time before you're sick of me."

He shook his head and stepped closer. He reached for my hand and grasped it in his, pleading with me with his eyes. "Blake, I'm not sick of you. I'm not going to get sick of you. I don't know where this is going, but I don't want it to end." He paused and looked up at me. "I love you, Blake."

I almost laughed. He loved me? No. Ian didn't love me. Maybe he thought he did, but he didn't. Not like that. He loved me as a friend, as a sister, but not like I wanted to be loved.

I looked at our hands joined together. How many times had I thought about the way his hands looked on me? Sliding across my skin. Turning me inside out. Making me beg for more. I loved his touch, just like I loved him. I couldn't continue, though. Not when he didn't really feel the same. If he could say those words so easily, I had to break free of him.

I stepped back and eased my hand from his. He stared at his hand as though he couldn't believe mine wasn't still there.

"I don't know what's going on, Ian, but I know this will end. You don't mean 'I love you' the way I want you to. You're not the kind of guy who wants forever. You want casual and fun and relaxed. I was okay with that, but I know I'm going to want more. And that's not fair to you. I know who you are and I don't want to change you, but I also know who I am and can't change me either."

"Why do you keep assuming you know me better than I know myself. That you know what I'm thinking and what I want?" he asked, his gaze as sharp as his words.

"I'm not assuming, Ian. I know you. Remember how you keep saying you know me? Well, I know you, too. You don't really love me. I've watched you with other women for years. You don't stick, Ian. You have no interest in it. And I thought I could handle it, but I have too much going on right now. My mom is trying to get sober, and I need to help her, and work is always crazy over the summer—"

"You didn't break up with Willie because summer was coming," Ian spat.

I drew in a breath and shook my head. "No, I didn't. Things were different with William. It wasn't like it is with us."

"Meaning?"

I shrugged. I couldn't tell him the whole truth. That

with William, I didn't care if I didn't see him for a few weeks, but with Ian, I wasn't sure I'd survive without him. Instead, I said, "William was easy. I always knew what I'd get from him and could count on him being there when I got busy."

He drew in a breath and crossed his arms over his chest. "What are you saying, Blake? Say the words. Spell it out for me."

I drew in a breath that hurt my chest and broke my heart. I looked up at him and held his gaze. His hazel eyes stared back at me with a matching pain in them. He would get over me. Ian would be back at O'Kelley's by the weekend, going home with someone new. Ian Jameson never stayed celibate for long.

"We're over, Ian."

IAN LEFT WITHOUT SAYING A WORD. I skipped girls' night because I wasn't in the mood to tell all of them what happened. He was still a friend, and he didn't do anything wrong. Everyone warned me to be careful with him because Ian wasn't the type who would get attached. They were all right.

He didn't fight for us. He just left. He proved that he didn't want me, and that made it a little easier. I knew I made the right choice.

I walked into Cracked early Monday morning feeling like a piece of me was missing. I kept trying to figure out what I forgot to do, but I couldn't think of anything.

Jean stopped me as I was filling coffee pots to ask what was wrong. I assured her it was nothing. Earl called out to me that I was in a daze, and I apologized and picked it up. Even some of the customers asked if I was okay.

When I took my break, Jean walked over and asked if I was okay.

"I'm good. Why?"

She shook her head. "You look like someone kicked your puppy. What happened? Finley? Karissa?"

I shook my head.

"Your mom? Ian?"

I forced a smile and shook my head again.

"Ian? Did he break up with you?"

"No, and nothing's wrong with Ian."

Jean examined me closely. "Something happened. I know you weren't crazy enough to break up with him."

"Why would that be crazy?" I blurted.

"Oh, Blake, you didn't."

"I did, but I'm not sure why that's so crazy, Jean. You and everyone else told me things would end with us. I just decided to do it before he did."

"Why?"

I shrugged and pursed my lips. I didn't want to talk about it. I didn't even want to think about it. Walking away from Ian was impossible, but it was the right thing to do.

"He loves you, Blake."

I outright laughed at that. "No, he doesn't. Ian loves Ian." I paused. "That was mean. I didn't mean for it to sound like he doesn't care about other people, but Ian doesn't get attached. He doesn't want a relationship. He likes being single."

Jean nodded. "He did, yes. He was always single because he wanted to be available when you finally were, too. Trust me, Blake, he loves you."

I rolled my eyes and dismissed what she said. Ian didn't love me. He barely even said anything when I ended things. If he wanted me so badly, he would have fought for me, not walked away without a word.

Nope. Jean was wrong. I knew it.

22

"How are things going with your guy?" Woody messaged me the next day.

I sighed. Woody would understand. He was in a relationship that was tentative, too. Although, I really hoped his survived.

COVEMOUSE

We're done. Broke up this weekend. How about you? Still going strong?

WOODY

Nope. She dumped me. Must be going around. I still don't get why.

COVEMOUSE

What did she say?

WOODY

She doesn't think I want to be with her.

COVEMOUSE

Have you ever told her you love her?

WOODY

I tried. She still dumped me. She doesn't
want to hear I love her.

COVEMOUSE

Maybe she wanted you to fight for her. My
guy just walked away. Without a word. I
know I made the right decision even though
it hurt like hell.

WOODY

How do you know he didn't want to fight but
felt like you wouldn't listen. Maybe he's
giving you time.

I shrugged. I wish it was that simple. Ian and I wanted
different things from our relationship. He wanted great sex,
and I did, too, but I wanted more. I had to admit that to
myself.

COVEMOUSE

He's not that kind of guy. If he wants
something, nothing stops him. He doesn't
want me.

WOODY

I still think you should give him a chance.
Maybe he's trying to figure out a new plan.

COVEMOUSE

Is that what you're doing?

WOODY

Absolutely.

COVEMOUSE

Well, good luck. I hope she takes you back
and falls madly in love with you.

WOODY

Me, too.

I was sitting in the square, enjoying the sunshine before the rain came that afternoon. It was the first test of my mural and the paints I used. I wasn't worried, but I was worried, so I was sitting outside staring at Ms. Georgia and hoping she looked the same tomorrow that she did today.

"Hey," Melody said quietly, sitting next to me in the pink Adirondack chair. The rest of the chairs were full, but I was still happy she said hello.

"Hey. How are you? Ooh, that's pretty," I said, pointing to her necklace.

"Thanks. I just picked it up at Island Designs. Olive said your friend is the designer."

"Trinity, yeah. She moved here not too long ago. She's really talented."

Melody nodded. "She is. I love it."

I smiled and tried to think of something to say to her. I didn't know Melody well, but Finley wasn't a big fan of hers. Ian mentioned Melody and Ramsey weren't doing well. Between the two of them, I had nothing to talk to Melody about.

"How's Amber?" I finally asked, right before I remembered she wanted another kid.

Melody smiled warmly and nodded to the redheaded girl running around the square, chasing butterflies. "She's great. She can't wait for kindergarten to start. We've been trying to get together with other kids her age so she knows more of them."

"That's a good idea."

She nodded. We were silent a minute, then she said, "I know Ian told you Ramsey and I are having problems."

"Oh, um…" I tried to come up with something, but I couldn't think of anything to say. "He did. I'm sorry. I know it's not my business. I haven't told anyone."

Melody nodded. "I appreciate that. I'm glad Ramsey has him to talk to. He needs a friend."

"You're lucky because you have Willow."

Melody snorted. "Willow isn't exactly Ramsey's biggest fan. If she had her way, I'd have already left him."

"Why?" I blurted.

Melody shrugged. "I'm not really sure."

We were quiet again for a minute.

"Can I ask you a question?"

I nodded.

"How hard was it to give Ian a chance?"

I sucked in a breath at her question, more than a little surprised by it.

"I'm sorry. That was really personal. I shouldn't have asked you about Ian."

I shook my head. "No, it's fine. I actually just ended things with him."

"You did? I'm sorry. I didn't realize. Can I ask why?"

I sighed. I wasn't ready to talk to my friends about Ian, but talking to Melody was safer. She wasn't as close. I was sure she liked Ian, but with her own relationship issues, she might understand how I felt.

I took a breath and stared up at Ms. Georgia. If she were still here, she would know what to tell me. She would be able to offer advice for how to get over Ian. I had no idea how I was going to, but I needed to try. No, I needed to do it.

"I got too attached."

"To Ian?"

I nodded. "He's a flirt. Everyone knows he is. I've been warned by so many people about getting involved with him, and I thought I could handle it. But I've gotten to where it's not just sex for me. I'm falling in love with him, and I can't."

"Why not?"

I scoffed. "Because he doesn't feel the same, and he never will. I know it, and so does everyone else."

Melody nodded. "Ian's always been a flirt. He hit on me when we were in high school. I almost hooked up with him instead of Ramsey. For years, I told myself it was for the best. But now…"

"You wish you were with Ian?" I asked, hurt and shocked.

Melody laughed. "God, no. Ian's great, don't get me wrong, but I totally understand. He's not a forever kind of guy. I just meant getting together with Ramsey was…I thought he was it for me. I really thought we'd be together forever. I never once regretted marrying him. But lately I've been wondering if I was wrong all along."

It hurt to hear her talk like that. Melody and Ramsey were always solid. They were the couple who walked through town holding hands, the people you could see doing the same thing when they were married fifty or sixty years. Instead, they hadn't been married fifteen and she was talking about ending it.

A part of me understood how she felt. With William, I never pictured our life together. I more or less accepted I'd be with him forever, but I couldn't imagine it. The picture wasn't there. We weren't close enough for it to really make sense, but I wanted it that way. I wanted someone who wouldn't make me forget myself. Someone who would be a companion but not who would take over my life.

Ian would take over my life. He was the kind of man I would lose myself for. I'd want to do everything for him and forget everything else.

I wondered if Melody felt the same way.

"I'm sorry, Melody. I always thought you two were perfect for each other."

She nodded. "Me, too. But all this with the baby…" She

stopped talking and smiled. "Hey, sweetheart. Do you remember Ms. Blake?"

Amber gave me a grin and said hello.

"Hi, Amber. I love your sparkly top."

"Thank you. It's my favorite. Mommy, can I have a snack?"

Melody pulled a bag of fruit snacks out of her bag. "Make sure you throw the package away when you're done."

Amber nodded and ran off with her snack.

"Sorry," Melody said.

I waved off her concern. "She's fine."

Melody smiled after her daughter and drew in a breath. "I hate the idea of breaking up her family."

"Ramsey refuses to talk about more kids?" I asked, knowing I was pushing.

She nodded. "He said he can't do it again. Amber wants a sibling, and I always wanted more than one kid. We waited a few years, but when we lost Steven, Ramsey refused to try again. He won't even talk about it. I feel like I have to give up what I want for what he wants."

I huffed a laugh.

"Why is that funny?"

I shook my head. "It's not. My mom…" I took a deep breath. "My mom used to drink. A lot. And until a few weeks ago, she would get drunk regularly. I know she has a problem, but she would stop drinking whenever she met someone new. She let men determine her worth and dictate how she lived her life. I never wanted to live like that, which is why I ended things with Ian."

"So you get it. Ian and Ramsey are the same. They're the kind of men who decide how something is going to be and we just have to fall in line."

"No, I'm not saying that. All I mean is that he's the kind of guy I'd give up everything for. He's someone I'd let take over for me. I'd want his approval so much that I would lose who I am."

Melody nodded slowly. "I spent a lot of years wanting Ramsey's approval. Maybe not approval, but his love. A part of me always felt if I didn't agree to what he wanted, everything would fall apart. But a baby is too important to me to roll over and let him have his way."

"I'm sorry, Melody. I really am. I wish I could offer you some advice, but I clearly don't know the first thing about a successful relationship."

"You were with William for a long time."

I scoffed. "Yeah, but he wasn't right for me."

"How did you know that?"

I smiled, thinking about Ian and walking in on him. "He never made me crazy. Everything was mediocre with him. I liked that until I knew something else could be better."

"Ian?"

I shrugged. "If that was an option, yeah, but it's Ian. I dated William for years because I knew he was a good guy and couldn't figure out a reason to end things. I paint simple, basic artwork because it's what people like. I'm boring and safe, and Ian is not."

Melody nodded. "Ramsey and I aren't the same either. It was one of the things I loved about him. He pushed me out of my comfort zone."

"Ian was risky and terrifying. He was someone I never thought I'd date. He scared me, and the way he made me feel is something I'll never forget. But that doesn't mean I can handle it forever. I don't want to spend the rest of my life worried that the gorgeous, skinny woman at the bar was able to grab Ian's attention and he decided he was done with the fat chick."

"You're not fat," Melody argued. "I gained forty pounds with Amber, and another ten with Steven."

"But I bet Ramsey's eyes still light up when he sees you."

She laughed. "It's more of a wary look I get from him now. He's waiting to see what kind of mood he gets from me before he speaks."

"Mommy, can we go?" Amber asked, running up to us.

Melody nodded and got to her feet. "Sure, honey. It was nice talking to you, Blake. Good luck."

"You, too, Melody."

She smiled and took Amber's hand and they walked away talking. I watched them go then sighed and left, too.

BETWEEN MY MOM and Melody telling me it was good Ian and I were over, and my friends telling me I should talk to him, I was more confused than before I ended things with Ian. I wanted to believe it was the right thing to do, but I kept second guessing myself. A part of me wanted to call him and tell him I was wrong, but another part of me knew I couldn't do it. He didn't want me. For months, he was calling and texting and showing up places I was. For the last few days, nothing.

Ian was done.

The morning of the Fourth, Earl was running a special to celebrate the holiday and Ms. Georgia. It was supposed to be my day off, but he asked if I could help out since he expected a big crowd.

It went by quickly since we were running food constantly. We turned tables over as fast as we could to get people in the door, but there were customers who waited almost an hour for a seat. By the time I headed out, I was dead on my feet and debated skipping the rest of the Festival.

I was sitting on the edge of my bed in a towel when a text came through from Finley asking where we were going to meet. Laura replied first saying she was headed to the square. Everyone agreed they'd meet there so we could watch the parade then sit together for the dance.

FINLEY

Blake?

ME

I'm not really in the mood for a party tonight. It's been a busy day.

KARISSA

Get your ass down here or we'll drag you here.

ELISE

You have to come.

LAURA

You're coming, no matter what.

I closed my eyes and groaned. The last thing I felt like was a party. Ian would be there, probably with someone, and I was tired and crabby.

ME

I won't be good company.

FINLEY

We don't care.

LAURA

Agreed.

ELISE

Yep.

TRINITY

No problem.

KARISSA

Come anyway.

I groaned.

ME

Fine. I'll be there in 20.

FINLEY

Yay!

I smiled and shook my head. They could get me through anything.

I searched my closet and finally came up with a dress that was loose and comfortable. I wore my favorite sandals. And I fixed my hair and put on a little makeup and a necklace I bought of Trinity's. I checked myself out in the mirror. I certainly wasn't eat-your-heart-out hot, but I was better than my normal see-what-you-dodged.

The square was crowded when I got there. I wanted to find my friends and avoid running into Ian, but it was a mob scene. It took me ten minutes to get to where they said they would be and another few minutes of searching in the area for them.

"The parade is about to start," Finley said when I finally got to them. She pulled me onto her seat with her and we sat back and enjoyed the parade we'd seen countless times.

Once the parade ended, the music started playing and the tables and chairs came out, and the party got started for real. It wasn't long before we were all on the dance floor and singing along with the rest of the crowd.

After an hour or so of dancing, I took a break and headed to our table. I needed a break to slow down and have a drink, and I needed to breathe for a minute, especially when a slow song came on and I had no one to dance with.

I hated being single. Not that being with William had been right for me, but I didn't know just how wrong he was until I let myself get involved with Ian. Ian showed me how wrong William and I were for each other, and even though I knew Ian and I weren't going to be together forever, I still ended up spoiled by him.

The entire crowd seemed to be having a good time. My friends were laughing and dancing together and with other friends. My mom even seemed to be having fun. She hadn't come to very many town events over the years, but she was smiling and talking to my high school math teacher, Mr. Peters. She hadn't had a drink in almost two weeks, and I definitely didn't think she was better, but it was the longest I'd ever seen her go without getting drunk, so it was progress.

I sipped my beer and told myself I was having a good time. I smiled and said hi to a few people I knew as they walked by. Finley tried to get me to join the rest of them on the dance floor, but I wasn't in the mood.

I checked my phone, but everyone I knew was at the Fireworks Dance. Except Ian. I hadn't heard from him since he blurted out that he loved me. Ha! He loved me. I still couldn't figure that one out, but I knew it wasn't true. He didn't love me. Not like that. Not like his parents loved each other. Not like Eddie loved Georgia. Not like he made it sound.

I searched the dance floor again, but he still wasn't there. I was surprised, but I was happy. I didn't think I could handle watching him with someone else. Not yet. Ian would move on, way before I did, but I wasn't ready for it yet.

He said the Fireworks Dance was his favorite event of the festival. I didn't even want to come in case he showed up, but he wasn't there yet. The night was long, and it wouldn't be long before Ian showed up. I couldn't be there alone. I had my girls, but I needed a friend who would be there for me.

I pulled my phone back out and clicked on the Book Boyfriends Wanted app. Woody. He was aware of the dance.

He talked about going with the girl he was in love with, but that plan fell through when they broke up.

I sent him a message asking if he was doing anything.

WOODY

Not a damn thing.

COVEMOUSE

Come dance with me.

WOODY

Um, what?

COVEMOUSE

I could really use a friend tonight. I know it's a lot to ask and you can say no, but I hope you're open to meeting me at the Fireworks Dance in MacKellar Cove.

WOODY

I'll be there in fifteen minutes.

I smiled and finally felt better. I kept my eye on the entrance, counting the minutes. I tapped my toe on the ground and tried not to make myself sick. I didn't think about reaching out to Woody since we'd been talking for almost two months, but now that I was sitting there waiting for him to appear, I was nervous as hell.

I alternated between staring at my phone and staring at the entrance once ten minutes passed. I didn't think to tell Woody what I was wearing and he had no idea what I looked like, so I waited and wondered if every guy who walked through the gate alone was him.

At sixteen minutes, I still hadn't heard from him. I thought about messaging him again, but then Ian walked in.

He was effortlessly gorgeous. I could tell his hair was wet even from the distance and remembered the way it felt running through my fingers in the shower. He wore a navy tee with khaki shorts and red flip flops, looking very patriotic. He looked around as though searching for someone, and I had to suck back a sob.

I turned away and drew in a breath. Woody needed to get there immediately. My phone was clenched in my hand so tight my knuckles hurt. I drew in another breath and jumped when my phone buzzed in my hand.

WOODY

I'm here. Where are you?

I wanted to run. Inviting him was a bad idea. But I couldn't do that to him. Maybe I could make up an excuse for why I needed to go. But first, I had to be honest.

COVEMOUSE

To the left of the entrance. At a table. I'm wearing a blue dress with red and white stars. Dark hair in a ponytail. I'm going to stand and look for you.

I hit send and turned to the entrance to find Woody. Ian was still there, staring at his phone. Great, so not only did I have to watch him with someone else, it was someone he planned to meet.

His head snapped up and his eyes locked right on mine. I tried to look away and find Woody, but Ian slid his phone into his pocket and headed straight for me.

I never should have stayed. I shouldn't have even come. But I wanted a glimpse of him. I wanted to remind myself of who he was. It was going to hurt like hell to watch him with someone else, but it was easier in the long run to rip off the band-aid.

I waited until he stopped right in front of me. I drew in a breath and swallowed roughly, praying my voice wouldn't shake. I promised him we'd always be friends, no matter what, and I had to keep that promise.

"Hey," I said, forcing a smile.

"Hey. Um, how are you?"

"Great," I said, my voice squeaking. I cleared my throat and tried again. "Um, good. Sorry. Good. How, um, how are you?"

He shrugged. "I've definitely been better."

"So, um…you're meeting someone here?"

He nodded.

"Blind date? I saw you looking at your phone."

He took a breath and shrugged. "Kind of. I'm meeting someone from Karissa's app. She said she needed a friend tonight."

The back of my throat tingled. I swallowed again, roughly. No. There was no fucking way.

"I wanted to tell you, Blake," he said.

"Tell me what?" I needed him to say the words. I wouldn't believe it until he did.

"I'm Woody, Blake. I'm the guy you've been talking to. The one you asked to come here tonight. The friend you needed."

23

IAN

lake's face went white. I knew it was going to be bad if she ever found out I was Woody, but I didn't know quite how bad until all the color drained from her face.

"Sit, babe," I said, gently guiding her to the table right behind her. She let me hold her elbow but shook me off as soon as she was seated.

"You're lying. How the hell did you find out about him?"

I shook my head and pulled out my phone. I unlocked it, opened the app, and handed it to her. She glared up at me, then glanced at the phone.

"What is this, Ian?"

"Read them, Blake. I couldn't have this if I wasn't the one you were talking to."

She finally took my phone and scrolled through the months of messages we traded. Her hands shook when she handed the phone back to me. "Why?"

I knew what she was asking. Why didn't I tell her? Why did I let it go on? Why was I such an ass?

"I knew you wouldn't talk to me so much if you knew it was me. I thought you'd figure it out really quickly."

"So this is my fault?"

"No, Blake, no," I said quickly, crouching in front of her. "Nothing is your fault, babe. It's all mine. I should have told you. Not that it would have mattered."

She glared at me. "What does that mean?"

I sighed. I was tired. I'd barely slept all week. Losing her destroyed me. And worse than losing her was hearing her tell me she thought I was lying about being in love with her. Like she knew me better than I knew myself.

I thought about losing myself in someone else, but even thinking about it pissed me off. I wanted Blake. There was no substitute for her.

"It means even if you knew who I was, you still wouldn't have believed me the other day. You still would have pushed me away. You still would have seen me as not good enough for you."

"That's not true, Ian."

I scoffed. "It is, babe. I came here tonight knowing you would hate me. I don't want a life without you, but I showed up because you needed a friend. I said we'd always be friends. No matter what. So I'm here for you, Blake. And I always will be, even if it fucking kills me."

"Why would it kill you, Ian?" she asked, as though she had no clue. Or maybe she still wouldn't let herself believe it.

I sucked in a breath and blew it out slowly. I pressed my lips together and stood. Her gaze followed me up.

"I love you, Blake. I've loved you for a long time. I've never gotten involved with other women because none of them were you. No one has ever been you. But you don't believe me. You don't trust me. And I guess I have to accept that maybe all that is just because you don't want me. So, yeah. It'll kill me to stand by and be your friend. To watch you meet someone else and know he's touching you. You're screaming his name. You're falling in love with him. But I'll do it because I want you to be happy, Blake. Even though it'll fucking kill me."

I didn't wait for her to reply. I simply turned and walked away. I'd do what I could to be her friend, but I needed a minute. Or a month. Or a few. I was too raw to have her mad at me because of the app when she'd already told me we were done. It was too much for one week.

I walked home slowly, trying to walk off the shitty mood I was in. All I really wanted to do was take a baseball bat to something. My head maybe?

The fireworks over the river screamed through the air and startled me. I jumped back and looked up at the sky. The explosion was loud but the pop and sparkle almost made me smile.

I should have kept walking, but the *ooh's* and *ahh's* of others drew me in. O'Kelley's doors were open, and the music was turned off so everyone could watch the show. I found myself following the rest of them inside and through the bar to the back where I stood with the crowd on the Riverwalk to watch.

For years I dreamed of watching the show with Blake's hand in mine. To hold her while the fireworks lit up the night sky. Kissing and touching her and having every right to do it.

I came close to having her. For a few weeks, I thought she was mine. I lived out all my fantasies except the one that really mattered. The one that meant we were together forever.

I stood near the entrance to the bar and watched, partly mesmerized and partly depressed. Eventually I closed my eyes and debated walking home. I wasn't fit for being around others. Not when I felt like shit and everyone seemed to have someone else to lean on. A hand to hold and lips to kiss.

A hand slapped down on my shoulder, startling me worse than the fireworks. I turned, ready to swing, but stopped when I saw Hudson behind me.

"Let me buy you a drink," he said simply, nodding to the mostly empty bar.

I nodded and followed him inside, taking a seat across the bar from him.

"Things fall apart with Blake?" he asked, not one to sugar-coat things.

"Yep," I answered, downing the shot of whiskey he set in front of me. "I almost had myself convinced she loved me. What a fucking joke."

Hudson nodded. "Blake's not an easy woman. She's amazing, but she's a tough nut to crack."

I glared at him. "Don't you dare touch her."

He lifted his hands and shook his head. "Wasn't even thinking about it. I was going to ask if you're okay."

I shook my head and laughed. "Not even close." I told him the whole story about the app and how I screwed up an already screwed up situation.

Hudson shook his head again. "Shit, man. That sucks. How are you going to fix it?" He poured me another shot and I tossed it back without thinking about it.

"I can't. It's over with Blake. I have to move on. Forget about having her in my life."

He hesitated for a second then nodded and rubbed his neck. "I wish I could offer some advice about that, but I sure as hell don't have any. Losing the woman you love will gut you."

I laughed. "That's pretty much how I feel. I think it would have been less painful."

He nodded. "True. Enjoy the good memories you have and try to find a way to move on. You've never had trouble meeting women before."

I laughed mirthlessly. "Because those other women were just sex. They were a temporary fix. I never wanted any of them. Not like I want Blake. But I fucked that up." I pulled out my phone. "I need to delete this fucking app."

"What app?"

I showed him Book Boyfriends Wanted.

"Is that a dating app?"

I nodded. "It is. It's the one I used when I was paired with Blake. Karissa made it. I guess it's good, but obviously not flawless since it screwed me."

"You're blaming the app?" Hudson asked with a chuckle.

I shook my head. "No, you're right. I'm the one who fucked up. But I don't need another reminder of how I lost Blake." I tapped the app and hit the X to delete it. My finger hesitated for a few seconds. I scowled at myself and touched it, erasing one piece of Blake from my life. It would take a while to get rid of all of her, but that was one step.

Hudson shook his head. Customers started to filter back in and wave for his attention. "It sucks, man. Sorry about you and Blake. Hang out for a bit. I'll be back."

I nodded and let him walk away. Nothing he could say would help. Blake was gone. I tried to show her how I felt, but at the end of the day, it didn't matter. She wasn't in love with me, and it was time I let go of her. I promised Georgia I would try, and I did. Now, I had to try to stop loving her.

Worried she might show up with Finley and the others after the dance, I left not long after the fireworks ended. I waved to Hudson and walked out into the cool night, letting the river breeze guide me home.

I let myself in, but everything still smelled like Blake. All week I'd debated washing my sheets and lighting some candles or something to erase her scent, but I couldn't bring myself to do it. Hell, even knowing things were truly done, I couldn't bring myself to let go of her completely. All I had left were my memories of her. I needed one more night with those memories.

I woke up the next morning with a killer headache. If I'd had anything to drink after the two shots at O'Kelley's, I might think it was a hangover, but it wasn't. It was losing Blake.

The last few Sundays I spent watching Blake paint, or just spending time with her. Her mural was done, and so were we, which meant I had an entire day to do whatever I wanted. Except the one thing I really wanted to do. See Blake.

I made coffee since Cracked was now off-limits for me. Even if I could handle seeing her, Jean would kick my ass. Everyone in town was going to think our break-up was my fault. Especially when they heard about the app. Blake was the sweet one who was loved by everyone. People looked out for her and protected her. I was the asshole who hurt her. No one would care or believe that I was the hurt one. They'd all blame me.

Just like I did.

I stripped my bed and cleaned my apartment. I seriously considered burning the whole place to the ground, but I knew that was pushing it. I stretched clean sheets over the futon, thankful I never bought a real bed for her, and scrubbed my home until the only thing I could smell was bleach.

I was still restless, so I went out to the shop. I had three boats in progress, and it seemed like a good day to get some extra work done. My contracts included a bonus if I finished a boat early, and without any reason to stop working, I had more than enough time to finish all three early.

I went to the one that was closest to done and examined the checklist. With Devon working with me, we had to have a system to make sure everything was getting done, and getting done the right way. He suggested a checklist, both to help him learn my process and to monitor the progress we made on each boat. So far, it was working perfectly.

I climbed into the hull of the boat and picked up the sander, where Devon left it. I could see the difference in the wood where he'd stopped and let myself get lost in the process.

At some point, I heard the door open and slide closed, but I ignored whoever it was. If they really wanted to talk to me, they could get my attention. If not, I was perfectly happy not talking to anyone all day.

I could feel eyes on me, but I pushed away the creepy feeling and kept on working. My pulse throbbed a steady, fast beat, alerting me, but I ignored that, too.

Eventually, two feet hit the inside behind me. Even with my back to her, I knew it wasn't Blake. Which meant it was the next worse person.

"What do you want, Fin?" I asked without turning around or shutting off the sander.

"To talk to you. See how you are."

"I'm fucking fabulous," I growled. "Go away."

"Are you really going to turn into one of those 'get off my lawn' old men?"

I shrugged and kept working. "Maybe. It'll keep people away."

"Ian!" she screamed.

I jumped and almost dropped the damn sander. My pain in the ass sister was not going to take a hint. She never did. Ever since we were kids, Finley did things her way. And if you didn't go along with it, you had to find a way to get over it because she wouldn't.

I turned off the sander and spun to scowl at my sister. If she was standing there with her arms crossed and her best protective sister look, I would have been able to handle it. She should protect Blake. I was the asshole who pushed myself on her at Georgia's party. I was the one who told her to invite me in. I was the one who kept going back for more and not letting her push me away. I was the one who made the entire thing happen. Blake should have been protected from me, if only so I would have been protected from her.

"What?" I snarled. If she'd looked at me like I was the enemy, it would have been easier. But she didn't. She looked at me like I was the victim. I was the injured party. I was the one who needed comfort.

I almost laughed. If Finley was with me, it was because Blake was completely fine. She wasn't upset. She wasn't hurt. She was good. Because she didn't care about me. We were over, and it was just another day for Blake.

I didn't wait for Finley to say something. I unplugged the sander and left it on the floor, then climbed out of the boat. Finley was right behind me, matching me step for step until I stormed into my apartment and decided I needed a beer.

I opened the fridge and froze. Even my fridge reminded me of Blake. Half a six-pack I bought for her since she didn't like my beer. Orange juice because she liked it instead of coffee on mornings she didn't get up with the sun. Half and half instead of just milk because she convinced me the tiny amount of difference in calories wasn't worth it to give up the better flavor.

I pulled it all out and set it on the counter. I put the beer on the table near Finley and said, "You should take those home. I won't drink them, and I don't need them anymore."

She didn't say anything. She just stood there as I dumped

orange juice and half and half down the drain. I would have dumped the beer, too, but getting rid of them worked.

"What do you want, Fin?" I asked, leaning against the counter and looking at her.

"I'm sorry," she said.

I shrugged. "Nothing to be sorry for."

She nodded. "You and I both know there is."

"Did you tell Blake not to love me? Did you tell her I was an ass and wasn't worthy of her? Because if you didn't interfere, then there's nothing for you to be sorry for."

"You know I didn't do either, but I'm still sorry, Ian. I was really hoping things would work out. I hate seeing you like this."

I shrugged again and filled a glass with water. My throat was dry and sore. I chugged the water then looked at my sister again. "I'll be fine. I've spent my entire life without Blake. I can handle it."

"She'll come around. She's really upset, and—"

"Don't," I barked. "Fin, just don't. I can't hold onto hope that maybe one day she'll want me. I convinced myself of that for years. That once things were over with Willie, she'd see that she was supposed to be with me. But she's not supposed to be with me. She made it clear that's not what she wants."

"Ian, you know how she is. Love scares her."

I laughed at that. How could I not? "Fin, love scares me, too. I think it scares everyone. Have you ever talked to someone who didn't have some kind of fear when talking about the person they love? But you know what, most of those people talk about losing the person they love. How that's their biggest fear. I'm living it. Right now, I'm living it. I've lost her. She's gone. And she's not coming back. I have to accept it and move on, Fin."

I met her gaze and saw sadness and resignation in her

eyes. She knew I was right. All her other words were empty platitudes, trying to help me feel better. She knew Blake wasn't going to change her mind about me. Which meant moving on was my only option.

"I gotta take a shower. You can show yourself out. And don't forget the beer. I don't want it here."

24

BLAKE

I did not want to go to girls' night. The idea of facing all of them after the humiliation of Ian's confession was too much. As soon as Ian walked away, Finley, Karissa, and Laura were there. Elise and Trinity weren't far behind them. They all demanded to know what happened.

I told them as much as I could choke out, then rushed off. I couldn't believe I was so stupid. Ian was Woody. The things I told him. The way we talked. How did I not realize they were the same person?

And what was I supposed to do with Ian saying he loved me? He kept telling me the same thing. Twice he'd said he loved me. But it was Ian Jameson. He didn't fall in love. He didn't stick.

I pulled up Book Boyfriends Wanted and went to the chat function. I scrolled back to the beginning and read every single one of the messages between Woody and me. Our promise to be friends. The things I told him that I never told anyone else. The things I admitted to him.

And then I reread all his words about being in love with

his friend. About the way he felt about her. How he wanted to know what she was thinking. How he cared for her but knew she was scared. How he had been in love with her for a long time but she didn't feel the same way.

I reread about him telling me they were together. How happy he was and scared that it would all end.

I sat there and cried. For weeks I told myself the woman he loved was a fool. That she didn't know what she had. That I would trade places with her in a heartbeat.

And I was her.

Everything I ever thought I knew was upside down. I'd spent months convincing myself that Ian and I were temporary, but he wanted us to be forever. I was the one who ended things. I was the one who pushed him away. I was the one who didn't believe him when he said he loved me. I was the problem.

I decided I would drive myself insane if I sat around my house all night, so I forced myself to take a shower and go to Book Boyfriends Unlimited. If I told them I didn't want to talk, they would let me sit there. I just needed to not be alone.

Everyone was already there when I walked in. They took one look at my red-rimmed eyes and oversized tee and knew exactly what was going on. I pressed my lips into a smile that I didn't feel. Finley cut me a piece of cherry pie, and Elise added a generous squirt of whipped cream. Trinity handed me a glass of wine filled to the top.

I smiled at my girls and sat back in my seat. I let them talk around me while I ate my pie and drank my wine. They were talking about the book we read, and I realized I did not read it the same way they did.

"Did you really think he was sweet?" I blurted when Elise said something about the hero being such a good guy.

They all turned to look at me. "You didn't?" Elise asked.

I shrugged. "I thought he was kind of full of himself. Like he expected her to just love him simply because he was the one who came to her rescue."

"Well, he's the kind of guy who puts others first. How many movies have the hero save the heroine?" Finley said.

"Yeah, and how many times have we said it's dumb? You can't build a relationship based on something like that."

"So, what should you build a relationship on?" Laura asked.

I clamped my mouth shut because God knew I had no idea.

"Sex," Elise said with a smile.

"Hell, yeah," Karissa agreed. "You gotta have good sex. But unless you have sex on a first date, there has to be something else. I'd say common interests."

"Yeah, but opposites attract. Didn't we all learn that in Hawaii?" Finley said with a grin.

"True. My most successful relationships have been with men I had less in common with," Elise said.

"That's because you like to pick fights and have make up sex," Karissa teased her.

The rest of us laughed as Elise nodded in agreement. Her smirk was priceless. "There's nothing wrong with some damn good make up sex."

"Very true," the rest of us agreed.

I felt out of place in the conversation. None of us had many successful relationships, but I felt like I was the least successful of everyone. I was with William for five years, but we didn't have any of the things they were talking about. The sex was mediocre, and we never disagreed on anything so make up sex was nonexistent. We had to care in order to be passionate.

But with Ian it was different. When we argued, it was fun and playful. And Elise was right. Make up sex was amazing when it was with someone you wanted to make up with. Passionate and emotional and powerful.

"I think you have to have some things in common. Whether it's the way you think or the movies you like or the team you cheer for. It doesn't really matter what, but you have to be able to agree once in a while and share things," Trinity said.

Finley nodded. "I agree with that. My parents are like that. They both always loved boating, and while it seems silly, they always seemed happier when they came back from going out on the water. Ian and I used to joke they went out there to have sex, but I think they just went out there to talk and get away. It was something they shared and a way for them to stay connected to each other."

Ian and I went fishing. When I was stressed, I always went fishing, and Ian did the same. Going together was better than going alone. Everything with Ian was better than being alone.

"I think it's also about the way he makes you feel," Elise said. "If you don't feel safe and loved, then it doesn't matter how much you have in common or how hot the passion is."

"Absolutely," Karissa said, reaching for Elise's hand.

We all knew how bad Elise's relationship with her college boyfriend was even though we didn't know her then. She hadn't shared much with me, but I knew enough to know he did everything he could to control her. I wasn't sure if he was abusive or not, but I guessed he was.

Trinity said, "I like to figure things out about him, too. Someone that I know really well, who there's no mystery with, I end up bored. The last guy I dated was a friend. We made that transition well, but it fizzled quickly. I knew all his stories and all his moods. I didn't have to figure anything out with him. We were just friends who had sex, and it wasn't enough for either of us. I loved him, but it ended up being awkward and weird."

"Not all relationships end up that way. I think friends can become lovers and it can be really amazing. That's what I hope to find one day," Finley said.

"Good luck," I mumbled.

They all looked at me.

"Are you okay?" Trinity asked, the only one brave enough to say something to me.

I gave her a smile and shook my head. "No. I don't think I am."

"Do you want to talk about it?" Laura asked.

I shrugged. "I'm not sure there's anything to talk about. Ian and I are over. He lied to me about who he was on the app. I thought he was someone I could trust, but I just don't know."

"How did you not know it was him?" Trinity asked, glancing around. When everyone else avoided her gaze, she added, "Sorry, but I kept wondering how you didn't figure it out."

I smiled. "I don't know. The things we talked about were different than we talked about in person. I told all of you about Woody, and none of you figured it out." I looked at my friends and found them looking away from me. "Did you know?" I asked.

When they looked at each other, then looked at me, I saw the guilt in their eyes.

"You did? You guys knew and didn't tell me?"

Karissa opened her mouth then snapped it shut. She traded a look with Finley who flashed puppy dog eyes at me. She sighed and leaned forward.

"I helped him set up his account, Blake. When you said you were paired with Woody, I knew right away, but I didn't think you would be so open with him if you knew it was Ian," Finley said.

I groaned. "You and your brother are the same. That was his excuse, too."

"Blake," Karissa said harshly. "Are they wrong?"

I opened my mouth to argue but had no words. I slumped back in my seat and glared at her.

"You can give me whatever look you want, but you and I both know you're not going to win," Karissa said, full of attitude. She raised an eyebrow and waited for me to sigh before she continued. "You can be mad at Ian and Fin, and me for that matter, but I think you're really mad at yourself. I knew who he was. As soon as you told us about him, I looked him up. I wanted to make sure you weren't paired with some guy who was going to hurt you. Even though you said you were only friends with him, I could see you were getting attached. When I saw it was Ian, I said something to Fin, but she already knew. I agreed with her. You wouldn't have been so open with Ian. You would have shut him down so fast, and you never would have fallen for him. So, you can be pissed off, but you need to accept that you're mad at yourself, too."

I scowled at her because she was right. All day, I'd been thinking the same thing. I couldn't believe I'd thrown away Ian not once, but twice. He told me he loved me, and I didn't say anything. I let him believe I didn't care.

They all looked at me for a long moment, then Laura said, "Well, if I get paired up with Dr. Allison, I don't want to know. And I don't want him to know. I just want him to fall in love with me without anyone else getting involved."

Everyone laughed and the tension in the room dissipated. I sat back and let them talk around me again. Karissa was right. I was mad at myself. I was so mad at the woman Woody was in love with because she didn't love him back. I didn't know who he was and could tell he was an amazing man. Not only that, but I ended things with Ian because I was so sure he was going to end things with me.

He got close. He changed things when we made love. It was always intense with Ian, but that night, the night after my mom said she was done drinking, everything was different. I could feel it. I knew it. And it scared the shit out of me.

I loved him. So much it terrified me. But when I thought about what scared me the most about loving him, it was the idea of losing him. Of letting him in all the way and watching him walk away.

But he didn't walk away. I pushed him away. I sat back and did nothing when the man I loved said he wanted me and loved me. He told me over and over again. For months he told me how much he wanted me. For months he showed me how much he loved me. He held me and comforted me and made me laugh and loved me. And I told him I didn't want him. I made that choice. I pushed him away. I ended things by not telling him how I felt. I let fear get in the way of everything.

"Am I incapable of love?" I blurted, interrupting the conversation they were having.

"What?" said Elise.

"Love? Am I broken?" I clarified.

"Why do you ask that?" Finley asked.

I looked around at the people I'd been closer to than anyone else my entire life. Finley that I'd known forever and thought of as a sister most of my life. Karissa and Elise who became fast friends of mine and just as close as Finley. Laura who joined our little group much later but was still a crucial part for her wit and care and occasional bossiness. And Trinity who we'd only known a couple months, but who felt like she'd been a part of our group as long as the rest of us. I looked at all of them and saw the answer written on every single face in the room.

"You do. You all do. I really am Buttercup, aren't I?"

"Where is this coming from?" Karissa asked the same moment Elise said, "Yes."

"See?" I cried. "Elise has the guts to tell me. I'm broken. There's something wrong with me."

"There's nothing wrong with you," Finley said. "But tell us what happened."

I laughed mirthlessly. "Nothing happened. That's the problem. Ian told me he loves me, and I couldn't say it. I couldn't even respond. He just walked away."

"Ian?" Elise blurted. "Ian Jameson?"

I nodded. "Yep. Ian Jameson, perpetual bachelor, said he loves me, and instead of immediately repeating the words, I clammed up."

"Maybe you just don't feel the same way?" Laura suggested.

I shook my head, unable to meet their gazes.

"My brother said he loves you?" Finley asked. "Last night?"

I could hear the smile in her voice, but I couldn't meet her eyes as I nodded. She told me she'd kill him if he hurt me. I laughed and asked what she'd do to me, but I never thought I'd have to find out. I never imagined Ian Jameson falling for me. I never dreamed of it.

But it happened, and I messed it all up because I was scared. Ian wasn't safe. Ian wasn't easy. Ian was…everything. Loving him scared the hell out of me because I would forever second guess everything. He was the kind of guy who made heads turn when he was walking down the street. The only heads I made turn were the ones who had to move off the sidewalk to let the wide-load pass by. We didn't match. We didn't fit. And if we stayed together, I'd forever be waiting for the other shoe to drop and Ian to realize he made a mistake.

That he should have fallen for someone else. Someone thinner. Someone prettier. Someone better for him.

"She's spiraling," Karissa said. Her voice was faraway, like she wasn't in the same room as me anymore.

"Oh, shit," Elise said.

"Blake!" Laura shouted.

I turned and looked at her.

"Blake, calm down. Breathe." She put a paper bag in my hands and brought it up to my face. "Deep breaths."

I followed her instructions and huffed into the bag, each breath bringing my pulse down and my sanity back. I finally drew in a shaky breath of fresh air and looked at the room around me. Five scared faces. Five people I loved who hadn't hurt me. Who hadn't asked more of me than I could give. Five people who gave back as much to me as I gave to them. I loved all of them, and they loved me, and it was okay.

"I screwed everything up," I admitted. "You guys have to help me fix it."

They shook their heads and laughed. "You know we will," Finley said. "I'd hate to have to kick your ass because you hurt my brother."

I smiled at her. "Me, too."

25

IAN

Ork was my only respite. Without Blake, I worked, I drank beer, and I slept. That was the extent of my life. I finally understood how Ramsey felt. Losing the woman you loved, and having her there but untouchable, was almost impossible.

I didn't leave home much because I risked running in to Blake. Finley tried to get me to go out, but I had no interest. Not when Blake was at every turn. I couldn't even go out in my own damn boat because of Blake. If I wouldn't get arrested for it, I'd blow the damn thing up.

I itched to get out. I wanted to take a break from everything. I hated being in the same town as Blake. For years, it was the best part of my day to run into Blake. And now...I couldn't face her.

I sat on my futon, happy I never got a bed, and scrolled through my phone. My recently watched shows on Netflix were all shows I watched with Blake. My texts were full of Blake. My pics were Blake. I couldn't get away from her.

I went to the kitchen and grabbed a beer, then went back to my room and flipped through the channels. When my phone dinged with a message, I picked it up without a thought.

BLAKE

I'm sorry.

Jesus. What the hell?

I screwed up. Can we talk?

I sat up in bed and held my phone. I wanted to tell her to go to hell, but it was Blake. I loved her no matter what she said or what she did. I ached to see her.

I'm outside, but we can meet somewhere another time if you'd rather. But I'm not going to disappear, Ian.

I'm home. Let yourself in.

I scrambled off my bed and went back to the kitchen with my beer. I hadn't shaved in days, and my black tee and gray shorts were only barely clean. I certainly wasn't doing myself any favors or showing her what a catch she let loose.

Her footsteps echoed through the shop as she walked closer. Each step increased my tension and made me want to throw up. I waited, staring at the door until she knocked softly then turned the knob to let herself in.

I leaned against the counter for support, gripping the edge so I didn't go to her and drop to my knees, begging her to give me another chance. She said she wanted to talk, so I'd let her, then smile and tell her we could still be friends. Fuck me, I hated it.

I hated it even more when she finally stepped into my view. She was stunning in a short, pool blue dress that hugged her breasts and flared out at her waist, ending high on her thighs. She wore those shoes that fucking killed me, the ones that wrapped up her ankles and onto her calves and made me want to unwrap her. Her hair was loose around her shoulders. She looked like she was going on a date.

I wanted to rip whoever she was dressed up for to fucking shreds.

"Hey," she said, giving me a tentative smile.

I nodded but didn't say anything. If I did, it was going to be something stupid.

"How are you?"

I shrugged. Again, something stupid was on my tongue. *I love you. Forgive me. I'll do anything if you'll give me another chance. Don't let me die alone.* You know, stupid.

She took a deep breath and my gaze fell to her breasts. They pressed against her dress and threatened to spill over the top edge. She hated her breasts, but they were fucking perfect. She was perfect. Every inch of her.

"I, um, I was hoping we could talk. Unless you're busy." She said the last part like it was a question, her voice rising at the end.

I shook my head but still didn't speak.

"Okay. I don't blame you for not making this easy on me. I think marrying your rival to save your life would be easier, but I can't be Buttercup anymore."

"What?" I blurted.

She shook her head. "Nothing. Never mind. We promised we would be friends, and I was hoping I could hold you to that because I really need a friend."

My throat burned and my heart threatened to beat out of my chest, but I nodded. Just once. I promised her we'd always be friends. It didn't matter that I hoped I'd never have to keep that promise.

"It's about a guy. And about me, too." She took another deep breath. "When my mom started drinking, I was embarrassed by it. I didn't tell anyone because I didn't want her to be the mom everyone laughed about, but I hated it. Then she stopped. She met a new guy and just stopped. Then they broke up and she started drinking again. Over and over again, she'd start and stop based on the guy she was dating. And over and over again, I saw her throwing her life away because of the way other people thought of her."

I loosened my grip on the counter and crossed my arms over my chest.

"I always worried about what other people thought because of her. I didn't want them to judge me because of her. I never realized I was doing the same thing she did. I let what others thought impact how I felt. I did it with my art. I did it with my relationships. I did it with falling in love."

I sucked in a breath. I didn't think I could hear what she had to say. I turned to the fridge and grabbed a new beer and drained half of it.

"I started falling in love last summer. I didn't want to admit it because I was still dating William, but this guy…he was everything William wasn't. He was funny and sexy and smart and he made me feel things I never felt with William. I knew things were over between us because a few hours with this guy was better than a year with William. But I didn't take a chance with him because I worried about what people would say. I worried about what he would say. I didn't want him to think I was trying to trap him in something he didn't want."

She said the same thing to me before. That she didn't want to trap me.

"He was the first one to make a move. He kissed me, and kissing him was better than sex with any other man. Kissing him was like jumping out of the boat on a hot day and sinking under the cold water. It was refreshing and new, but it was so much more because it was with a man I trusted and cared about. More than I was ready to admit."

I swallowed thickly, not counting on what she was saying until she came out and said it.

"But then I started talking to this other guy. He was also funny and sweet, and he was in love with his friend. I was so jealous of her because he seemed great. I couldn't imagine how someone wouldn't want to be with him. It wasn't that I was in love with him, but a guy like him was too good for someone to throw away. Why couldn't she see that?"

I smiled when she chuckled. God, she was beautiful.

"At the end of the day, though, I was exactly like that girl. I was that girl. I was too worried about how I looked. How I felt like I was fooled. How I wasn't enough for him. How I was going to end up hurt when he decided all my fears were true. And I told him we couldn't be together."

For the first time since she walked in, I let a little bit of hope in.

"My biggest fear was letting him in and losing him. I convinced myself, because of my mother, that letting someone in and losing them was more painful than not letting them in at all. She'd always drink the most right after a break-up, and I reasoned that it didn't make sense to even get involved with someone if it was just going to result in pain. So I ended things before I could let myself get hurt. Except I got hurt anyway."

"I'm sorry, Blake. I should have told you about the app. I never should have lied to you. Don't let my bad choice influence the rest of your life. You deserve love, babe."

She smiled and nodded. "I didn't believe that for a long time. That I deserved love. I thought love was possible for everyone else, but not for me. I wanted safe and easy. I wanted passionless and unemotional. It meant I wouldn't run to the bar when things went wrong. That I wouldn't blow up my life."

I wanted to yell at her, but she said she wanted a friend, and a friend was supposed to be supportive. A friend didn't tell her she was wrong and that love was supposed to be all those things, but if it was right, it was worth it.

"Then I realized, thanks to Fin and the others, that I'm not my mother. And not only that, but I'd already lived through my worst case scenario and survived it. And the worst part of all of it was I didn't have to go through it. If I'd pulled my head out of my ass, I could have saved myself the pain of losing the man I love. I could have saved both of us that pain."

I met her gaze and sucked in a breath. I saw the pain in her eyes that I felt over the last week. She felt it, too.

"I never should have pushed you away, Ian."

I shrugged. "I wasn't the one you wanted. It's worse if it's not right and we drag it out."

"But it is right, Ian. We're right. I didn't want to believe it because I was scared. You're not the kind of guy who wants forever—"

"But I—"

"I know," she said, holding up her hand. "I know. You told me. And I wasn't ready to hear it. I couldn't believe it. Ian Jameson couldn't love me. He couldn't want me. He couldn't choose me. Not when I was me. I wasn't enough for you."

"You are," I assured her.

She smiled. "It's not going to be something I'll have an easy time hearing, but thank you."

"It doesn't matter what other people think of you or of us, Blake. All that matters is what we think."

She smiled and took a step toward me. "Well, I think you're the only man who's ever made me scream his name. And I think you're the only man who's ever made me want to throw caution to the wind. And the only one who's ever made me feel safe and dangerous in the same second. And who's ever made me think I could do anything. Who's ever believed in me more than I believe in myself. Who's there for me and supports me and loves me in ways I never even dreamed were possible. But I know you're the only man I've ever loved and the only man I ever will love."

"You can't promise that," I said.

She smiled. "I can because you're it for me, Ian. I was always attracted to you, but I never saw you as a possibility. You were untouchable. But when I walked in on you in Hawaii, I couldn't get that look in your eyes out of my head. I didn't sleep with anyone else after William because every time I closed my eyes, I saw you. I dreamed about the things you would have done to me if I hadn't closed that door between us."

"Fuck, Blake," I groaned. "All I wanted to do that night was touch you. I was so fucking hard. I didn't sleep the rest of the trip because of the way you looked at me."

"You never said anything," she said softly.

"You were still with Willie. I don't like him, but I wasn't going to put you in that position."

"Why did you take so long to tell me how you felt?"

I smiled. "I didn't think you were interested. But Ms. Georgia...She made me promise I'd make a move by her birthday."

She snorted. "Nothing like cutting it close."

I laughed. "I was sure you'd turn me down."

She choked out a laugh. "Why?"

I shrugged and my smile faded. "I was kind of right."

She took another step toward me. "I'm sorry, Ian. I want to make that up to you."

"Oh, yeah? And what did you have in mind?"

She grinned. "Well, for starters, I'm not wearing under-wear beneath this dress."

I groaned and my cock throbbed.

"But more importantly than that, I love you, Ian. I've loved you for a long time, and I'm sorry for being too scared to tell you, but I want to tell you every day for the rest of my life."

I tugged her into my arms and let her feel the effect her words had on me. All her words made me ache. "I love you, Blake."

"Good," she said against my lips. "Then maybe I can borrow your couch. Permanently."

"Huh?"

"Move in with me, Ian. I don't want to spend another night without you, and your futon is killer on my back."

"I'll give you back rubs every night. And foot rubs. And whatever other kind of rubs you want."

She laughed and pulled me back in. Finally, finally, she was mine. And I wasn't letting her go.

AFTER BLAKE AND I CELEBRATED, twice, she told me she had one more thing for me. She pulled on one of my old tees and walked out of the apartment into the shop. I started to follow her, but she came back in a few seconds later holding a canvas behind her back.

"I was really inspired when we first got together, and I created some new paintings. I have them in my closet because I didn't want anyone to see them, but I wanted one for you. I painted this yesterday. It's...well, you can see."

She pulled it out from behind her back and showed it to me. The colors struck me first. Blues and grays with splashes of pink. Passion poured off the canvas in the pink. Her lips, my hands, my tongue. I could tell it was us without even thinking about it. She was riding me in the painting, her curves shaded in gray, except where my hands dug in and pink highlighted where we touched. My tongue on her breast. Her lips parted in pleasure. My hands holding her hips.

I set it gently on the chair next to me and grabbed her. I carried her to my room and repeated the painting for round three.

WHEN WE EMERGED AGAIN, she told me we had to go.

"Why? I was going to keep you naked for the rest of the day. The rest of our lives if I can manage it."

She shook her head and reached for her dress. "Fin, Rissa, Elise, Laura, and Trinity are going to O'Kelley's. They told me to meet them. They want to know if you forgive me."

I kissed her slow and deep, pouring everything I felt about her into the kiss. I slid my tongue alongside hers and enveloped her in my arms. I tilted my head and stroked deeper into her mouth, licking and teasing and tasting her until she moaned and wrapped her hand around my cock.

I stepped back. "I thought we had to go," I protested.

"You're evil," she said with a pout. "We've been apart for days, and you're teasing me."

I kissed her nose. "Yeah, but you know what?"

"What?" she asked, still pouting.

"We're never going to be apart again, babe."

She looked up at me with the most beautiful smile. "Yeah?"

I nodded. "Yeah. Because you're mine, and there's no way in hell I'm letting you go ever again."

"Even when I stop trusting us?"

I nodded.

"And when I convince myself you should be with someone skinnier or prettier?"

"No such thing."

She rolled her eyes, so I scowled and nodded.

"And when I let my mother get to me?"

"Always, babe. You're mine, and I'm yours, Blake. Forever."

"Forever?"

"If you'll have me, but that's my plan. I've loved you for years. Forever sounds almost long enough."

She smiled and nodded. Her eyes were watery when she closed them and lifted onto her toes for another kiss. We didn't pull back from that one until long after I carried her to my room.

EPILOGUE

MELODY

I sat at the bar at O'Kelley's sipping my wine. It was one of those days. Ramsey was home with Amber, and I was supposed to be meeting Willow. She was late, as usual.

The door opened, and I glanced back to see if it was my sister. Instead, it was Blake and Ian, holding hands and grinning like they just won the lottery.

I blew out a breath. Guess they worked things out. I wanted to be happy for them, but it was hard to find it in me to celebrate someone else's love when my own was tentative at best.

I knew it was my fault. Ramsey wasn't the kind of man who would sit back and watch me do something dangerous. He was solid, and he protected me. But he didn't understand. I couldn't shake the desire for more kids. And he wouldn't budge.

"Hey," Willow said, finally joining me. "Sorry I'm late." She nodded to Hudson and pointed to my wine. "What are we drinking to tonight? The end of your marriage?"

I rolled my eyes. My sister was my rock forever. We were

best friends, but my little sister did not like my husband. She never had, and I didn't know why. "No," I said firmly. "I'm not ready for that yet."

Willow shook her head and grabbed my wine glass. She swirled it then took a sip. "He's always been an ass. I don't know why you don't just leave him."

"Because I have a daughter to think about," I countered.

"You know staying in an unhappy marriage for your kid is not going to teach her anything good," Willow said just as Hudson walked up.

He stilled but pretended he wasn't listening to our conversation as he poured Willow a glass of wine and refilled mine. He left the bottle on the bar in front of us and pressed his lips together in a smile for me.

"I still love him," I admitted. "I'm not ready to give up hope that we can work this out."

"It's been over a year since you lost Steven, Mel. He hasn't budged. Why do you think he's going to change his mind?"

I shrugged. I didn't know if he would. I was fairly sure he wouldn't, but I'd been in love with Ramsey since I was sixteen. We dated for a year, then broke up when he went to college, but once we settled back in MacKellar Cove, we got back together and stayed together. For almost twenty years, I was in love with him. It wasn't easy to walk away from that. To not roll over and see him. To not watch him kiss our daughter. To not grow old with him.

"There are plenty of other guys out there. Let me see your phone."

"Why?" I asked.

"There's a dating app that you should get."

"I'm not getting a dating app, Willow. I'm not single."

Willow shrugged like it was no big deal. "You should try it. I think you'll find someone else. Someone far better than Ramsey."

"What is your deal with him? Why do you hate him so much?"

Willow rolled her eyes. "Because he's not good enough for you. He never has been."

I drew in a breath and closed my eyes. We'd had the same conversation for years. I didn't know why Willow felt that way, and she always refused to explain. She was adamant that Ramsey wasn't who I thought he was, but I knew she was wrong. He almost came between us, but Willow finally accepted that Ramsey wasn't going anywhere. Until now.

"There's a cute guy looking over here. I'm going to go say hi to him. I'll be back."

I nodded and watched her walk away. The dark haired guy she stopped in front of smiled and asked her to dance. I wished I could be as confident with men as my little sister, but I never had it. I was always self-conscious of my large breasts and flabby belly. Ramsey made me feel beautiful, but he hadn't touched me in months.

I turned back to my wine and took a sip. I just refilled my glass again when someone sat in Willow's chair.

"Hey," Blake said.

"Hey," I replied, smiling at her. "I see things with Ian are better."

She nodded, that happy grin making a reappearance. "They are. I know he's not perfect, but we love each other."

I snorted. I couldn't stop it. I hated crapping on her good mood, but I was cynical on a good day. And I hadn't had many good days lately.

"Things aren't better with Ramsey?" she asked, her smile fading away.

I shook my head. "Nope. He won't talk about having another kid. Just tells me it's not up for discussion."

"I'm sorry, Melody. What are you going to do?"

I shrugged. "I wish I knew. My sister thinks I should leave him."

Blake gasped. "Are you thinking about that?"

I shrugged again. "Honestly, I'm not sure what my other options are."

"But you love him."

I nodded. "I do. And as much as I'd love to believe it, love doesn't conquer all. Love sucks balls sometimes."

Blake pressed her lips together, and I felt like a complete piece of shit.

"I'm sorry, Blake. You're all shiny and happy and I'm over here making it sound like you should walk away now before life craps on you."

She huffed a laugh but didn't argue.

"I really hope you and Ian have better luck than Ramsey and I. If half of marriages end in divorce, I guess we'll be the ones taking that bullet and you might survive."

"I don't want that to happen, Melody."

I smiled and nodded. "Me, either, but I'm having trouble seeing another choice."

Blake opened her mouth then snapped it shut. Hudson came over to see if we needed anything. Blake ordered another pitcher of beer.

"Are you guys celebrating?" I asked.

She shrugged. "Um, yeah. We're sort of celebrating Ian and I getting back together. And me pulling my head out of my ass. I almost let him walk away because I was scared."

I nodded. Hudson set the pitcher in front of Blake. She thanked him and smiled at me.

"Do you want to join us?"

I laughed and shook my head. "I'm clearly not good company right now. I think I'm just going to head out. Have a good night, Blake."

She nodded. "Yeah, um, you, too. Maybe we can get

together sometime. Have a drink? All four of us, or even just you and me. If you're interested?"

I smiled. She was trying to be nice, but she didn't really mean it. I nodded and told her that would be good, then left. I sent my sister a text letting her know I was going home so she didn't worry, then walked to my house.

The light from the TV in the living room flickered through the curtains. The porch light was on. Amber's bedroom had a soft glow from her nightlight. From the outside, my home looked happy. Bright flowers along the front walk. A happy, yellow front door. Gray siding and two vehicles parked side-by-side. It was only once you got inside that you realized there was nothing perfect or happy about my home.

I let myself in and closed the door behind me. Ramsey drew in a sharp breath and jumped up from the couch, where he'd clearly been sleeping in front of the TV. Amber's toys were everywhere because he never made her clean up. I could see the sink full of dishes from where I stood. And he was just sleeping on the couch.

"You're home early," he said, glancing at his watch.

I nodded. "I didn't feel like watching Ian and Blake make out all night. Or Willow flirt with half the men in the bar. I'm tired."

He nodded and sat down again.

I closed my eyes and took a breath, then started picking up toys. I could feel him watching me, but I didn't look at him. Once all the toys were cleaned up, I went to the kitchen and unloaded the dishwasher and filled it up with the dirty dishes. I turned and found him leaning against the doorframe.

"I was going to do all that," he said.

I nodded, not wanting to fight with him again.

"Are you ignoring me now?" he asked.

I sighed. Guess I wasn't going to get my way. As usual. "I'm tired, Ramsey. I just want to go to bed."

"But you're pissed at me. Like always."

I tried to tamp down my anger, but I couldn't. It boiled over and I threw my hands up. "Yes, I'm mad at you. I went out for a few hours, and I come home and have to work. I'm always cleaning something up because you don't do it, or I'm taking care of something because you don't do it. I'm exhausted. Everything is the way you want it."

"Is that really what you think? Because nothing about us is how I want it."

I crossed my arms over my chest and glared at my husband. "Oh, yeah? And how do you want it?"

He looked at me and said the six words I never thought I'd hear from him.

"I think we should get divorced."

THANK **you** so much for reading Blake and Ian's story and coming on a whole new journey with me! I wanted to get back to a truly curvy girl romance series, and I absolutely love these characters. Now, if only I could figure out how to make Karissa's app real, everything would be perfect. Am I right?

Melody and Ramsey's story is next, and I am so excited about it! Months after Ramsey asks Melody for a divorce, they're still trying to figure out what normal looks like. Things with them aren't over just yet, but rebuilding a failing marriage can't be as easy as starting over. Start reading His Curvy Wife today!

. . .

LOOKING for more from Blake and Ian? Subscribers get a free, exclusive bonus epilogue of their wedding day! Only available to subscribers! Sign up now!

You can also find out what happened in Hawaii. Subscribers get His Curvy Secret for free!

LIKE A LITTLE EDGE with your romance? She's a curvy woman who's all but given up on love. He's her best friend's brother and a sexy, badass former SEAL. Together, they have to find his brother, and maybe each other. Freedom is available now.

ABOUT THE AUTHOR

USA TODAY Bestselling Author Mary E Thompson spent most of her childhood wishing she had a few less curves. She hid in the pages of books because her favorite characters never cared what size her clothes were. Now, neither does Mary, and she writes stories that celebrate women like her. Real women who have curves, chase dreams, and find love, because we should all be happy, no matter our dress size.

Mary spends her non-writing time with her husband and two kids, watching too much TV, cheering for her home-town football team (Go Bills!), and hiding chocolate from her family.

Visit https://MaryEThompson.com/ to sign up for Mary's newsletter, **Romancing the Curves**. Subscribers get free ebooks and other fun stuff, like exclusive, members only content and giveaways, plus are the first to know about new releases and sales!